ONE

THE letters came after I had been back at college for three days. They were in my pigeon-hole when I came out of breakfast and I took them to my room to read.

They had both written, presumably by agreement, so that I would get both letters at once. Obviously they had timed the whole thing carefully to coincide with the end of the vacation. It made me realize what a strain the last few weeks must have been for them.

I opened Mother's first because I always saved Dad's till the last in any batch of letters, just as I saved the best piece of food on my plate for the last mouthful. It was quite short and rather stilted, not at all her usual chatty style. It asked me not to think badly of either of them and explained that these things happened through no one's fault. Dad's was longer and took all the blame while hoping I would understand. I didn't believe either of them.

Still, it was a shock. Probably I had only myself to blame for smugly assuming that they would always tolerate the un-spectacular discontent of their marriage. Martin was already off their hands. My departure was, now I came to think of it, an obvious signal for them to resume their separate lives.

After a while I stopped staring foolishly at the letters and put them back in their envelopes. Life had not stopped. The sun still shone, the birds still sang and all the rest of it. There was probably a poem about this very subject which I ought to know. All the same, it was strange to think of my parents on the point of functioning separately at their age. I did not think of them as old, but in my mind they were certainly beyond the age when freedom of choice was theirs by right. I suppose the whole thing added up to surprise on my part at the first independent action I had ever seen them perform.

Anne came in while I was still trying to clarify my new status. She was fresh from the benefits of having a fiancé in London; she looked crumpled, fatigued and happy. My face must have expressed more than I realized, for she stopped half-way through saying, 'Anyone miss me –?' and changed to, 'Whatever's the matter?'

The language of shock was distressingly plebeian, I thought. Half of my brain was treating this experience as a prose appreciation, and the critical thumbs were decidedly down.

'I'm the product of a broken marriage,' I said pompously, because I wanted to test the sound of the words. 'Now read on.' And I handed her the letters. They were, I felt, social documents; my parents had not exactly taken a scalpel to their naked souls. Anne looked at me sharply, lit a cigarette, and began to read while I stared, very hard, I remember, at a shaft of sunlight which had umpteen particles of dust in it, dancing for all they were worth.

Anne read slowly. It was an irritating fault, but she had many good qualities and was an easy room-mate. Eventually she put the letters down, both out of their envelopes.

'Oh, honey,' she said in her lovely soft voice, 'I am sorry. What an awful thing.' And she offered me a cigarette. I took it gratefully, having run out the night before, but I felt guilty because I had taken the happiness out of her face.

'Nobody missed you,' I said. 'Did you have a good time?'

'Never mind about me.' She was frowning. 'This is awful. There was nothing like this brewing up last term, was there? What about the vac? Did you get a hint then?'

I shook my head. 'No more than usual. They've – they'd been jogging along for years. I suppose I just never thought they'd do anything about it.'

Anne was twisting her engagement ring round and round and dropping ash on the carpet. 'Does Martin know?'

PENGUIN BOOKS

A SHARE OF THE WORLD

Andrea Newman was born in Dover in 1938 and brought up in Shropshire and Cheshire. In 1960 she graduated from London University, where she married while still a student, and then worked as a civil servant and a teacher before becoming a full-time writer.

Her publications include *Mirage* (1965), *The Cage* (1966), *Three Into Two Won't Go* (1967), *Alexa* (1968) and *An Evil Streak* (1977). *A Bouquet of Barbed Wire* (1969) was dramatized by her for London Weekend Television and *Another Bouquet* . . . followed in early 1977. Her most recent novel, *Mackenzie*, was originally written for the BBC television series screened in autumn 1980. She has also contributed to other television series such as *Tales of Unease*, *The Frighteners*, *Love Story*, *Seven Faces of Woman*, *Intimate Strangers* and *Helen, a Woman of Today*.

Andrea Newman is divorced and lives in London.

A SHARE
OF THE WORLD

*

ANDREA NEWMAN

PENGUIN BOOKS

Penguin Books Ltd, Harmondsworth, Middlesex, England
Penguin Books, 625 Madison Avenue, New York, New York 10022, U.S.A.
Penguin Books Australia Ltd, Ringwood, Victoria, Australia
Penguin Books Canada Ltd, 2801 John Street, Markham, Ontario, Canada L3R 1B4
Penguin Books (N.Z.) Ltd, 182–190 Wairau Road, Auckland 10, New Zealand

—

First published by The Bodley Head 1964
Published in Penguin Books 1979
Reprinted 1980, 1982

—

—

Made and printed in Great Britain
by Hazell Watson & Viney Ltd,
Aylesbury, Bucks
Set in Linotype Juliana

I shrugged my shoulders. 'I imagine so.'

'Look,' Anne said, becoming decisive, 'you must ring up Peter. He'll make you feel better. You can't just sit here and think about it.'

'The cheap rate doesn't start till six,' I said.

'Oh, for God's sake,' said Anne, reaching for her handbag.

'Besides, he'll be at work,' I added.

'So what?' Anne demanded fiercely.

'So his father will be sitting opposite him while I pour out my heart,' I said, 'and you know how his father loves me. And besides, d'you suppose my parents want Peter's parents to know all about their private lives?'

'They can hardly be all that private any more,' Anne said savagely.

'Well, I can't do it,' I said. 'Not till this evening. I must get him alone.'

We sat then in silence, regarding the floor. A clock struck somewhere and I jumped up. 'I've got a lecture.'

'You're not going to bother with that?'

'Why not? I'm not doing any good here, am I? What difference will it make if I sit here another hour?'

'Oh dear,' said Anne, discouraged, 'I do so want to help and I'm only making it worse.'

I wanted to hug her but I was too inhibited. 'Bless you,' I said, 'you're doing wonders by just being here. I'll be all right.' I picked up my file and my gown and made for the door, but I felt as though I had forgotten something. It was all so muddling, like a theorem in geometry.

'The thing is, Anne,' I said, 'I just don't know how to behave. What does one do? It's like somebody dying; you don't get enough practice at it and the etiquette's all strange. I feel so silly and self-conscious. It's caught me on the wrong foot. I know there isn't a right foot, but that's how it feels. Whatever I do is false. Should I cry? Should I have hysterics? Should I take it on the chin and all that? Whatever I do feels like putting on an act.' I heard my voice talking much too quickly and then I was frightened because I don't like losing control and it seemed too early for that somehow. I don't know why I had this idea of saving it up. Anyway, it scared me, so I smiled at Anne and shut the door and went quickly to my lecture.

It was on Chaucer, who had limited appeal for me. I listened at first, because it was comforting to hear someone else's voice talking about safe, far-off things, and then I put dots on my paper and drew lines between them all until I had a lot of squares and then I drew lines between all the corners to join them up until it was all very complicated indeed. Then I looked at the incredible number of triangles I had created and decided there was nothing more I could do with them. After that I wrote CHAUCER in large letters and decorated them in pseudo-medieval style. It looked rather good. I wrote *Troilus and Criseyde* underneath because that was the subject of the lecture, and it looked so stark that I had to decorate that, too. The girl next to me was scratching away with her pen and I felt sorry for her because she was trying so hard to get every word down and she obviously couldn't succeed. I wrote, 'Is it worth it?' in my normal handwriting and nearly passed it to her, but I didn't because it looked so plain and feeble underneath the triangles and the ornamental names. Clearly I had passed my peak and all else would be an anti-climax. I switched to contemplation of Chaucer and how strange it was that we should all be sitting here learning about him when he had been dead for hundreds of years. I looked at the material of my gown and wondered if its previous owner had had to study Chaucer too. Perhaps she had been a mathematician and had done clever things with numbers that were not really there. Some of them had told me about that. They had not been able to explain it to me but they seemed to find it very exciting. From this I proceeded to enumerate all the other lectures that my gown might have sat through, which took me a long time. And then it was ten o'clock and the lecture was over.

I did not want to go back to Anne and her sympathy. At the doorway I caught up with Marty, who was shuffling along, shrouded in her gown, her black hair in rather a splendid mess on her shoulders. She looked very white and her eyes were half-shut. 'God, I feel lousy,' she muttered. 'Ruth came in at twelve and we talked till half past three. I wouldn't be here, but the damn birds woke me at six. Come and have coffee. You don't look so hot yourself.'

Marty's room was a glorious jumble of colour. She flung everything down and Ruth cleared it up. They had worked very hard at their cushion covers and bottle lampshades and created a black and orange colour scheme with dashes of white and moss-green. The normal college furniture looked ridiculously self-conscious in its bizarre setting. I began to feel better. Marty's world was permanently a little crazy.

'Of course, it seemed worth it at the time,' she went on, 'but then it always does.' She had a low, rich voice which achieved a remarkable blend of amusement and self-pity. At times this could be exasperating, but today I found it attractive.

'What did you do before Ruth came in?' I asked. Marty's life was always awash with drama. I had not seen her alone since term began, for one crisis had followed another. It was a miracle that she ever got to the few lectures that she did attend. They should have created a special award for her.

'Well, it all started so peacefully,' she said, bending over the coffee. She was one of the few people in college who always had real coffee in abundance. 'I washed my hair and put my feet up and was just going to start on Durrell when Tom arrived with some records. So I had to stop and make coffee, and we played all the records and talked about being just good friends and all passion spent, which was quite entertaining, and then someone came and told me I was wanted on the phone.'

She paused to pour out the coffee and be questioned.

'Who was it?' I asked.

'Louis.' She waved her hand dramatically. 'So we had it all out again and it took about half an hour. When I got back to Tom I didn't know what to say, so I didn't. But he must have got the message, he took off pretty rapidly after that. And just as well, because twenty minutes later Louis arrived.' She stopped, and the relish went out of her monologue. This was serious. 'Oh, Lois,' she said helplessly, 'I thought it was all over, I thought I was safe, but now it's all started again. I must be crazy, I swore I'd never get into this mess again. What is the matter with me?' She pushed her hair on to the top of her head and let it fall down. 'You are lucky,' she added, 'you and Peter. And Anne and Keith.'

I did not want to be diverted back to myself, or Anne. Marty, a good listener only when her funds were exhausted, interrupted herself occasionally to ease her conscience. 'Go on,' I said.

'Well, it was all marvellous again,' she said. 'Just the same, only better, after a month apart and thinking it was all finished and everything. What I can't understand now is how I ever dreamed I could do without him. He wanted to stay, but I said no. I pointed out how Ruth felt about him and he was all for having a showdown with her, but I said we could hardly expect to turn her out of her own room. He was awfully good about it, Lois, he didn't lose his temper, quite – that does show he's trying, doesn't it? In the end I promised I'd go round there tonight and he left like a lamb at ten. And I went to sleep till Ruth came in.'

Marty's voice, flowing over and into me, was like warm alcohol, soothing and restorative.

'What did you tell Ruth?' I asked.

'I wasn't going to tell her anything,' Marty said, 'but she guessed. Then it started. She went on as if she were my mother. That's why we stayed up till half past three. All for my own good, of course, but, my God, destructive! By the time we got to bed she had me so punch-drunk I honestly believed I was going to ring Louis up and tell him I wouldn't ever see him again. Honestly. Of course, this morning I came to my senses. But I couldn't look Ruth in the face. She still thinks I'm going to tell him. God knows how I'm going to get out tonight. What do I tell her? Do I leave her a note? "Changed my mind again; don't hold it against me"? Or do I just sneak out and say nothing? You don't think –' the idea flashed on, clear as a neon sign – 'you don't think she'd report me, do you?'

'Of course she wouldn't,' I said; 'that's just your girls' boarding school outlook. Midnight feasts and ragging the prefects. I know Ruth disapproves, but she's only expressing her opinion. She wouldn't act on it.'

'I suppose not,' Marty said vaguely. 'Anyway, I'll soon know, won't I?'

'Look here,' I said, 'Ruth's your friend. She wouldn't get you sent down, however much she may hate what you're doing.'

Marty smiled. 'The way I feel now, it wouldn't matter if she did. It would be worth it.'

'I'm glad you're so happy,' I said. And I was.

'What do you think, Lois?' Marty asked. 'Am I doing the right thing?' She never acted on opinions but she liked to hear them. It was like collecting stamps and then never looking at them again.

'Well,' I said, 'I think Louis is very bad for you but I know how I feel about Peter. I couldn't give him up and I think he's wonderful and presumably you feel the same about Louis.'

'Not exactly,' Marty said, screwing up her eyes. 'I think he's a bastard, but you're right about not giving him up.'

At this point the door opened and Ruth came in, obviously from her lecture. With superb composure Marty said to me, leaning back in her chair, 'Well, go on, when did you see Peter?'

'Not since last term,' I said truthfully, prompt but uneasy on my cue. 'His parents took him off on a cruise all vac and all I got was picture postcards.'

'What a bloody shame,' Marty said indignantly. She lit another cigarette; she was too busy being casual to remember to offer me one. 'Ruth, isn't that a bloody shame? Lois hasn't seen Peter all vac.'

Ruth's light green eyes were darting to and fro between us. She was very tall and thin, but large-boned so that she appeared rather more clumsy than elegant.

'Hullo, Lois,' she said, reminding me we had not met since last term. 'I *am* sorry. Did they do it deliberately?'

'Oh, yes,' I said. 'It's called "taking his mind off that girl".'

'Oh, well, it's their money they're wasting,' Ruth said briskly.

I had forgotten how kind she could be and my gratitude stirred guilt feelings at the part Marty was making me play.

'I'd better be going,' I said, rising.

'Just let me throw on some make-up,' said Marty quickly, 'and I'll come with you. I need a few things from the shops myself.' She rapidly smeared foundation across her nose and below her eyes, transferred lipstick from one lip to the other and outlined her eyes with grey pencil. 'There,' she said brightly under Ruth's thoughtful scrutiny, 'almost human.'

'Well, I do need some cigarettes,' I said, as we walked down the path. 'We'd better go out now; Ruth's sure to be watching.'

'She suspects,' Marty said, teeth clenched so I could scarcely hear her.

I was not so sure. 'Obviously she knows you've been telling me about it, but I can't see why she should suspect you've changed your mind.'

'Because she knows me so well,' Marty said irritably. We walked on in silence, the sun very warm on our backs. 'Oh, God,' Marty went on in her most despairing tones, 'how am I going to keep out of her way all day? She's got two more lectures – it's a mercy she's so conscientious. But that still leaves about three hours to get through and I can't live in the bathroom.'

12

By this time we had reached the shops and I bought my cigarettes, feeling rather guilty because I was suddenly bored and irritable. It was becoming difficult to concentrate on Marty's misfortunes. This was my usual reaction to a long bout. Later on I would be interested again.

'I must leave you,' I said. 'I'm going to telephone.'

Marty smiled absently, absorbed in calculations of evasive action. I went into the phone-box and started thumbing through the directory. What a lot of people there were that one did not know. What if one rang them up and embarked on a long recital of personal woe? It was a situation ripe for treatment by the new American humorists. 'Say, you don't know me, I'm at college the other side of town, but I got such a shock in the mail this morning, I gotta talk to somebody. Know what I mean? D'you ever get a shock in the mail?' And so on. It would probably be funnier if Shelley Berman did it. Funnier, in fact, done by anyone but me; not that I hadn't had my moments. But still, life and soul of the school magazine is one thing and funny-man to a nation quite another. I went on looking at names and trying to fit faces to them; some of the names were extremely improbable. I stayed there until I noticed a man outside rattling pennies while carefully avoiding my eye. I came out.

By this time it was twenty to twelve and I had a noon lecture. What a good thing that the letters had not come on a Friday, with nothing to attend after eleven. I walked slowly back in the sunshine, remembering my first arrival the term before last and the enthusiasm with which I had said to myself, 'This is it. I'm at university.' Everything I had noticed seemed charged with deep significance. It was rather like dying and reaching the Other Side. Very definitely the end of a long journey, if not paradise.

After the lecture there was lunch, and by that time I was quite hungry. Afterwards I had coffee with Anne and made her talk about Keith. She said cheerfully, 'This three-year engagement is a bind.' Anne was twenty, older than most of

13

us, and she had already known Keith for three years. Keith was due to graduate next summer, a year ahead of Anne; he had done National Service before going to college. Anne and Keith had something I could understand; they seemed to function from the same basis as Peter and I did. It was harder, I felt, to understand Marty's point of view, not that that prevented me from sympathizing with her.

Anne had a two o'clock lecture and when she had gone I began to plan the rest of the day carefully. I had to get through until six. It was an almost physical ordeal, rather like clenching your teeth or tightening your knuckles. It suddenly struck me as funny that Marty and I were both trying to kill this particular afternoon. Perhaps that was why I had so soon been irritated by her. There was more than a phone call waiting at the end of her day. Perhaps I was simply envious.

I started to become very busy. It was not safe to go to the cinema because you never knew what you might blunder into. Safer to take refuge in the bathroom as Marty had suggested. I had a very leisurely bath and came out in time for my three o'clock lecture, the last one of the day, unfortunately. I listened to some of it and it was quite good.

We came out at four when tea was nearly over. I went along to our room and found buns and bread ready for toasting. Anne had collected them as usual before going to her four o'clock lecture. I made tea into quite an event for myself. But after half an hour I was becoming restless. An hour and a half still to go. Time was definitely passing at a slower rate. I slipped across to Marty's room in the other building, but I did not dare to knock in case Ruth answered and started to ask me questions. Instead I wandered down to the bathroom where there were sounds of splashing and singing. I called, 'Marty,' but there was no reply; perhaps she did not hear, or it was someone else in there. Maybe it was Marty and she thought I was Ruth. I wandered back to our room again. There was an afternoon chill on the courtyard and building. I prowled round the room, fingering Anne's history books. With terrible, reluctant fascination I looked at the clock. I had only disposed of twenty minutes.

College was extraordinarily dead at this time of the afternoon. Last term Peter and I had called it our favourite time, waking from sleep after love-making, still with the whole evening ahead. Without him it was almost unbearable. I snatched up my things and rushed to the bathroom where I succeeded in washing my hair in half an hour instead of ten minutes. Five-twenty; quite an achievement. Surely the next forty minutes were not beyond the reach of my ingenuity? I borrowed Anne's hairdrier and set to work on my hair. Luckily, it was thick and reached almost to the bottom of my neck so it took a little while to dry. The hairdrier was pleasantly warm, like a cure for neuralgia. I turned on Anne's radio, too, and it played gloriously brash, cheerful noises. I began to allow myself the luxury of planning what I would say to Peter. There was nothing more I could do to myself except renew my make-up. My nails, unlike Anne's, were not worth manicuring.

At ten to six I brushed out my still warm hair and backcombed it a little. It never worked as well for me as it did for other people, but it was a help. I sprayed the result with lacquer and turned away from the mirror to find some change. In the end I had to raid our gas-meter money. And then I started to look for an empty phone-box.

There were three phones in college for students' use, but they were greatly in demand and I had to do two complete circuits before I found one free. None of the booths was soundproof and the triviality of the conversations enraged me. I wondered guiltily, though, how often I had had this effect on somebody else.

At ten past six I was installed and asking for Peter's number. Now it seemed as if I had hardly had to wait at all. I could feel peace creeping towards me. The male operators had come on for the night shift and they sounded so good-tempered I did not grudge the minutes I had to wait before the number started to ring. I knew it would be all right as soon as I heard his voice.

Peter's mother answered. I almost loved her.

'It's Lois, Mrs Fairley,' I said. 'Please may I speak to Peter?' I always tried to be specially polite to her.

'I'm sorry, my dear,' she said in her cool, distinct voice, 'I'm afraid you can't.'

I could not believe it. Whatever her reasons, she could not be so cruel tonight.

'It's very important,' I said. 'Please.'

'I'm sorry, my dear,' she said again, very casually, 'but he's out. He went to a show in town straight after work.'

I swallowed hard. It was incredible. How could he have gone out when I had lived through the whole day to telephone him at six o'clock?

'Can I give him a message?' Mrs Fairley asked me. I had not stammered since childhood, but I did it then.

'N-no,' I said, and shut up, too frightened to thank her.

'Very well, then,' she said crisply. 'I'll tell him you called. Good-bye, Lois.' And she hung up on me.

I stayed in the phone-booth for about five minutes after that with my head on the cold black metal of the box. I felt very sick. I kept repeating Peter's name and it seemed to help, but not enough. When I felt it was safe to stand upright again, I came out. I almost ran to our room. I wanted Anne badly now.

She took one look at my face and jumped up. 'My God,' she exclaimed, 'whatever's happened?'

I shook my head. 'He wasn't there, Anne. He'd gone out; he'd gone to the theatre. His mother told me.' My voice was decidedly unsteady and I felt an awful confusion between tears and laughter. Anne put her arm round my shoulders. 'Oh, Anne,' I said helplessly.

Anne was really very sensible. Once she saw that I did not want to break down, she pushed me into a chair, gave me a cigarette, a writing pad and biro. 'You write to him. Get it all off your chest,' she said. 'It's the only thing to do. You'll feel much better. Get him to come this weekend if he can.'

I wrote and wrote. It was easier to put on paper than I had imagined. I described the whole day, starting with the letters and ending with the phone call, and gave him a phone number and a time to ring me the following night, whether he was coming or not. But I felt pretty sure he would come as I posted the letter.

Anne wanted me to go in to supper, but I couldn't. My stomach had just achieved an uneasy equilibrium. I read the evening papers in the Common Room while she ate and met her as she came out. It seemed vital we should not be separated for longer than was necessary. During supper, the paper had served as an Anne-substitute. I was becoming very neurotic, I noted disapprovingly.

Back in our room (very womb-like now) Anne made coffee for us. I drank without tasting it. 'Anne,' I said, 'I'd like to get drunk. I never have and I think it's a perfect opportunity. How much do you think it takes?'

'Not all that much,' Anne said. 'Just a fair old mixture. Give me five minutes and we'll find out.'

She came back loaded with bottles. 'There we are,' she said cheerfully. 'Just about one of everything.'

I stared at her. 'Whatever did that lot cost you?' She shook her head. 'Remember me? I'm a rich girl and occasionally I appreciate it. Like now.' She put the *Verboten* notice on the door, produced two glasses and we began.

I have very vague recollections of that evening. Anne drank only a little, but she kept my glass filled and each time the contents tasted different from before. I remember thinking Anne was very like a doctor and I think at one point I asked her, 'Why didn't you read medicine, Anne?' at which she laughed and said she couldn't imagine. Anne's face began to blur, after a long time when I was nearly giving up hope, but her general shape remained lovable and safe. I knew I hadn't

17

gone on long enough, though, because I could still remember why I had started. Anne seemed to sense this, for she said, 'Come on, honey, drink up. Not far to go now,' and I said weakly, 'Oh, Anne, does it always take as long as this?' But presently, perhaps only three drinks later, I began to feel so ill that all I knew or wanted in the entire world was to be sick and go to sleep, and that was a good feeling.

TWO

THE sound of knocking first adapted itself to my dream. I was inside a cupboard on the sea-front and knocking to get out. Anne was trying to open the door. But the knocking went on even after I was standing beside Anne on the sand and I opened my eyes and saw darkness and heard Anne's steady breathing. Someone was knocking at our door. I was very resentful at waking up and my head ached considerably, but I crawled out of bed, keeping more or less horizontal, because it seemed inhuman to wake Anne. I groped my way to the door, wondering what time it was, and remembered then that with the *Verboten* notice on the door no one should have knocked at all, so it must be an emergency. I wished I felt fitter for it.

It was Ruth. She was still in her day clothes. She made no apology or introduction but simply said, 'Is Marty there?'

I peered at her. We could only just recognize each other by faint moonlight through the landing window. I said, 'No,' wishing I did not feel as though someone had cracked my skull. I could not imagine why Ruth thought Marty was with us. The entire course of the previous day was still obscure to me.

Ruth said, 'Do you know where she is?' and her voice shook. Then I remembered: about Marty, about myself. I took a deep breath and stepped backwards, crashing into some bottles as I did so. I said, 'You'd better come in, Ruth.' It was obviously hopeless for me to try to shield Anne from this. I switched on a bedside lamp.

Anne woke up gradually, protesting. 'What's the matter?'

she said, very slowly, as if unwrapping her mind. 'Lois? Are you all right?'

'I'm fine,' I reassured her. 'It's Ruth.'

'Oh, Ruth,' Anne struggled up on one elbow and blinked. 'Isn't it awfully late?'

'She's looking for Marty,' I said.

'Marty?' Anne repeated. I felt semi-hysterical.

'Do you know where she is?' Ruth repeated urgently, but with less hope, I thought.

We were silent. I was about to speak, realizing Ruth would have to know, but she saved me the trouble. She sat down very suddenly on my bed and said quietly, 'Then she's done it. She's gone to him.'

'What?' Anne groaned plaintively, more bemused than ever. I had forgotten she was two instalments behind on Marty.

'Marty's gone back to Louis,' I said briefly. Ruth was shuddering like an animal after a wetting. Anne relapsed on to her pillows with a long, deep moan. 'Oh, God,' she said, almost to herself, 'I'm so tired.'

A moment later she was the other Anne once more, springing out of bed, putting the eiderdown round Ruth's shoulders, lighting the gas to make coffee. 'I'm sorry there's no milk,' she said absently, and offered Ruth a cigarette.

Ruth shook her head.

'Ruth doesn't smoke,' I said, as Ruth seemed incapable of speech. I took one myself, grateful that Anne, prepared for a marathon, had bought a box of fifty along with the drinks.

Ruth suddenly looked at me straight in the eyes, disconcertingly, and said, 'She talked to you, Lois. What did she say?'

I knew Ruth had to be told the truth, but I had no idea how much of Marty's conversation to repeat, nor, at this particular moment, were the details of it very clear. I was conscious, however, of a certain resentment that Marty had chosen the simplest escape route and left me to cope.

'She talked for about an hour,' I said, 'but really it just boiled down to the fact that although she knows he's no good she can't resist him. I'm terribly sorry, Ruth. She was very upset; she couldn't think how to tell you.'

'I had her convinced last night,' Ruth said. 'I really did.'

'Oh, yes, I know,' I said. It seemed important to reassure her on this point. 'She said so. It was only this morning she changed her mind.'

'I should never have left her,' Ruth said. Her voice was quite expressionless. 'I should have stayed with her every minute.'

'I don't think it would have made any difference, Ruth,' I said gently. Anne put a cup of coffee into her hands and to my surprise she drank it at once, like an obedient child.

'It might have done,' she said, returning the cup to Anne, but still looking at me. 'She used to listen to me.' Tears suddenly flooded her eyes; it was uncanny to see them appear and overflow so rapidly. She did not blink, and they poured down her cheeks; it was absurd, exaggerated, and all the more shocking because it was what I had so nearly done myself. I almost envied Ruth.

Anne put her arms round her and rocked her back and forth. I knew Anne was doing the right thing but I was embarrassed. Anne had been very good to me, but now it seemed that she was becoming a kind of universal mother. Poor Anne, I thought. Perhaps she had had a more trying twenty-four hours than any of us.

Ruth was clinging to Anne and weeping against her nightdress. It made an incongruous scene, for they had just been politely friendly before, acquainted only through Marty and me, never left alone together, not through antipathy, but because they had little to communicate.

Presently Ruth sat up and began to wipe her eyes. Anne gave her some tissues and she blew her nose. Then she started to talk. The fit of tears seemed to have switched on speech again.

'He won't make her happy, you know,' she said with a kind of proud certainty. 'He didn't before. Last term, before it all finished, she was terribly unhappy. He wasn't even faithful to her. He had other girls when she wasn't there.'

I remembered Marty walking up and down in her room last term saying to me, 'Damn it. Sod it. If only I could get out of this bloody place every night I could stop him doing it.' But it was too risky even for her.

'He knew how I felt,' Ruth went on, 'but he only laughed. He said I was jealous. Marty laughed too when he said that. She knew how ridiculous it was. But she couldn't have told him, could she? She wouldn't do that – she's loyal really, in her way. She understands.'

I felt the heat of embarrassment creeping over my face, but Anne sat pale and quiet, holding Ruth's hand.

'You see,' Ruth went on, 'he must have thought I wanted him. That's why Marty laughed. He's so conceited. If only she hadn't gone back. She could have beaten it. She hadn't seen him all vacation. The worst was over.'

I felt suddenly impatient with Ruth. She obviously had no idea what she was talking about. I had not seen Peter all vacation either.

'She was very good in the vac,' Ruth added, almost smiling to herself. 'She only had one man and he was an old friend, so it doesn't really count, does it? Not for someone like Marty.' She sounded like a schoolteacher making excuses for a favourite pupil who had cheated in an examination. I wondered if I had heard her correctly. In two terms of friendship with Marty I had understood that Louis was the great experience of her life and he had been preceded only by an intimate, but physically unrewarding, friendship with Tom. My head still ached. I wished Ruth would stop talking and go away. I felt that we ought not to be hearing what she said.

'I've got to stop her,' Ruth said feverishly. 'I've got to break it up this term. If it goes on till next year I won't have a chance; we'll be in separate rooms. Then he'll come in any time he likes. But how did he know I was out the other night? Did Marty tell him? That's the awful thing, you see. I daren't leave her for a minute. How am I going to manage?'

She went on like this for some time, becoming more and more distracted, until Anne said gently, 'Ruth, try to calm down. You ought to get some sleep.'

Ruth looked at her wildly and said, 'Yes, I ought. D'you suppose she's asleep, though?'

I shuddered.

Anne said, 'Would you like to stay here tonight? You can have my bed and I'll have cushions on the floor.'

Ruth shook her head. 'No, I'll go back, thank you, Anne. All her things are there, you see. It's better really.' She stood up, smiling graciously at us. 'You've been so kind, both of you.'

After she had gone we both lit cigarettes with simultaneous shaky gestures.

'My God,' I said, 'that was quite something. Talk about broadening one's horizons.'

'Yes,' Anne said seriously. 'Poor Ruth. It's very sad. But it may only be a delayed adolescent phase. She may grow out of it.'

'She sounded pretty far gone to me,' I said. 'What if she doesn't grow out of it?'

'Then I suppose her only hope is to meet someone like herself,' said Anne.

I was silent, wondering why I had never really suspected before. Dozens of things Marty had said about Ruth now acquired a new meaning.

THREE

On Friday Peter phoned to say he couldn't come. Anne had departed, confident I would not be alone, to spend the weekend with Keith, his flat-mate being away. Presumably Peter did not like to run up bills on his parents' phone, for we only had six minutes. Usually he rang from a call-box and we talked endlessly. This time, at least three minutes were taken up with explanations and repetitions of them, as the line was not very good. It was an involved account of business meetings and dinners and promises to his father. I wanted to say, 'But I'm so lonely and I need you : isn't that more important?' In the two years I had known Peter, however, I had never won an argument involving his parents and now I knew better than to try. So I just said, 'I understand, but I miss you, darling.' I tried to see the problem in proportion. One day Peter would have to put me before his parents, but he was young; there was plenty of time. They might even come to like me. It was easy to understand that Peter very sensibly did not wish to antagonize them when one day the whole business would belong to him.

'I miss you too, sweetie,' he said. 'You're having a rotten time; I wish I could be with you. But next weekend I'll make it, I promise.'

'You better had,' I said, trying to sound cheerful. 'I'm getting awfully hungry.'

He sighed. 'I know, darling. It's been a long time.'

It had, too. Five weeks : the longest period of abstinence I had known since our affair began. It had been quite an education for me, though the kind I would willingly have done without. Last term Peter had visited me every other weekend and the fortnightly intervals, bearable because unavoidable, made the walk from the tube to college quite uncomfortable, though the excitement of the reunion was a compensating factor. Five weeks, however, was too long. In a fortnight I could spend one week feeding on weekend memories and the other preparing for our next encounter. But in five weeks there was a drear middle period, leading nowhere, in which the hollow feeling grew and spread, without hope of relief. Before, I had naïvely imagined that I enjoyed sexual inter-course simply because I loved Peter. Now I knew I had become an addict. I became short-tempered as the weeks passed. I was reluctant to go to dances because, although I knew it was Peter or no one for me, I did not want to find out if there was any hardship involved in refusing a stranger.

I worked very hard that weekend. There were exams await-ing us at the end of term but I had never expected to start preparing for them so soon. At this rate I should get an excellent degree, I thought.

I wrote to my parents, telling them I understood, but be-yond that I could think of nothing to say, so the letters were very short. Just then they seemed too remote, as people, for me to worry about them. I posted the letters on Friday night, though the post had gone, just to get them out of the way, and on Saturday there was a letter from my mother. She asked if I would like her to visit me in order to discuss everything. It was the first time she had treated me as an adult by asking my permission, and it made me feel uncomfortable. She also warned me that if the separation culminated in divorce my father might marry again. I did not like the way she put this. It sounded like a challenge, straight, one woman to another : I have lost him, but so have you. Then I knew that my father was already living with someone else and that was why he had not written again. Some things blur with time and it is hard to recreate the intensity of them, but I really do remem-ber with precision how I wished then that Peter were with me.

I read the whole of *Troilus and Criseyde* again that week-end, even pausing to look up words in the glossary, something I was normally too impatient to do. I waded through pages of Old English translation, too. It was all very soothing in its remoteness. Modern poetry would not have helped at all.

In the afternoon of Saturday I got a telegram saying, 'Bloody shame chin up writing love Martin.' I was touched and grateful, but at the same time it seemed odd to me to send such an urgent message as a telegram, symbol of crisis, two days after the event. It was possible, though, that our parents had not written to both of us on the same day; more likely that Martin was quite simply preoccupied. He had been very quiet during the vac, so I knew nothing of his private life, but he had written a great many letters.

College was usually quiet at weekends. People went away, officially or unofficially, or entertained in their rooms. A few studied; perhaps many, I don't know. You can only judge from your immediate circle. Others, maybe the majority, went to theatres, dances, concerts, and returned to gossip and sleep. It is always hard to know whether you represent the norm in any community. At college perhaps most of the population retired to bed early and alone, attended lectures, wrote essays before the eleventh hour, got up for breakfast, discussed work and clothes rather than sex and religion. I cannot tell. Such behaviour would have been odd in our group, but how could we know how odd we seemed to others?

On Sunday evening at about nine, Marty came into my room. Anne had not yet returned. Marty looked beautiful, in a dark green linen suit she had made herself, her hair drawn back and up into a high French pleat. Her face was very care-fully made up, too. Louis at least had a good influence on her appearance, I thought, before remembering I had a grievance to nourish.

She sank into a chair, very relaxed and happy, smiling to herself.

'How are you?' she asked. Her weekend made her considerate, too.

'Fine,' I said shortly. Then she gave me the chance I needed. 'I thought I'd call in on you before facing Ruth,' she said cheerfully. 'I need strengthening. Got any coffee for me?'

'We could have done with some strengthening, too,' I said, 'when Ruth rolled in here at one in the morning looking for you. It's a pity you didn't manage to face her before you went.'

'Oh, God, I am sorry,' Marty said promptly. This enraged me because it seemed too automatic to be sincere. I felt twice as angry as I had been when Ruth was actually there. Jealousy, no doubt: Marty's weekend versus mine.

'I don't believe you,' I said. 'You must have known what would happen when you cleared off. You deliberately left us to pick up the bits. It wasn't very entertaining for either of us. Quite frankly, I'd rather not have heard half the things Ruth said.'

Marty had been watching me carefully and I saw the look of concern in her eyes change to one of calculation. She lit a cigarette, dropping the match on the floor.

'Like that, was it?' she said. 'True confessions. "I was a teenage pervert" and all that.'

'Don't you care?'

'Oh, Lois, calm down. It's not my fault you've led a sheltered life. Of course I care; I'm very fond of Ruth. But I'm not a queer, so I can't help her. I haven't played those little games since I was at that convent boarding-school you always make fun of. I don't suppose Ruth would really do anything – not much, anyway – but I wouldn't chance getting into bed with her to find out.'

'Nobody's asking you to,' I shouted. 'You might just show a little common humanity, that's all.'

'Oh, Lois, be realistic. That's not what Ruth wants. If I can't love her, at least I can make her suffer. From her point of view, it's the next best thing.'

Suddenly I felt very tired and quite out of my depth. 'Is it?' I said. 'I don't know. Maybe I don't understand any of it. I just know she was in a dreadful state when she came to us and I hated every minute of it; and I don't think it was at all fair on Anne.'

Marty frowned. 'Let's leave Anne out of it. You don't mean that, it's just a moral whip to beat me with. Anne's tough and she loves coping; that's why she's so good at it. But I'm not and neither are you. That's something we've got in common. I'm not concerned with Anne, but I am, believe it or not, concerned with our friendship. If I've done the dirty on you (and I know I have really) I'd like to apologize.'

Beaten, and rather glad of it, I put on a pan for coffee.

'Lois?' Marty said. 'Something's wrong, isn't it? I should have realized on Thursday but I was too bloody self-centred to notice. It's more than not seeing Peter, isn't it?'

To my own amazed horror, I promptly burst into tears and when Marty came over to me I grabbed both her hands and hung on, as if to a raft. I howled with dreadful noisy abandon for about two minutes until I felt suddenly exhausted, drained and peaceful. Marty took her hands away, stroked my hair in passing, turned off the gas below the bubbling water and made coffee. She lit a cigarette from the stump of her own and passed it to me.

'It wasn't like you to get so angry with me,' she said, 'so I knew it must be more than Ruth. What's happened?'

I told her all about everything, in much more detail than I had told Anne, and gave her the letters to read. When she had finished with them she said thoughtfully. 'You'll know a lot more when you see your mother. I should let her come.'

'Yes. Anyway, I don't think I can politely stop her.'

'Lois, I really am sorry. When I think how I rambled on all about me on Thursday and all this had happened. I'm a rotten friend. It's lucky you had Anne. I should never be bitchy about her.'

'She's been marvellous,' I said honestly, 'but it's a great

relief to talk to you. I couldn't have talked much on Thursday, though; it would have made it worse, so don't feel too guilty. And if Peter had come this weekend I'd have been fine. It's just the combination of bad luck that's got me down. I'm afraid I must have been envying you rather badly.'

'Envy me while you can.'

'Oh, Marty, don't say it's gone wrong already.'

Marty smiled. 'No. It's heaven. But I'm not such a fool as to believe it'll last for ever.'

I was curious. 'Would you never consider marrying Louis?'

Marty actually laughed at this. 'Oh, Lois, be serious. Of course I wouldn't. Which is just as well, really, since Louis would never consider marrying me.'

'If he would,' I asked, 'what then?'

Marty's face became serious. 'I can't see me marrying anyone,' she said. 'I haven't enough positive qualities. I think you need to be a very stalwart character.'

'I don't follow you,' I said.

'Well . . .' Marty paused, waving her hands in the air. 'You need so many good qualities to make a success of it. I think so, anyway. Like patience. I haven't got any. I'd make a lousy mother. And I don't think I could promise to be faithful all my life.'

'But you're faithful to Louis . . .'

'When he's there, yes. But not when I thought it was all finished.'

'I know,' I said. 'Ruth told me. An old friend of yours.'

'My first,' Marty said.

'I thought Tom was your first.'

'Oh, no . . .' For some reason this amused Marty enormously. 'I taught him all he knew. No, Ray was my first. But I didn't get my little gadget till I met Louis. You ought to get one, you know.'

I shrugged my shoulders. 'Peter looks after all that.'

Marty laughed. 'There's many a mother who said that before the happy event.'

'Oh, well,' I said, 'maybe I'll go after we're married.'

'You may always meet someone else, of course,' Marty said. 'Have you thought of that?'

I was annoyed. 'No, I haven't.'

Marty said gently, 'I'm sorry. Do I sound very callous? I'm really only generalizing from my own experience. I probably envy you marrying your first love and all that.'

'That's something I've always wanted to ask you, Marty. If you do get married, will you tell your husband?'

'You do sound coy. I presume you mean about the other men I've had. No, I won't, because it won't be his affair. I certainly wouldn't want to hear about all the girls he's had. On the other hand I could hardly pretend to be a timid little virgin, so I imagine he'd get the picture without much trouble.'

I was silent. Marty made me feel inexperienced. However, I had provoked a flood of reminiscence.

'Ray's improved a lot,' she said. 'I used to think he was marvellous. I didn't know any better till I met Louis. Then I really learnt something.' She drew her knees up to her chin and shivered.

'Don't do that,' I said. 'I haven't seen Peter for five weeks.'

'Sorry,' Marty said. 'I'll tone it down. I know how you feel. That's why I went back to Ray. I felt awful after finishing with Louis. Ray's very sweet. Now I know what people mean when they say they're just good friends. He's getting married next year.'

'Oh, Marty, really . . .' I said in disgust, yet somehow fascinated.

'What's the matter?' Marty asked, widening her eyes. 'His girl lives in Scotland. What do you expect? I'd finished with Louis and I felt terrible. Ray was lonely. I went to a party at his place and after everybody'd gone we talked and then we went to bed. It was splendid. He must have learnt a lot from her. After that we had several dates a week.'

'Do you always go prepared to parties?'

Marty appeared genuinely surprised. 'I certainly do. Once I didn't and I worried for two whole weeks. I've never forgotten it.'

'Does Louis know what you did in the vac?'

'No, but he knows me. And he wouldn't dream of asking because he knows what he did in the vac and he'd hate me to ask. But we'll probably chuck it all at each other in the next row we have.'

'You're certainly prepared for the worst,' I said.

Marty smiled at me. 'I'm so happy I can afford to be. That doesn't mean it won't break my heart when it comes. But I'm so alive with Louis, you see. I can live so intensely. I know that's a corny line, but it's true. I get drunk with him. That's why I can't stop talking. I'm so full of Louis.'

'In every possible way,' I said.

Marty giggled. 'Oh, good,' she said, 'you're getting crude. It's only a question of practice. I think women are basically much cruder than men, only society encourages them to cover it up and men to let it out. Did I ever tell you how when I was fourteen I was so inhibited I had to go in a cave to shout all the bad words I knew before I could use them? And when I think now how feeble they were, and how few, I could weep!'

There was a pause and we smiled at each other, comfortable in our dissimilarity. We drank what was left of the coffee cold, and lit fresh cigarettes.

'Just one more,' Marty said, 'and then I must face my doom. I ran out of nerve on Thursday but now I feel fortified.'

'All the same,' I said, for we were accustomed to *non sequiturs*, 'I don't think I could sleep with anyone I didn't love.'

'Good for you,' said Marty. 'I hope you never have to.'

FOUR

I HAD a lovely week preparing for Peter. Anne was working hard after taking the weekend off, but we still found plenty of time to talk. She was going away officially the following weekend to attend her sister's birthday party. She did not like Barbara very much and regretted the fact that she and Keith would have to be on their best behaviour.

'I doubt if we'll get any time alone,' she said, 'and what's more, we'll be made to feel the whole time that it's up to Barbara to redeem the honour of the family by marrying an MP or an MFH or something.'

'Don't Keith's prospects count for anything?' I asked.

Anne shook her head. 'My parents live very much in the present. The future doesn't impress them. After all, it may never happen. They argue that Keith may fail his degree, and then what? And they've never really liked the idea of women working after marriage. They only sent me to university to meet the right type. I'm afraid my flag started drooping when I missed out on Oxford.'

'Never mind,' I said, 'it's only for the weekend.'

'That's the best thing about college,' Anne said. 'The freedom to live your own life. I really don't fit into my family.'

'Did you . . . before you met Keith?'

'I suppose so. Yes.' Anne smiled. 'But did you have to remind me?'

I was already thinking of other things.

'Anne . . .'

'What?'

'Suppose our parents knew what was going on at college?'

'Do you think they don't?'

'Oh, Anne, surely . . . They'd say, they'd do something . . .'

'Such as what? Don't forget, once they send us away they're helpless. I think a kind of self-protecting double-think sets in. Logically, they must suspect; emotionally, they can't accept it. They don't ask and we don't tell them. All quite simple and civilized. They don't want to pry and we don't want to worry them. Provided we don't go home pregnant there's no reason why the subject should ever be discussed.'

'I suppose you're right. But it's hypocrisy, isn't it?'

'A virtue, if you ask me.'

'That's funny – not something I expected to hear from you.'

'Oh, look –' Anne frowned. 'Don't get me wrong. I'm basically honest. But I think a certain amount of hypocrisy is vital between parents and children and that's what we were discussing. It's only another name for respecting each other's rights and privacy.'

I sighed. 'It must be very difficult being a parent, especially of teenagers.'

'Oh, I've no doubt it is,' Anne said. 'At least it doesn't happen suddenly – not the teenage part, anyway.'

The week passed slowly, like any space of time advancing towards delight. But I was not impatient; I savoured the delay. It seemed a long time since I had had so much to look forward to. I had only one letter from Peter, telling me about trains and with just a few words of love at the end. I read it over and over. I had a blonde rinse to lighten my hair to the shade he liked.

There is an unreality about summer days at college. Even though you have work to do, this is fluid and adaptable to your chosen routine. In an ordinary job, the summer must pass you by; head down, at your office desk or shop counter, you are only given the tag-end of it, in the evening, when it is already cooling and the scent is a little dusty. At college you can sunbathe religiously on the roof, or lie in a deckchair in the quadrangle between old stone buildings, watching the light making the grass sparkle. The print dances in the book on your lap and you peer at it behind dark glasses. And then at the end of term you are given three months of vacation. I always felt that someone had made me a present of the summer and a vacation job, though necessary, was almost sacrilegious. Never again in my life would I have the chance of watching so much time trickle warmly past. As in childhood, the weather seemed charmed, as I look back on it now. Illusions are precious; there are so few of them to keep.

A letter came from Martin during the week, but it was mainly concerned with the doings of someone called Rick, who, it seemed, was a marvellous chap and practically certain to get a double first and be the cox in next year's Boat Race. Rick did worth-while things with his vacations, such as touring the Continent with about fivepence in his pocket while he, Martin, remained miserably at home, playing gardener or postman according to the season. Later on in the letter Martin said it was a shame about our parents, but maybe they would be happier apart. In a postcript he invited Peter and me to the May Ball. At a loss how to answer all this, I put it on one side, mentally reserving the weekend as my excuse. Besides, Martin would feel more comfortable if it were my turn to write.

On Saturday I got up at nine, missing breakfast but reinforced by eleven hours' sleep, and spent an hour on my appearance. I sprayed myself freely with Peter's favourite scent.

'Is Peter going to stay the night?' Anne asked.

'I don't know. I hope so, but he may think it's too risky.'

'I suppose our luck's bound to run out some time. Hotel then?'

'I don't know.'

'I'm sorry Keith's room-mate isn't away again or you could have his flat as we won't be there.' Remembering where they would be, Anne made a face. 'Spare me a thought, won't you?'

'Maybe it won't be as bad as you expect.'

Anne just shook her head slowly and emphatically.

Keith came to call for her before I was ready to leave for the station. He was very brown from an outdoor vacation and made Anne look very fair and fragile, though she was in fact quite sturdy.

'Hullo, Lois, have a good weekend,' he said before he was quite through the door. We shook hands. 'It's your turn to be happy while we suffer for our sins,' he added.

Anne took over on the hair I was unsuccessfully back-brushing.

'You are a gloomy pair,' I said, laughing. I already felt a little dizzy from expectation and to think of Peter too often was distinctly uncomfortable.

'You may laugh, honey,' said Keith, 'but you don't have to face a young lady you put across your knee and spanked only a month ago.'

'Why? You never told me . . .'

'Oh, she pushed Anne into the swimming-pool,' Keith said carelessly. 'Fully dressed. But I won't deny I'd been looking for an excuse.'

They grinned at each other. The affection between them was tough and bright and obvious.

'They don't like me, do they, your folks?' Keith said, deliberately accentuating his northern accent, and Anne giggled and said, a poor copy, 'No. They don't.'

'Hey, Lois, this term's got off to a cracking start, hasn't it?' Keith said suddenly. 'Marty's gone back to her gigolo and it turns out she's sharing a room with a queer. Ever thought of getting in touch with the Sunday papers? Be one way of augmenting your grant.'

'Oh, Keith,' I protested, 'you can't call Louis a gigolo.'

'Nonsense,' said Keith briskly. 'Chap's a bloody frog, isn't he? They're all the same, these foreigners, coming over here and sleeping with our sisters. Horse-whipping's too good for 'em.'

'Oh, Keith, shut up,' said Anne, wiping her eyes. 'Not

everybody appreciates your sense of humour and Marty is Lois's friend, after all.'

'Quite true,' said Keith solemnly. 'Can't blame the girl for sleeping with a gigolo if she's only got a queer for company. Girl ought to be locked up. Beat it out of her. None of this psychiatric muck. They're getting too soft these days; that's why we're losing the Empire. It's all this decadence, y'know.'

We both choked and spluttered. Keith looked round with an air of innocence.

'Just getting into trim for my true blue Tory weekend,' he said. 'Anne's mother is only waiting till the hangman retires, you know. Been after his job for years, weaving a rope from her own hair.'

He blew me a kiss from the doorway, his arm round Anne. 'Have a good time, love,' he said in parting.

I was at the station half an hour before Peter's train was due. The arrival board told me it would be ten minutes late. I sat in the hall and stared at this information for a while, but the other people there seemed so calm and bored that they depressed me and took away my excitement. I went outside again and wandered around looking in the cheap jewellery shops. This led me on to thoughts of rings and hotels until I went back to the station and went to the lavatory from sheer nerves. After that I stared at my reflection in the ladies' room mirror. Anne had done my hair beautifully and I dared not touch it. I lit a cigarette and wandered around the station. It did not reflect any of the dramas enacted on its platforms. Stations never do. They are drab and depressing, even a little pompous. I doubt if anything can be done to improve them. Keith would probably say they are part of our British heritage and should be left undefiled by the beast called Progress.

When the train did arrive I could hardly believe it was the train, my train. It looked so ordinary. Why was it not festooned with flowers and ribbons? Then began the awful business of searching through all the heads and hurrying bodies. He was never among the first. It was terrible if there was still no sign of him when the crowd started to thin out. Then I always started to invent reasons why he was still in his compartment: wrestling with a suitcase, arguing with the guard.

I saw him. With a lurching heart, I stood and gasped as with cold-water shock. He looked just the same, only, after six weeks and so much concentrated yearning thought, the physical sight of him was like a blow. He seemed sharper, clearer, more dramatic than all the others around him. They were dead automatons and Peter the only living man.

I stood and watched him hurry towards me; he saw me a moment after I saw him. I wanted to enjoy his steady approach, so I only ran the last few yards and then we were hugging each other.

'Hullo, darling,' Peter said and kissed me. We walked quickly back along the platform. I felt weak with relief.

'Oh, darling,' I said, 'it's so wonderful to see you. I was afraid something would happen to stop you right up to the last minute.'

'You are silly,' said Peter. 'I promised, didn't I? Come on, let's go and have lunch.'

'Oh,' I said, surprised, 'I thought we'd have it at college. I got you a ticket.'

'Well, you can get a refund. It's always something ghastly on Saturdays and I want to take you out.'

Eventually we found somewhere Peter considered clean enough to eat in and I had chicken and Peter had a steak. I studied his face. I thought he looked pale and tired, not rested after his holiday.

'How was the cruise?' I asked.

He made a face. 'Oh, bloody. A bore.'

'Have you been working too hard?'

'Why?' He looked up sharply.

'You look worn out.'

'Oh. Yes, it has been a bit rough. Dad's been turning on the heat.'

'Does that mean no more weekends?' Strengthened by his presence, I thought I could hear the worst but I did not really expect it, even so.

'Well, I don't really know. It might. For a while, anyway. Dad's got a lot of plans for expansion, giving me more responsibility and so on. You won't want to hear all the details.'

'Oh, well,' I said, 'I suppose it's all for our good eventually.'

'What about you, darling?' Peter asked. 'I'm sorry I wasn't there when you needed me. Anything new?'

'I had a letter from Mother, another one. It seems my father's got someone else.'

'My God, already?'

'Well, I don't know when it began, but Mother says he may remarry if they get divorced.'

'Oh, if. Then it isn't settled. That's something.'

'She didn't say, but I imagine it is really. She wouldn't hang on to Dad just to be vindictive and he may want to marry this someone else.'

Peter laid down his knife and fork. 'Well, I must say you sound very calm about it, darling.'

For some reason I felt angry and disappointed, so I answered with a remark I had never imagined I would make.

'You forget,' I said. 'I've had a week to get used to it.'

Peter did not retaliate and I felt guilty at once.

'I'm sorry, darling,' I said. 'But I've been so lonely and miserable, and things have been jumping for everyone else.'

'Oh, really,' said Peter. 'Tell me more.' He sounded genuinely interested, so I brought him up to date on Marty and Louis and Ruth, throwing in Ray for good measure. He listened attentively, but when I had finished he said abruptly, 'Your friend Marty seems a bit of a tart.'

I flinched. 'I don't think so.'

'You mean she does it all for free? That's the only difference I can make out.'

'You've never liked her,' I said stubbornly.

Peter shrugged his shoulders. 'I suppose that's true. I can't get used to your being friends with these people, somehow.'

'What do you mean – these people?'

'Well, they seem a pretty loose lot at your college.'

'Marty and who else?'

He was silent, saying at last, 'Well, there's that girl she shares a room with . . .'

'Ruth. She doesn't do anything loose, she just suffers.'

'God! It's just like a Russian comedy. Aren't there any normal people there at all?'

'Plenty. Only I don't know them. Anne's normal, though. What about her?'

Now we were both quiet, shocked. 'Peter,' I said eventually, 'do you realize we've been fighting, all about nothing, and you've hardly got off the train and we haven't met for six weeks?'

Peter took a deep breath. 'Sorry, darling. It's my fault. I shouldn't criticize your friends.'

We clasped hands across the table. 'Let's go,' I said.

We took a taxi to college and went straight to my room. I drew the curtains and put the *Verboten* notice on the door. We clung to each other and kissed as desperately as if we were parting already instead of meeting with the whole weekend ahead. Then we undressed quickly and got into bed, between the sheets, properly, as we always did because it seemed to make it more like being married and less like a love affair. We were both very excited; the first touch of skin on skin after so long apart is supremely thrilling. But I had looked forward too much to this love-making and it was over too soon. Peter was too quick for me. I had hardly settled down to enjoy it and luxuriate in it (for great excitement can almost be an impediment to pleasure) before his climax came. I nearly wept with disappointment; I went on moving, unable to accept defeat. Peter apologized. I hated him. I turned on my side, quite unable to indulge in our usual aftermath of tenderness.

Peter lit a cigarette. I lay with my face to the wall, violently hating him, wrestling with the pain. We had never had such a disastrous failure.

He said, 'Anything I can do?'

And I snapped back, 'Don't be so bloody stupid.'

He sighed heavily. 'Sorry, darling.'

The worst was over, I suppose, after about twenty minutes, and ten minutes after that I turned to Peter and put my head on his shoulder.

'Sorry I was so beastly,' I said, 'but I felt awful.'

'I know. It was my fault.'

'No, just too long since the last time. Can't blame you for being quick after six weeks.'

'I'll try and make it up to you next time,' Peter said.

If all had gone well I would have been asleep by now, but as it was I suddenly felt restless and full of energy. 'Come on,' I said to Peter, 'let's get up and go for a walk.'

He put his arms round me again before we got dressed. 'You're very lovely, did I ever tell you?' he said.

My hair was a little spoilt from bed, so I put a scarf over it and we went out, holding hands.

'My mother wants to come for a weekend,' I said, 'to talk about it all.'

Peter said casually, 'Is there any hope of them patching it up?'

'I shouldn't think so,' I said, surprised. 'Why?'

'Oh, no reason. It would just make it easier for you.'

'I wonder if it would? I think I'd only be waiting and watching for the next time. It's funny, you know – the sort of thing you imagine could never happen to you, like suicide or abortion.'

'Oh, darling, what a comparison.' Peter sounded vaguely uneasy.

'Well, you know what I mean. It's essentially someone else's misfortune. Marty's parents were divorced, and then her father died and her mother married a clergyman. I often wondered how far that explains Marty.'

'I don't see why it should explain anything.'

'Oh, Peter, surely. Everyone knows that broken homes affect children . . .'

'Yes, darling, but they can be made an excuse for bad behaviour too, don't you think? I would say your friend is just promiscuous by nature and it's no good trying to blame her parents.'

I protested. 'I said it, she didn't. She hardly ever mentions them. Anyway I'm not sure you can be promiscuous by nature.'

Peter lit a cigarette, striking the match so roughly that it broke and he had to use another. 'Oh, darling, what rubbish,' he said.

To my own surprise I stopped and stamped my foot. Some passers-by glanced at us curiously and I was reminded of childish tantrums but still felt unashamed.

'Look, Peter,' I said, 'we're going to have to decide something. Either we drop the subject of Marty completely or we'll have to have a full-scale row about her.'

'It's a deal,' Peter said, and we walked on. Presently he said, 'I'm spoiling this weekend, aren't I?'

'Of course you're not.'

He sighed. 'Bless you. Can I make it up to you? Let me take you out to a dinner and a show.'

I suppose I showed no sign of delight, for he said anxiously, 'Please, darling. Don't you want to go?'

'Yes,' I said, 'but I thought we were going to have a quiet evening in my room. We don't usually go out when you come for such a short time.'

'I know, but I want to show you off.'

I felt a pang of disappointment; at the same time I was excited. 'All right,' I said, 'it's always nice to go out with a rich boy.'

'Shut up, woman,' said Peter. But he sounded more cheerful.

We had to go back to college because I insisted on changing to do Peter justice. I put on a dark silky dress and high-heeled pale shoes and took a lot of trouble with my hair. Peter watched and hugged me when I had finished. 'Gorgeous,' he said.

' "Thank you, kind sir," she said. Sure you don't want to change your mind and stay in?'

'Don't tempt me.'

'Why not? Go on, let me.' But he was already holding the door open for me.

'D'you know,' I said, 'you're the only man I ever met who could give the appearance of evening dress while wearing a lounge suit.'

We had a taxi into the West End, which reminded me of an old grievance.

'Do you think your father will ever let us have the car for one of our weekends?' I asked.

'I doubt it. He's convinced I'd go in for speeding on a long trip.'

'You should have your own car,' I said. 'Then you could use it any time you like.'

'Cars cost money, darling.'

'I know that, but you're not poor, are you? If you are, what are we doing in this taxi?'

'Lois, there's a slight difference between taking the occasional taxi ride and buying and running your own car. I may be the boss's son but I'm still only a trainee and I don't get paid a millionaire's salary.'

'If only millionaires ran cars,' I said, 'there'd be no parking problem, would there?'

'Well, you know what I mean,' Peter said, not laughing. 'Don't go on at me, darling.'

'Sorry,' I said, feeling suddenly lonely. 'That's our third fight in six hours, isn't it? It all goes back to having a flop in bed, doesn't it? I suppose I'm still subconsciously resentful and you're subconsciously guilty, and there you are.'

'For God's sake,' Peter said, 'cut out the psychology.'

I persisted. Sometimes there is no limit to the stupidity of the young. 'But it's true,' I said. 'That's the most logical explanation.'

Peter ran his fingers through his hair. 'For Christ's sake, Lois,' he said, in a loud voice, 'cut it out.'

'Don't shout,' I said coldly.

There is a dreadful fascination about a row with someone you love. After the first pain of wishing you had not begun, you seem to encounter a new flood of energy and a perverse satisfaction in inflicting wounds. The reckoning comes later.

Peter passed me the evening paper, open at the entertainments page, and I indicated the shows that appealed to me. We got tickets for the five-thirty matinée at the first of them; in fact we were just in time. But we did not start to repair the quarrel until the first interval. Peter took me for a drink. We both had brandy and clinked glasses.

'To us,' I said, 'with all our faults.'

'Are you enjoying the show, darling?' Peter asked me.

'The music's lovely,' I said, 'but that chap isn't nearly as handsome as you.' Absurdly, I wanted to cry. 'Peter,' I said, 'd'you think we'll fight like this when we're married?' It seemed a long while since we had discussed that future time. Six months ago it had been our most engrossing topic of conversation.

The bell rang for the second act, and Peter, without answering, took me back to our seats. They were excellent seats, the best we had ever been in. I lapsed into a private dream of our future, after we were married; how important and secure I should feel as Peter's wife. I peered at my bare left hand in the semi-darkness. I resented it more and more since Anne had become engaged. We had always agreed that there was no point in a long engagement and we could not be married until I graduated at twenty-one. But that was more than two years away and I felt a spasm of rebellion. Perhaps we were being too sensible. Anyway, I was already Peter's mistress (I loved this old-fashioned word), so surely I deserved a ring? Then I felt awful; guilty of reducing our love to a mercenary basis.

In the next interval I said to Peter, 'If you'd bought me a ring we could have gone to an hotel.'

Peter said, 'Sorry, darling.'

'But we can still go if you like,' I added. 'I can keep my gloves on.'

'What, at breakfast?' Peter asked.

I laughed. I thought this was the first joke Peter had made that day, and stupidly I said so.

'Do you normally count them?' he asked sharply.

'No,' I said, 'but I'm counting fights, so be warned.' I tried to keep my voice light but I was frightened.

'Hope you're sound on double figures,' he said grimly. And then the bell rang for the last act. I felt rather confused, probably through brandy on an empty stomach. I reached for Peter's hand towards the end of the show, expecting to be rejected, but to my surprise he took hold of it in a clutch of desperate strength. I loved him very much then and wished that we could melt into each other through our sticky hands and become one person instead of two who kept having fights.

Afterwards we stepped outside into the light, chilly dusk of a spring evening. Peter hailed another taxi and gave the man the name of our special restaurant. It was warm and leather-smelling in the taxi and our latest row seemed to have evaporated like the others. We clung together and kissed as London whirled and tramped and hooted past us. I said, 'We've been doing what Hemingway calls misunderstanding on purpose,' and Peter nodded and kissed me again. 'Oh, I love you, I love you,' I repeated between kisses; it was like hearing someone else speak, as if something alien inside me were trying to make up for lost time. 'Darling,' said Peter and I gazed deep into his eyes and felt drunk with gazing. 'Let's have a very quick dinner,' I said.

We drank wine with our dinner and were very gay. I felt

wonderfully confident once I started making Peter laugh again. I told him about our lectures and seminars and imitated my rather eccentric tutor. 'I wrote a marvellous essay on Donne,' I said, 'all due to us, darling, all our favourites. He was quite pleased with it, only he's prejudiced. He feels early Milton isn't getting a fair look in these days; the Metaphysicals are sweeping the board. I think he feels each new batch of students ought to reinforce his own good taste and when we disappoint him he abandons us.' I went on in this vein for some time.

We arrived back at college complete with champagne to drink in bed. I tried to assume that Peter would stay the night, but I was afraid to ask and postponed it till some favourable moment.

'Now,' said Peter, 'for what you really deserve.'

At first I was very conscious of his skill and care, but soon pleasure took over and I was conscious of nothing but that. This was what I had longed for in all our weeks of separation; this fulfilled and refreshed me. It was not until he was sure of my delight that Peter seemed to relax and participate completely. I wished it could go on for ever, poised on the very edge of climax, yet I longed to fall over it, too, and hurtle down to peace. We arrived together, still fairly rare for us, for we had not had unlimited opportunities for practice and those we had were often far from ideal. I watched Peter's face; it was only at moments like this that I felt he really belonged to me.

Peter buried his face in my neck and stroked my hair. This was the time I loved best of all. I thought how wonderful it would be when we were married and could have times like this whenever we wanted to. I felt so contented that even the edge of the two years' wait was blunted for me.

All too soon Peter sat up and we drank some of the champagne. I thought it was perfect. Then Peter glanced at his watch.

'My God!' he exclaimed. 'It's five to ten.'

'It doesn't matter,' I answered, still drugged with happiness. 'You're staying, aren't you?'

'I can't, darling,' he said, scrambling up and into his clothes at fantastic, almost comic speed.

'No one will come,' I protested. 'Anne's away; none of my friends will come with the notice on the door; there's only the porter and there's no reason why he –'

'No reason – but he might, all the same.'

'But you stayed last term,' I said, desperate, almost ready to cry.

'We were crazy to risk it,' said Peter, straightening his tie. Already he seemed more remote in his beautiful clothes. I threw on bra and pants, slacks and sweater, just as the bell rang for all visitors to leave the building, and we charged along the corridors together and out through the main door under the half-amused, half-disapproving eyes of the porter.

The night was chill now, and I felt I had plunged into a cold bath. It was incongruous and wrong.

'I did so want to sleep with you again,' I said, 'as if we were married. Not just to make love and separate. I was so sure you'd stay.'

'You could be sent down, darling,' said Peter. 'Only the other day I read about a girl at Oxford. They only rusticated the boy, but they sent the girl down. I didn't want to risk that again.'

I remembered then what Anne had said about luck running out, but I still felt cheated.

'Then why no hotel?' I demanded. 'You could have bought me a ring this afternoon.'

'No, darling, it's risky. You could meet anyone. All sorts of people visit London and it would be just our luck to run into someone.'

'I suppose you're right,' I said sulkily. 'I just hate your being sensible, that's all.'

Peter sighed. 'I'm afraid I've got to be,' he said. He sounded very old.

46

'Cheer up, darling,' I said. 'Tonight was so gorgeous and there's more than half tomorrow before your train.'

Peter said nothing but squeezed my hand and we walked up and down the road from college, past couples kissing good night in the shadows.

'I feel so much better,' I said. 'Really set up.' I expected Peter to make one of the crude jokes we liked, but he didn't.

'You'll finish the champagne, won't you, darling?'

'Of course I will,' I said. 'Catch me wasting something like that.'

We walked to and fro in silence for a while and I envied the people in houses, with homes of their own, lights and television and furniture, comfortably taking each other for granted. I knew Peter and I would have a superior relationship to theirs, but at least they were enjoying their second-rate happiness now.

'Darling,' I said, suddenly anxious, 'will you get anywhere to sleep so late at night?'

Peter seemed to be jolted out of some private reverie. 'Oh, I expect so,' he said, 'but it is a point. Maybe I ought to go now in case I have to try a few places. Then you could get an early night.'

'What time shall we meet in the morning?' I asked. Then as Peter didn't answer I said, 'Will nine-thirty be all right?'

'Nine-thirty,' said Peter. Then he took me in his arms again and kissed my mouth and my eyes and held me very close. 'Sleep well, darling,' he said. 'I love you.'

It was only as he was walking away that I realized it was the first time he had said the words during the whole day. I went back to my room, smelling hotly of sex and sweat, drank the champagne, got into bed and fell asleep too suddenly for thought.

FIVE

In the morning there was no Peter waiting for me at nine-thirty. I waited on the steps for fifteen minutes. Then the porter came out of another building and walked towards the main entrance.

'Morning, Miss Mitchell,' he said. 'Did you find your letter?'

'Letter?' I repeated.

'Pinned on the notice-board,' he said, going on past me. 'Must have dropped through the letter box real early. No stamp – Sunday, of course.'

I retraced my steps. True enough, pinned on the notice-board where I had rushed past it in my excitement was a letter to me. It was in Peter's handwriting and I opened it expecting to find a change of plan, nothing more. It is strange that you seldom have premonitions when you should.

It was the first letter of this type I had ever received.

Dearest Lois,

I don't know how to write this letter but I must and I'll be on the train when you read it. I'm sorry it had to be another letter, after the ones you've had from your parents, but I think it's easier for both of us than saying it all face to face. Maybe I'm just a coward. If so I'm sorry.

The first thing I want to say is that I wasn't lying when I said I loved you. I couldn't say it before and I was afraid you'd notice. I did mean it, only it was a different sort of love from what I used to feel for you. It's very hard for me to explain and you're so analytical – it would be better for you to be writing this to me. Believe me, darling, I wish to God you were. But this is the best I can do. I still find you very attractive, as you must realize. And I still feel very fond of you and admire and respect you. None of that has changed. But I no longer feel miserable when we're apart or count the days till I see you. I lied about last weekend. I stayed away on purpose to try to sort out my feelings. But I decided I ought to see you again first and I did plan to talk it over with you. Only at the last minute I couldn't. What it adds up to is this. I no longer feel strong enough for all the fighting that lies ahead if we are to get married. I can't picture our life together as clearly as I used to. My parents haven't tried to influence me but I know they feel very badly about your parents, and they care a lot about my taking over the business one day and because of that about whom I marry. But you must believe they've never tried to turn me against you. It's just that I find I'm more their son than I thought I was.

There is another thing too. I don't want to lie to you, though maybe I should. While I was on the cruise I met someone. Her name is Angela. I'm not in love with her but I feel I could be one day. I feel I could be happy with her or someone like her, and without any effort. She's away in finishing school in Switzerland so it may come to nothing, but if I can feel like this it's obviously not right of me to let things go on between us the same as ever.

We're both very young and you could easily have met someone you preferred to me in your first term at college. I wish you had. I wish I didn't have to write this letter. You deserve a lot better than me. I often used to think I couldn't keep pace with you, anyway. I don't know half the books you've read, for a start. I suppose I'm just lazy. And I don't get on with your friends. This is probably my fault, I'm very prejudiced, I suppose. I thought it all over on the cruise. I only had vague ideas before and tried to squash them because we were usually so happy. It's been a wonderful two years, Lois, and I'll always be grateful to you.

All the things that irritated me came to the surface today, that's why I behaved so badly. And I had a guilty conscience because I couldn't come out with it. Perhaps you'll feel I had no right to go to bed with you, in the circumstances. But I couldn't avoid it, without telling you the truth, and besides I wanted to, as I think I've explained. And the second time was vital, to make up for the first, I'd have felt ten times worse to have left you like that. I hope you understand and don't feel I've behaved too badly. Believe me, I didn't mean to cheapen you or take advantage or anything like that. You're a beautiful and wonderful person, Lois, and I hope one day you meet someone really worthy of you, and when you do you mustn't let anything we've done stand between you. I'd have made you a rotten husband anyway. I think perhaps you built me up in your mind into a better person than I really am. I don't think I can offer you half as much as you really want.

I've read this over, and I sound like a pious bastard. Maybe I should just have said, 'Well, I fell out of love and that's that.' After all it could happen to anyone in any relationship. But it didn't feel as simple as that to me. You've made me very critical of the truth and I felt there was more to it than that and you deserved an honest explanation, as far as I could provide one.

Take care of yourself, darling, and forget all about me. And don't worry. There is nothing to worry about. I was specially careful.

I wish it had never come to this, especially now, with your parents and everything. But I couldn't get through tomorrow and if I did I think you'd hate me more afterwards. I hate myself quite a bit anyway.

Peter

Being jilted was something that only happened to other people, too.

SIX

It was half-term before my mother came. That is to say it was a weekend half-way through the term which my mother treated exactly like a school holiday, although at college it was unrecognized as such. She declined to be met at the station, somewhat to my relief, and arrived at college by taxi. It appeared prudence and marriage had departed together. She had returned to secretarial work after a brisk refresher course (which showed admirably prompt self-organization, I thought) and my father was naturally sending her a proportion of his salary as well.

It was strange that my mother should pay her first visit to me in these circumstances. Last term they had both planned to come, but my father had succumbed to flu.

I hugged her instinctively and took her along to my room. She had lost a little weight but was still fairly plump and she had the same powdery scent when I kissed her cheek.

'You're looking well,' I said, without much thought. She certainly did not look ill or tragic.

'Bearing up,' she said. 'But you look a bit peaky. Been working too hard?'

'I expect so.' I put on the kettle. 'I'll make you some tea. It shouldn't take long.'

She surveyed the room, specially tidy for the occasion. 'Well,' she said critically, 'you're very cosy here. How d'you like sharing a room?'

'It's fine,' I said. 'Anne's very easy to live with.' I had told her this several times before; she must be nervous.

'And am I going to meet this Anne?' she asked.

'Yes, of course. She's out shopping but you'll see her at lunch.'

'Will she be here all the time?'

'Oh, no, she's going away for the weekend, visiting her parents,' I said quickly.

'Oh, good,' said my mother, 'then we can talk.'

'We can talk now,' I said.

She seemed flustered. 'Well, you know what I mean.' She fumbled in her bag and produced a packet of cigarettes. So she was no longer using the case my father had bought her a few years ago. We each had a cigarette and sat on opposite sides of the fireplace, not quite looking at one another.

'Lois, what's the matter?' she asked suddenly. 'Is it this business?'

I shrugged my shoulders. 'I'm naturally not overjoyed.'

She frowned. 'It's more than that.' Then quickly, with maternal instinct or something equally repulsive, she found the spot. 'Have you quarrelled with Peter?'

I got up, wishing there were a fire to poke or some other violent, mundane action to perform. 'It's over.'

'Oh, Lois, I am sorry. How awful for you. When?'

'Oh, earlier this famous term. Does it matter?'

'I'm sorry. Don't you want to discuss it?'

'No.'

I seemed to have discouraged her from all conversation and made her feel awkward. She sat in silence, fidgeting with her hands, while I made the tea. Living on coffee, I had forgotten how the smell of tea nauseated me. I poured out one cup and gave it to her.

'Aren't you having any?'

'I don't like it – don't you remember?'

At that moment Anne came in. I was so relieved I nearly embraced her.

'Hullo, Mrs Mitchell,' she said warmly, holding out her hand. She looked golden and confident, wearing a yellow

52

dress. Yesterday she had been to the hairdresser and her hair was at its best.

'This is Anne,' I said.

They shook hands and my mother said, 'I must congratulate you, mustn't I?'

'There's no law –' I said, but Anne flashed me a disapproving look.

'No – I hope you'll be very happy,' said my mother.

'Thank you very much,' said Anne.

And then I heard myself saying, 'Don't put a jinx on Anne, Mother.'

I was as shocked as they were. They both stared at me and I felt there should be someone else for me to turn and stare at.

'Sorry,' I said. 'Don't know what's the matter with me.' I had felt numb for a month and there was a fascination about saying dreadful things just to see if any feeling penetrated.

They resumed their pleasantries to fill the gap.

'May I see your ring?' my mother asked, and Anne held out her hand.

'Lovely,' said my mother. 'An unusual choice, opals. Easy to see you're not superstitious.'

'They're my birth stone,' Anne said.

'Oh, really?' said my mother. 'Then they must be lucky for you, mustn't they?'

And then – by mercy of the powers, the fates, the gods – the bell rang for lunch. We sat with Marty and Ruth. Anne was very warm and interested in everything my mother said, and Ruth was very polite and correct. Between them, I thought, they covered the range of model daughters pretty well. But it was to Marty that I really owed a bouquet. She had the knack of rapidly discovering what amused someone new and then playing on it. She adapted herself splendidly to my mother, arranging lots of harmless little jokes in a long, satiric account of our first days at college and the endless confusion of bells, meals, corridors, notice-boards and lectures. We all took turns in waiting on my mother.

'It's really only a kind of highbrow Lyons,' said Marty, and my mother laughed happily. I felt hysterical and had to fight my impulse to leap on to the table, trampling on the dishes, and give my mother a potted biography of each of her companions.

Ruth was very subdued. Since that night in our room I had seen very little of her but on the few occasions we all met it seemed odd to watch her and Anne behaving like polite strangers again. Marty, after one star-splitting row with Ruth, had embarked on a policy of deliberate subjugation mixed with occasional bursts of brief but unexpected kindness which apparently had the effect of reducing Ruth to tears.

'Once in a while I stay in and let her brush my hair,' Marty had said, 'but when she gets too sentimental I start talking about Louis. That shuts her up. I'm paving the way for him to come here in the afternoons. I like making love in college; it's more exciting somehow. Hearing the virginal footsteps along the corridor makes quite an aphrodisiac. We've got a good few virgins in our corridor; you can tell from their constipated expressions. If they only knew. I bet they'd like to watch. I bet Ruth would like to watch. She'd pretend to be Louis.'

I had protested, fascinated, but queasy in my stomach.

'No, Lois, it's true. Face facts,' she said. 'I know, because the first time I wanted to go to bed with Louis he was making love to another girl. You see, I went home with his roommate, and Louis was already in bed with this girl, so Jerry and I got into the other bed. Then when we'd finished we had some more to drink – we were all pretty high to start with – and danced a bit and eventually we changed partners and did it again, only this time we timed it so we could watch each other. It was terribly exciting.'

'But hell,' I said, 'weren't you embarrassed?'

'I told you,' said Marty patiently, 'we·had enough to drink. As soon as I saw Louis doing things to this girl I knew I wanted him.'

'You're perverted,' I said.

She shrugged. 'What does that mean? Only that it doesn't appeal to you.'

'But it's abnormal,' I protested.

Marty shook her head. 'Not necessarily. You'd need a survey to prove that, and very honest answers. Anyway, what does it matter if it works? If you don't feel ashamed of going to bed with someone, why feel ashamed of making it more exciting? This is only one of many methods.'

'I don't know,' I said, 'but all my instincts are against it.'

'So were mine once,' said Marty. 'Have you not discovered yet how fascinating the thing that revolted you can be?'

And then I was frightened and disturbed.

'I'm going to telephone Louis,' Marty had said. 'I get a pain just thinking about it.'

'Okay for you,' I said, 'but where does that leave me?'

Her face changed, becoming serious. She took hold of my hand in both hers.

'I'm not heartless,' she said. 'I want to help. Sex is the great healer, not time. At least, it's a whole lot faster than time, I've always found. I can't talk to you about Peter because I only want to say what sods men are and that won't help you. I've only once been in love with someone I lost for good and I know what it feels like and nothing anyone says is any good, the only thing is sex with someone else and it doesn't much matter who it is.'

'Someone you lost for good,' I repeated. 'But you got Louis back.'

Marty's eyes were very dark and bright. 'I know,' she said. 'I was talking about Ray.'

The shock made me forget myself.

'Oh, Marty, I am sorry. I had no idea –'

Marty smiled savagely. 'Well, why should you? I don't go

55

round wearing a placard on my back. What's the matter? Surprised I wasn't always a tough little girl? You don't get born with a skin as tough as mine, you know; you grow it carefully, day by day, and sometimes people help you.'

After lunch we had coffee with my nice little friends, as my mother called them afterwards in private, and then I took her on a tour of the college. She seemed fascinated by the lecture halls.

'You don't have far to come,' she observed.

'No,' I said. 'It's good being residential. So long as you wear a gown you can practically sneak in in your nightie.'

We wandered round the library, empty on a Saturday afternoon as usual except for two true students. Even the swinging of the doors seemed an intrusion on their silence. The library was very cool and smelt of books and furniture polish. My mother stared around her and I wondered if she had ever been in a place like this before. The young are very snobbish, especially about the opportunities their parents give them.

'Do you like it here, Lois?' she asked as we walked away, back into the sunshine. 'Are you glad you came?'

'Oh, yes,' I said. 'It's a splendid opportunity.'

This seemed to shut her up for a while. I took her on a tour of the gardens which really looked quite good at this time of year.

'Have you thought any more about what you're going to do eventually?' she asked, as we were inspecting a flowerbed.

'No,' I said, 'but I've got two years to chew it over. And in our third year they give us career booklets.'

We walked on past the clump of plants Marty always said excited her because they smelt of sweat.

'I'm sorry,' my mother said, 'that you're having such a bad time this term.'

'Oh, well,' I said, 'into each life some rain must fall. Maybe I'm getting the whole rainy season over in five weeks.'

There was a note from Anne in our room. 'I'm off,' it said.

'Ask your mother to have my buns at tea-time. I enjoyed meeting her. Try to be kind, won't you? I think she's very unhappy.'

I screwed it up and threw it in the waste-paper basket. 'Anne says you can have her buns at tea-time,' I said.

'Please sit down, Lois,' my mother said. 'I do want to talk to you and so far you've been avoiding me.'

'I haven't left you for a minute.'

'No. You know very well what I mean.'

I sat down unwillingly. 'Can't we postpone it till this evening?'

'No,' said my mother. 'I'd rather get it over. I don't find it easy either.'

There was a pause and she began again. 'It's not your father's fault,' she said, 'not entirely. A lot of it's mine. Things can just die, but when you're married it can take a long time and you don't always notice in time to do anything about it. And sometimes you couldn't do anything about it anyway if you did notice. You couldn't change yourself sufficiently. Do you understand what I'm talking about?'

'Yes,' I said.

'I don't mean it's always like this, for everyone,' she went on. 'I don't know. I've tried to avoid divorced people since it happened. I don't want to join them – it's like a dreadful army somehow.' Her mouth quivered. 'I'm still very fond of your father and I don't want to discuss him with a lot of other women.'

'You don't have to discuss him with me either,' I said.

'I know, but it's not the same thing at all. You're my daughter. I've a right to explain my point of view to you. You'll be going to see him, I don't doubt, and you've always taken his part.'

'Well,' I said, 'since we're being so frank, it was always you and Martin versus us.'

'Yes,' she said meditatively. 'In a way it was. But I didn't mean it to be. I suppose that was my first mistake – giving too much attention to Martin as soon as he was born. But your father was always out so much. I had to make some life for myself.'

'You shouldn't have married a reporter,' I said, smiling. 'They're as bad as sailors.'

'It must have seemed very glamorous to you,' she said bitterly. 'But it isn't, you know. It was irregular hours and meals at any time of the day or night and all sorts of people dropping in and a hard-drinking crowd they were.'

The words washed over me, unreal. I looked at my mother: pale, plump, grey-haired, though once she had been fair and slim like me. I should have to be careful when I grew older.

'I'm fifty,' she said suddenly. 'It's not an easy time of life for a woman.'

'It's all right, Mother,' I said. 'I've read the women's magazines. I know what you mean.' Maybe I was cruel and Anne would have been ashamed of me, but I couldn't feel anything. She looked at me then.

'You're very hard,' she said.

'I'm sorry,' I said. 'I don't mean to be. It just comes out.'

'You're unhappy,' she said. 'And you're young. That's what makes you hard.'

I had the feeling that we were talking not to but past each other.

'Your father's only forty-five,' she said presently.

'I know,' I said. She seemed to be obsessed with ages.

'He thinks he's young enough to start again,' she said, very sadly. 'I don't know how he can fool himself. This girl won't stay with him. She's only nineteen, she'll find someone of her own age and then he'll be all alone.'

I felt uncomfortable. 'Then is it worth divorcing him?'

'It's what he wants,' she said. 'I won't stand in his way. Let him find out for himself if that's what he wants. Maybe he's right and she will stay with him. He said he wanted to find out if he was still alive. That's a funny thing to say, isn't it?'

I nodded, sick. I did not like the spectacle of pain, hers or anyone's.

'He was always a very demanding man,' she went on, 'and I suppose I disappointed him. But there's more to life than just that. There's more to a marriage than just that. You'll find out. Men and women are so different about these things. You young people think it's everything and you're going to live happily ever after.'

I shook my head. 'Please don't say any more.'

'I'm sorry,' she said. 'You don't want to hear. It's quite natural. But I can't talk to my friends. If they're married I'm an embarrassment to them and if they're divorced they want me to join in, become one of them, and I don't want to.' She fiddled with the clasp of her handbag, opening and closing it so often that I wanted to scream or strike her.

'I don't blame that girl too much, you know,' she said. 'He'd been restless for a long time, years. But I thought it was only a phase. I was tired – I didn't want to bother. And you don't feel threatened, you know, after so many years. We had a lot of happy times. I suppose it must be my fault, marrying a man younger than myself.'

'Surely not,' I said, suddenly moved to comfort her because she looked so tired and old. 'Five years can't make that much difference.'

'I don't know,' she said, shaking her head. 'Everyone warned me at the time, but I wouldn't listen.' She smiled faintly, looking at me. 'There you are,' she said. 'That proves I've been young once.'

From that time on I was very gentle with her, just as Anne would have wished me to be. I made tea and we toasted bread and buttered buns carefully. Between tea and supper I took her for a walk and we looked at the shop windows. She talked about her job; she enjoyed going out to work again but she found it tiring and it meant she couldn't keep the house as she liked it. She was wondering whether to get a woman to come in; just two or three mornings a week should be enough and it surely wouldn't cost so much. She told me about some of my old school contemporaries with whom I had lost touch, most of whom were either away at college or busy getting engaged. A few had married and started families. It all seemed very remote. The whole world was unreal; I wondered if we were perhaps on the wrong side of the glass in the shop windows.

After supper we went out to a film. It was an old one, the reissue of a musical. My mother used her handkerchief frequently and I pretended not to notice. Afterwards we went back to college and had cocoa and an early night.

In the morning we went to church. I had not been since Easter and it left me untouched though I could remember having a kind of fervour until a few years ago. If there is anyone there, I thought, he doesn't give a damn. But my mother seemed absorbed. Perhaps she was going to turn to religion, like Marty's mother. I knew my father would not be at church. No doubt he was in bed with his nineteen-year-old girl. Marty's age.

'Do you go to church often, Lois?' my mother asked as we were coming out.

'No,' I said.

She said no more. I think she felt she was not in any position to offer me advice, though I don't see much moral difference between being unhappily married and actually separated.

We had a good Sunday lunch in hall, after a glance at the papers, and then she ordered a taxi. She was going on to Cambridge to see Martin.

'Don't come to the station – it's ridiculous,' she said.

'All right,' I said.

It was the appearance of the taxi at the end of the road that actually initiated our leave-taking. We hugged each other and I felt the faint stir of instinctive blood affection.

'Cheer up,' I said. 'Look after yourself. I'm sorry if I've been a beast. I'm kind of dead inside at the moment.'

She smiled. 'I know the feeling. Don't worry. It's been a help to see you. I understand, you know.'

The taxi drew up at the bottom of the steps and the man took the case. She got in, then leaned out of the window.

'Here,' she said, pressing a small piece of paper into my hand. 'Your father's address. I thought you'd like to have it.'

And the taxi moved away.

SEVEN

THE term dragged on to its end. I did not do brilliantly in sessionals but I passed. Two people whom we did not know were asked to leave. We were all shocked by this. Looking at my own exam papers, I could not really see why I should be allowed to stay either. Absence of distractions had not proved the aid to learning I had hoped for. My brain had been numb and slow-moving. Marty did better than I did. She had a quicker intelligence, but I think it was more than that: she was always concentrating intensely, on the few occasions when she studied, so as to be free for Louis at the earliest possible moment. I had nothing to hurry for and my work spread itself accordingly.

Anne did very well. Her life was happy and on an even keel. Everyone was very pleased with her. Of the four of us it was Ruth who sank. She had come to college as a brilliant student, the winner of an Exhibition. But in the exams she was scarcely above pass standard. I felt concerned for her, though she herself seemed apathetic about her results.

'It's your fault, you know,' I said to Marty.

'Rubbish,' she said.

'It is. You made her so unhappy she couldn't work.'

'She did it to herself. She's made that way. If it hadn't been me it would have been someone else. She's responsible for her own life just as I am for mine.'

Ruth went around like a beaten dog. She was banished from the room she shared with Marty every afternoon and Marty usually stayed in with her one evening every week.

The actual day varied but you could always guess it from the look in Ruth's eyes.

'It's like being worshipped by a spaniel,' Marty said.

It was useless arguing with Marty and we could hardly raise the subject with Ruth unless she brought it up, so we did nothing. Marty's mother came one weekend to visit her, without the parson husband. It seemed he had turned Marty into a militant atheist and she lost no opportunity of arguing with him as violently as possible.

'There's no more suffocating vice than Christian charity,' Marty said once.

Marty's mother was a stout, dark woman with thin features. She was very efficient in all her movements and seemed fond of her daughter but in a wary, suspicious manner, keeping her distance, rather like an animal trainer who has already been mauled once or twice. It was hard to imagine how she could have produced a daughter like Marty. Perhaps the dead father had influenced her unduly. Marty never spoke of him but kept his photograph in her room.

Near the end of term we packed our trunks to travel home ahead of us. Only the prudent began preparations in time; for the rest of us it was frantic, small-hour work, stuffing in rubbish and all, because there was no time to sort it out. Tightly strapped and barely closed, our trunks were helped clumsily into the corridor like drunken men.

Three months of vacation seemed too long to me now. I had taken a job for a month and vaguely divided the rest of the time into a month of study and a month of rest. But I had, of course, intended to concentrate on Peter. Now I did not want to leave London and my friends. Anne and Keith were going to Paris for a month and then south. 'If we're not too broke,' Anne said. Louis and Marty were going to Spain. Even Jeanne, a new acquaintance who lived on Marty's corridor, was going abroad with her fiancé. 'It's going to be a terrible strain,' she confided in me. 'But I'm sure we'll survive. It makes all the difference if you really want to, doesn't it? I do so want a white wedding and I'd feel a fraud if – if we'd done anything beforehand. It's only two more years and we'll be so busy it will pass quickly. At least,' she added, 'that's what I keep telling myself.'

'Oh, well,' Anne said to me afterwards, 'we can all remember feeling like that.'

We were sitting in our room on the last night of term, drinking coffee. It was about one o'clock in the morning.

'Oh, Anne,' I said despondently. 'It's over. Our first year.'

Anne gave me a cigarette.

'Isn't it funny, Anne,' I said, 'how time passes? It's two months now since I got that letter, a year since I was at school. We've been here for three terms. I don't feel much cleverer or anything, but one third of our time here has gone.'

'You've had a hellish term,' Anne said gently.

'I've had two months of nothing,' I said. 'I think that's worse than all the letters. I really understand why Marty went back to Louis even though she knows he's no good. He makes her feel alive. Funny thing, that's very like something my mother said my father told her before he went away. I really understand it now. I don't feel alive, Anne. I'm wishing my whole life away.'

'I think we all live in the future when we're young,' Anne said, 'but you do it more than ever when you're unhappy.'

'It's so unreal,' I said. 'Each minute ticking past. What do they all add up to? Sometimes I think: if I just sit still long enough I can watch my whole life go by me and get to the end. Only not here, of course. They'd need the room in two years' time for someone else.'

'I know,' Anne said. 'It's like the man who said he didn't have to do anything but die. Only thing is, of course, you'd get so bored.'

I nodded. 'Anne, I honestly don't mean to wallow in self-pity. It's feeble and it doesn't help.'

'I know, honey. Go on.'

'But everything seems so pointless. I was so sure Peter and I'd get engaged next year and married the next. I didn't envy or resent anyone. I suppose I was too smug and the gods took their revenge. But now I really do resent the pointlessness of everything. I'm going to be here for as long as I'd known Peter and I've no idea what I'm going to do with myself except work. I can't look forward to getting a job because I don't know what I want to do. I can't imagine how I'll ever pass finals but I suppose I will because most people do. But what then? Will there ever be any point in anything again?'

Anne said, 'Don't hate me, but you'll have to meet someone else.'

'Now you sound like Marty.'

'No, I'm talking about love. You need an emotional centre to your life and I'm very sorry that sounds like a quote from an article on Togetherness. You're swinging round without a pivot or something. I'm sure there's a lovely technical analogy if only I knew it. And, of course, Marty does have a point as well – there is the physical angle. You can't be expected to lose a satisfactory relationship and not even notice. That's the price we all risk paying. Suppose something went wrong between me and Keith. How would I manage? Oh, it's lovely and smooth if you marry your first lover but if you don't, what then?'

'You're telling me?' I said vehemently.

'Sorry,' said Anne. 'But I do understand. I've often thought about it. It didn't deter me, but I did think about it.'

I smiled. 'It's been nice sharing a room with you.'

We had already been allotted our rooms for the coming academic year. There was an element of choice, but it depended on age and status. One year the eldest came first, and the next year the youngest. Scholars and exhibitioners always had a good choice. Ruth had a lovely room in a new wing with built-in cupboards, white paint and central heating. We all envied her, but she was joyless about it. Anne had chosen an attic room, narrow, almost L-shaped, far away from all authority but still in the main building. Marty had a ground-floor room with a french window and so did I. Many of the rooms were in halls of residence across the road and only the law-abiding took rooms near the dons. This was a little unreasonable. There was at least one don in most of the halls of residence and in fact they did not interfere, on the whole, except when provoked by excessive noise late at night. But they still succeeded in giving some of us an uneasy feeling.

I took a ridiculous number of books home that summer, swearing to work, convinced I should have nothing else to do. I went straight to my shop job and found it surprisingly soothing. It was pleasant to work among non-academic people and things. Superficially it made life feel much simpler. And it was good to feel my wages, such as they were, in my hand at the end of the week. But the old pattern reasserted itself. The other girls on my counter talked incessantly about boy-friends. Mavis was engaged but her fiancé was violent and very jealous. If he thought she had spoken to another boy he beat her; then he was sorry and cried and begged her not to leave him. She wouldn't either. In slack times we talked endlessly about him and I tried to make her see that he was not likely to improve after marriage. It was useless. He was her boy and she had stuck to him all through his National Service and now he was working on the buildings and getting good money. I think she was rather proud of her bruises. Carol was very different. She said Mavis wanted a caveman and had got one and it was no good talking to her. She herself ran several boyfriends, one against the other. She seemed to revel in involving herself in perilous situations and withdrawing at the last possible moment. I feared she would end up raped and murdered. If her stories were true she certainly asked for it. But maybe we were too good to miss as a willing captive audience. 'Oh, well,' she used to say, 'it's a great life if you don't weaken,' and occasionally when my long face provoked her, 'Cheer up, love, you're a long time dead.'

In the evenings I arrived home before my mother and prepared the evening meal. Very often we had salad as we both felt lazy after work. It was warm but not sunny weather and I was involved in the July sales rush which drained me of vitality. The house seemed eccentric without a man in it. Martin was hitch-hiking across Europe with his friend Rick, sending us a series of jubilant postcards. My mother and I ate suppers, washed up, ironed clothes, played cards. We watched a lot of television, I remember. I wondered then what people like us had done before it was invented. We talked only of trivialities, for which I was grateful. I waited. While still at college I had written to my father and arranged to see him.

My mother, never a great reader, had joined the library and changed books every weekend like a religious observance. I accompanied her to church and answered repetitive questions about college and looked at repetitive faces. Small town. How I longed to be back in London and safely anonymous. But till the start of term, even if there I would be worse than anonymous. I would be desolate.

My mother had moved into the spare room and single bed. There was only a thin wall between us at night and I heard her moving restlessly about and the switch of her light going on and off at odd hours. I lay awake and thought: I'll never let it happen to me, never.

I was already disturbed. Old urges were reawakening. A numb mind does not guarantee an undemanding body. I was frightened. I bathed a lot and went for walks.

In the evenings and at weekends when it was fine we sat in the garden. We did some gentle weeding and mowed the tiny lawn. I thought sometimes: this is my life going past. It is made up of such infinitesimal moments such as now when I touch this blade of grass or now when I study an insect or put on sunglasses. This book, which took somebody years to write, I can devour in an afternoon (or perhaps not at all if I feel lazy). But how many times did its author stop to look around him and wonder and watch his life trickle away?

At night I frightened myself by feeling the bones of my face under the flesh and skin. It was macabre to think that there was a skull. Unless they burnt it, it would lie in earth one day and might even be dug up. I imagined somebody examining it and making learned assumptions. But it would be my skull. I was looking out from those eye sockets now. I had the mask of a young girl over my bones.

And so the time passed until I saw my father.

EIGHT

HE met me at the top of the steps. I had rung the bell and waited. It was a windy day and the breeze blew dust and paper bags in my face and disarranged the hair I had washed myself for him because he liked it loose and natural, not stiff from the hairdresser's.

When he opened the door we stared at each other incredulously for a moment before flinging out our arms.

'You've come,' he said. 'You're really here.'

We both laughed.

'I could have come before,' I said, 'but you're as booked up as the dentist.'

'I've been working hard,' he said, 'and going out a fair bit.' Then he looked hard at me. 'Besides, I was frightened,' he said suddenly.

I swallowed. 'So was I.'

He let out a huge sigh. 'Good. Then we start even. Come upstairs.'

He took the stairs two at a time in the way I remembered and I ran after him. My dress had a straight skirt which narrowed my stride.

'Two rooms, kitchen and bath,' he said, 'on the wrong side of town. Do you approve?'

I looked around me. So this was what the more sensational newspapers would call a love-nest. Like most furnished flats it was rather crowded, but none the less clean and tidy. Philippa must be an adequate housekeeper. There were a few paintings and sketches tacked on the walls. My father saw me looking at them.

'Oh,' he said. 'Those are Phil's.' And so her name was spoken between us for the first time.

'They're very good,' I said.

'She's at art school up the road,' he said, with a mixture of pride and diffidence. 'They think quite highly of her.'

I took a deep breath. 'May I see the rest of it?'

'Yes, of course.' He opened the kitchen door. It was a small room but very clean and tidy and there was a refrigerator.

'It's very nice,' I said.

With an almost defiant gesture he threw open another door. 'This is the bedroom,' he said. 'The bathroom's through there and the lavatory's on the landing. It's rather an odd lay-out.'

I looked round the room, once I had dragged my glance away from the enormous, old-fashioned double bed. All the furniture was very dark and heavy. There was brown lino on the floor and a patterned carpet square in the middle. I nodded. I could think of nothing to say.

'I'm sorry,' he said. 'This must all be bloody difficult for you. I'm not finding it easy either.'

He was wearing an old velvet smoking-jacket I had given him years ago for Christmas. That helped a little.

He shut the door suddenly and went towards the sideboard. 'Will you have a drink?' he said. 'Or is it too early for you?'

'No,' I said. 'I think a drink's just what I need.' I managed to smile at him. 'No offence meant.'

He nodded. 'I know. Gin be all right? There is vermouth for it.'

'Fine. Lovely.'

'Good. Would you like to get some ice from the fridge for it?'

I went into the kitchen. The fridge was packed with food, all carefully wrapped up in transparent bags. They were certainly not living out of tins. The shelves, too, were loaded with all kinds of things: spaghetti and macaroni and coffee and peanut butter and rice and mixed herbs and fruit and cheese and tomato purée.

The ice hurt my hand with its coldness before I got it out of its tray. I took it and put some in our drinks and we sat in big, hard armchairs facing each other.

'Well,' I said nervously, 'here's to you.'

He looked older, more grey than I remembered despite his apparent increase in energy.

'You didn't write very often,' he said reproachfully.

'No,' I said. 'I couldn't think what to say.'

'I owe you a king-size apology and explanation, don't I?' he said, smiling wistfully. His smile was the youngest-looking thing about him: positively childlike and ingratiating. It was funny how if you loved someone, you could accept their faults; they became almost attractive.

'You needn't,' I said. 'I've already had one from another quarter.'

'All the more reason, then,' he said.

I shrugged my shoulders. 'You know I'm on your side. She knows it, too. How's that for a cosy situation?'

'I'm sorry,' he said. 'I've behaved very selfishly, haven't I?'

'Not really. If it had to come, this was the obvious time.'

He was silent for a moment. 'I think it did have to come,' he said, 'but I'm sorry about the letters.'

In spite of myself I shivered. 'Yes, that was bad.'

'It was very bad luck. We thought it was all settled and then it wasn't and by the time it was again you'd gone back to college. There was no other way. But it was due to our own clumsiness and indecision.'

In spite of affection this irritated me. 'Oh, well,' I said lightly, 'it's three months ago now. Let's forget it.'

Then, of course, he had to say, 'How's Peter? Did he help to cheer you up?'

I started to laugh. 'Funny you should ask that. He was a riot. He wrote me a letter, too.'

'My God, you poor baby,' said my father. But he looked so helpless that I could not stop laughing.

'It's all right,' I said when I was calmer. 'I have some very good friends and they were marvellous. The odds on this happening to me at least once are enormous, you know.'

'But you would have written to me, when it did, if things had been different,' he said. 'Wouldn't you?'

'Of course,' I said honestly. 'But they weren't and I didn't, so let's forget it. It was a long time ago, too. It won't kill me.'

I felt restless now and got up to wander around the room. There was not a lot of space to move in. I leant across the dining-table to look out of the window. My father got up, too, and refilled our glasses. He began talking again, rather quickly.

'I've done something everyone laughs at men of my age for doing,' he said. 'I expect your mother said it wouldn't last.'

'That's right,' I said. There were two children in the street below me. They were bouncing a ball against the shell of a ruined building.

'She's wrong,' he said. 'She's been very good about the divorce but it's only because she thinks she'll win in the end and I'll be left alone, too.'

'I don't think so. I don't think she has any idea of revenge.'

'I don't know,' he said. 'I've hurt her badly. I don't know her any more. Hurt people can be cruel.'

Now I turned round. 'I don't understand,' I said sharply. 'I love you dearly but I don't understand one bloody word you're saying. You'd been married to Mother for more than twenty years and now you calmly tell me you don't know her any more. Well, I just don't understand you. You sent me a letter – a letter after twenty years. "Sorry, but I have to go. Love from Father." That's nice, isn't it? That gives me a really cosy feeling.'

He was angry too. 'That's not true,' he said. 'I tried, I did my best.'

'You could have come to see me.'

'I wanted to. But there was Phil. She had to face her parents. How do you think they felt? I couldn't leave her to do that alone. It's my fault she's in this mess.'

I sat down suddenly and drank the drink he had given me. 'How about you and me getting tight?' I said. 'I did that, you know, with Anne, after I read my letters. She was splendid. We must have drunk every drink in creation. I was lucky to have a rich room-mate, wasn't I? And brother, if you really do get lung cancer from cigarettes, then I'd better book my bed right now.'

'Stop talking like that.'

I stopped. My father caressed my hair with his hand. 'You certainly know how to hurt me,' he said, 'and I deserve it.'

I said nothing. If anyone else had spread himself under my feet like that I would have stepped on him.

'Now listen to me,' he said, drawing up a stool so that he had to look up at me. 'I've behaved badly. I know that. I've been selfish and undignified. Between your mother and me, it's our own affair. We've both knocked the nails in. But I have a right to explain to you.'

Everyone seemed very conscious of their rights where I was concerned. I wondered what would happen if I said, 'Don't I have the right to live with you as well as my mother?' I seemed to be the only person not allowed to be melodramatic. But perhaps this was fair after all. In the normal course of events, though right now I could not imagine meeting anyone, I would be leaving home. In the next two years I would spend only ten months in my parents' house. If I had been going to marry Peter I would have been asking my father to stay for two years so that I could have ten months with him. Probably two years were even longer at forty-five than at eighteen.

'I have a real chance now,' my father was saying, 'to see what I'm made of. A fresh start. I can find out if I'm capable of having the kind of marriage I've always dreamed of. Your

73

mother and I made a mistake. We didn't realize it at first and we didn't admit it for a good while longer. We've wasted a lot of time. But when I met Phil I realized I couldn't spend the rest of my life only half alive. Our marriage had been dead for years. There may be many people like us, dragging along, without hope, resigned. Some of them don't want to break away. But I did. When you meet Phil I hope you may realize why. She's a wonderful person.'

It was not an unusual conversation really, after all. Just a man in love wanting to tell me about the girl he loved.

'Where is she now?' I asked.

'At a friend's house, a girl she knows at art school. But I've only got to phone her,' he said eagerly, 'and she'll come home.'

People are very careless in their choice of words.

'She only went out because she thought you might prefer to see me alone,' he added.

'That was very sensible of her.'

'She's a very understanding person. She left a marvellous dinner for us, too. You will stay, won't you?'

Now was the time for me to climb up onto my dignity and pour down scorn. But adolescent appetite is proof against most things and I was curious. 'Yes, I'll stay,' I said.

We had borsch first, which I did not enjoy, but after that there was a wonderful casserole of chicken with all kinds of flavours and vegetables I did not recognize. Then we had fresh fruit salad and cream. My father heated the coffee.

'There is brandy if you want some,' he told me.

'Thank you,' I said. 'Why not? But aren't you rather stretching your salary?'

He smiled faintly. 'It's called living for the moment. Not a prerogative of the young.'

He moved nimbly to and fro between living-room and kitchen, dealing with dirty plates, glasses, coffee pot and clean cups. I did not help. I had never seen him so domesticated. I thought there was something pathetic about the whole situation, but almost immediately I wondered if I had thought this merely because society had trained me to do so. It was very hard to judge it on its merits, whatever they might be.

'Does all this seem revolting to you?' he asked suddenly, anxiously.

'No,' I said, thinking: what a stupid question to ask.

'I'm glad,' he said, 'because you and Phil are the most important people in my life.'

I smiled.

'You're thinking, "But not in that order",' he said with sudden insight. 'But when you marry you'll put that person before me. It's the only way. It doesn't mean I love you any less.'

'I know,' I said, 'but please can we talk about something else?'

'Of course,' he said, frowning. 'Shall I telephone for Phil? Would you like to meet her?'

I shook my head. He showed his disappointment clearly on his face. I made a big effort.

'Another time I will,' I said, 'but I can't right now. I'm not up to it.'

'I do understand,' he said, not looking as if he did, 'but you mustn't turn this into an ordeal. You'll like her, I know you will, once you get all preconceived ideas out of your head. She's not a home-wrecker.'

I wondered if I were being silly. If I lived in Hollywood or somewhere this would all seem quite natural to me and I should probably take it in my stride. Phil and I would be the greatest of friends, exchanging girlish confidences and bottles of nail varnish.

'All right,' I said, 'I believe you. And I will meet her some time. But now I've got to go.'

'Must you? It's early yet.'

'I think so. You can phone as soon as I've gone.'

He took this calmly. 'I'm sorry I can't run you to the bus,

but the car's in dock. Otherwise I'd have come to meet you in it, of course.'

'Awkward for you,' I said. 'You need it for work.'

'Oh, they said they'd have it ready for me tomorrow.'

We walked downstairs together, slowly, amid the smells of other people's dinners. He held my hand.

'You will come again, won't you?' he asked. 'You can phone me here.' He gave me the number.

'Do you have to see Mother any more about the divorce?' I asked.

'Oh, no,' he said. 'The lawyers are seeing to all that.'

Now we were on the doorstep and there was no more to say.

'Damn,' he said. 'It's starting to rain.'

'It's not far to the bus stop,' I said, 'and I've got a scarf.'

'No umbrella? I must get you one.'

'No, please don't,' I said. 'I always lose them.'

Absurdly, I wanted to cry. I kissed him good-bye on both cheeks and he hugged me tight. He smelt just the same. It is ridiculous how much the scent of a person can upset you.

'Good-bye, baby,' he said. 'Come again soon. I miss you, you know.'

I said nothing to that; I was afraid of myself. I ran down the path and waved from the gate.

It was a long time before the bus came but I did not mind the rain. It was cool and clean. When I got on the bus I went upstairs to the front seat and smoked. The rain on the window made everything blurred. But I was warm and comfortable and isolated, in transit between two destinations. I would have liked to ride on the bus for a long, long time.

NINE

AT the end of the week I went to a dance with Margaret, one of my still unattached school acquaintances. She had come to see me one evening and had been shocked by the spiritless way I was allowing my vacation to pass. I agreed to go because it seemed easier than refusing and also because I was a little curious, not having been to such a function for some time. At college, always waiting for, or recovering from Peter, I had never bothered to attend students' dances. Before that, he and I had often gone together. It was more than two years, in fact, since I had been to a dance as an unattached female, accompanied by only a girl-friend.

I was a fool to forget what it was like. Too hot or too cold (seldom just right), these places are large but always over-crowded if successful so that you can scarcely move. Occasionally there is a bad night with only ten couples, who could easily give a display in the space at their disposal, but the atmosphere is so frigid that nobody wants to move. You take your choice.

You queue to pay your money amongst crowds of other girls, elaborately dressed, scented, made-up. They are all hopeful while pretending not to care. They are the ones who will jive defiantly together for hours if necessary, to show the world that it is of no importance to them whether or not boys invite them to dance. They will go to the cloakroom in pairs to reclaim their handbags, repair their faces, and discuss their conquests – or failures. They will disappear at a glance so as not to spoil an opportunity; and reappear when needed. 'Well, I'm going home with my friend.'

The boys stand in clusters at either end of the hall or along the walls. They talk and laugh and keep each other supplied with cigarettes. The idea of dancing is as remote as cannibalism to most of them – more so to some. Their cigarette ends join the french chalk on the floor; the many small, dim lights in the hall cast a faint sheen on their thickly plastered, shiny hair. Occasionally one breaks free to invite a girl he has chosen, after prolonged scrutiny. If the hall has no bar, most of them disappear before the interval and return perhaps an hour before the Queen, considerably livelier, even spoiling for a fight. They go home raucously, whistling, shouting, cat-calling, their ranks thinned by the disappearance of those who have retired earlier in the evening to parked cars with the girls of their choice.

After two years of partnership it is strange to sit alone or with another girl, keeping a pleasant expression on your face as the magazines tell you, since no one wishes to dance with a misery. You must also insert into this expression some indication that you do not care if you do not dance all evening; you are perfectly happy to sit and regard the others and make penetrating and witty comments to your friend – as long as she is there. Laughter, the great weapon. But you cannot laugh by yourself, for no one wants to dance with an idiot and everyone knows that only idiots laugh at nothing.

I danced with a very thin, nervous boy who, when he found out I was at university, shut up completely. I don't know what he thought I might say or do. Then I danced with a Scot who invited me to guess where exactly he came from. I said Glasgow. I could only think of Glasgow and Edinburgh in any case. It turned out I was right and he was so delighted he bought me a Coke to celebrate. I was afraid he might stick with me all evening and it would be my own fault for accepting a drink, but after a long silence he suddenly jumped up and excused himself. After that I had an American partner. 'My girl friend went to the powder-room,' he said, 'and she said, "Why don't you dance with the prettiest girl in the room while I'm gone?" So I came right over.'

I smiled. As a line it made a change; it might even be true. He was beautiful, though quite unlike Peter: blond and tanned, with the added advantage of uniform. We had three dances and he made amusing conversation the whole time. I was sorry when he went away; I would not have minded spending the rest of the evening with him.

Margaret came to tell me we would not be going home together. 'Is he nice?' I asked.

'All right,' she said indifferently. 'Better than nothing anyway.'

I was pleased. At least it meant I could go home early by myself and no questions asked.

August began; my job finished and with it the fine weather. Rain poured down for a fortnight and I sat and watched it, vaguely studying. Then Martin came home unexpectedly. I was absurdly glad to see him; he was a novelty, a break in routine. But he seemed depressed and reserved.

'Where's Rick?' I asked. 'I thought you were going to bring him back with you.'

Martin stared out of the window at the rain. 'I was,' he said, 'but he had to go home. His mother's ill. She's a widow.'

'Bad luck,' I said.

'Yes. Yes, it was.'

'Well, write and ask him to come later, if he can. I don't think you're doing your brotherly duty by me; I could do with a new boy-friend.'

Martin looked at me sharply and then glanced away again. I had the ridiculous impression that he was actually blushing, very slightly, under his new tan.

'Or isn't Rick my type?'

'What d'you mean?'

'Martin, you're being very dense. Would he appeal to me? You don't need a translation, surely.'

'I don't think he would.' He said it with great finality and I thought he sounded relieved.

'All right then. That's all I wanted to know.'

A week later he got a letter from Paris which he answered immediately. A couple of nights afterwards I went into his room on my way to bed and found him packing.

'Where are you off to?' I asked.

He did not look up but went on stuffing things into a haversack. 'Back to France.'

'When?'

'Tomorrow.'

'Will Rick be there?'

'Yes.'

'Why ever didn't you travel back together? Was your letter from him?'

No answer.

'Martin, did he ever leave France at all this summer?'

'No.'

'But his mother doesn't live there, does she?'

'No. Now will you stop asking damn fool questions?'

'If you like,' I said. 'I'll tell you a story instead. My friend at college, Marty, shared a room with a girl called Ruth. We all shared in first year. But Ruth had a thing about Marty and she nearly went mad every time she had a date.'

Martin was silent but he had started to fold his clothes very carefully before he put them away.

'Isn't that an interesting story?' I asked.

'Fascinating. Now if you don't mind too much I'd like to go to bed. I've got an early start in the morning.'

I changed direction. 'Does Mother know you're going?'

'Yes. I told her.'

'I think it's mean of you. She needs you. You do her far more good than I do. I think you could spare her more than a week of your vac.'

'I'll be back in September.'

'Is that a promise?'

'Oh shut up, Lois, for God's sake. We're not kids any more.'

I sat on the bed to prevent him getting in, remembering how years ago he would pretend to be asleep when I wanted to talk to him.

'What do you think about it all?' I asked. 'I thought you might come and see me at college, but you never did.'

'There didn't seem much point. It was all settled and there was nothing we could do.'

'It might have helped me, that's all.'

Martin sighed. 'I'm sorry, Lois. But it helped me to keep right away from family, even you. Maybe it was selfish of me. It was just how I felt. I was sorry you couldn't come to the May Ball. I thought maybe we'd talk there.'

I smiled. 'I'd have looked silly without a partner.'

'Yes. That was rotten luck for you.'

'Oh, well,' I said. 'Never mind me. You still haven't told me what you think about Mother and Dad.'

He looked away. 'I feel sorry for them. I think marriage is overrated and people expect too much. They can't keep it up.'

'Well,' I said, 'is that what they teach you at Cambridge?'

He flushed. 'You asked me what I thought. I don't think there's enough friendship in marriage. You asked my opinion and that's it.'

I said, 'You might be right. What does Rick think about it?'

Martin said roughly. 'I haven't asked him. Come on, Lois, get up. I want to go to bed.'

At the end of August Mother and I spent a week by the sea. There was a wind most of the time but the sun shone quite a lot. We did not want to do very much so we sat on the beach reading magazines and ate huge meals at our hotel. I looked at the sea as it sparkled in the distance and thought how deliciously long and flat it was, stretching across the horizon. I had begun to see my father again before we came away but still avoided meeting Philippa. I was interested, however, to hear that she was Jewish and her family had severed all connection with her on being informed that she was involved in a divorce case. Some of her more orthodox friends, too, had been alienated by her behaviour. Perhaps my father hoped to persuade me to meet her by arousing my sympathy.

I had received cards from Anne and from Marty. Her card provoked an odd look from my mother since it bore the single word BLISS in enormous letters which nobody could pretend not to see. By the same post, unfortunately, had come a letter from Ruth, full of agony and enquiry. I was surprised that she had my address. She begged me for news of Marty, saying she herself had heard nothing. I wrote and told her that Marty seemed to be enjoying herself and had only sent me a postcard.

Martin returned a few days after we got home from our holiday and I was surprised and pleased to see him exerting himself in my mother's direction. She warmed and unfolded beneath his attentions; they had long talks together. I took to studying in my room : time was short now, a little over a fortnight. I had been very lucky all vacation : I had not seen Peter once. Already he was beginning to seem part of a beautiful episode very far in the past. I did not know if I were making a slow or quick recovery but I knew that I had to recover sometime. The uncomfortable fact remained that I had not made love for five months and I wanted to. But I had seen no one who attracted me sufficiently or who, for that matter, was sufficiently attracted to me. I was hopelessly divided in my mind. I wanted physical satisfaction, and soon, but for two years I had convinced myself that it only came with love. And I was not ready for that.

TEN

AUTUMN in London. The true season in its rightful place; bright days, windy, rich-smelling and warm. I felt terrific surges of energy and an utter disinclination to work. It was good to renew friendships and sit on beds into the far hours of the night, talking or listening. We drank coffee and smoked cigarettes and played the gramophone. Marty had brought back flamenco music from Spain and Anne had some French love songs. They were very bad for me.

We surveyed the freshers as they felt their way around college. They were, incredibly, ourselves of a year ago. We helped them, condescendingly, when they lost their way in the web of corridors, and noticed with regret how soon they ceased to need our help.

Marty was shocked at my celibate vacation. 'I was sure you'd come back cured,' she said. 'You must be mad.' She was very brown.

'I'm a lot saner,' I assured her. 'Just give me time.' I did not want to disgust myself.

Marty was eager to tell me about her holiday. At one stage she had been ill with food poisoning and Louis had gone out alone. He had been unfaithful to her.

'How did you find out?' I asked stupidly.

'Oh, don't be naïve,' she said. 'He couldn't make love to me that night when he came back. He'd only just crawled out of this girl's bed. So I told him as soon as I was better I'd be unfaithful to him and then we could start again together.'

'How mathematical,' I said.

'Rubbish, I couldn't miss a chance like that with someone

like Louis. He's so jealous. He suffered agonies, not knowing when I was going to do it. I had such difficulty getting away from him; he hardly let me out of his sight for two minutes. In the end I phoned him from the other man's flat so he'd know exactly. He was nearly hysterical; it was fantastic, he was desperate to stop me. Isn't it funny it didn't occur to him to get the other girl back? Now if she'd answered the phone it would have served me right.'

'You are extraordinary,' I said, but I was very interested and perhaps less shocked than I would have been a few months ago.

'Phoning Louis and hearing how upset he was made it much more exciting with Ramon,' said Marty. 'I wanted to leave the phone off the hook but he wouldn't let me. Spaniards are very puritanical.' She giggled.

'What happened when you went back to Louis?' I asked.

'He beat me up,' said Marty calmly. 'The moment I walked through the door he slapped my face. I thought he'd never stop. Finally he started banging my head against the wall. He was screaming rude French words at me all the time. I only knew a few of them. In the end I fainted and when I came round he was kneeling on the floor beside me, weeping. You can imagine the rest for yourself.'

'It's not like you,' I said, 'to leave anything to my imagination.'

I had forgotten how quickly her mood could change. Her face was now soft and Madonna-like, full of calm beauty.

'It was such a lovely reconciliation,' she said tenderly, 'I don't want to discuss it.' And she smiled at me, almost hurtfully complacent.

I now had quite a regular, recurrent pain when I thought about sex as such, but it tended to disappear when I thought of going to a dance with the deliberate intention of picking up a stranger with whom to have intercourse. I envied men then for the first time. They could masturbate or go to prostitutes. I was a prisoner of my own inhibitions. Previously I had always enjoyed being a woman.

I rehearsed it all in my mind. The world seemed full of men eager to have intercourse with Marty, but I was sure I would have difficulty in finding one to oblige me. Even if this were an unsound idea, the fact that I believed it would obviously impede my progress. I foresaw all kinds of snags. The men I met would all be honourable, or engaged, or impotent. Or I would find a likely one, only to panic and back out myself at the last moment. I think I was more frightened of that than anything. Suppose when the man had undressed to his underpants I had a spasm of revulsion and bolted? What would I be wearing at the time? I contemplated visions of myself fleeing along countless corridors – nude, dressed in my underclothes, carrying my outer garments, wrapped in a bath-towel. It was painful and ludicrous at the same time. People in films and books always met someone else. They only had difficulty in keeping the numbers down. People like Marty always met someone else, too. I had no doubt that even Anne, if her engagement were broken, would manage to meet someone else quite soon and, being Anne, would manage to fall in love with him before falling into bed. What was the matter with me? By what miracle had I ever contrived to have an affair with Peter? And yet I clearly remembered that I had needed a great deal of persuasion.

'How can you expect to meet anyone,' said Marty patiently, 'if you never go anywhere?' She was now resigned to the fact that she was dealing with an idiot. 'Besides, it's no good going out grimly determined to be raped. It's almost as bad as being grimly determined to get married. Men want to hunt and it puts them off. Just go to a dance to meet people and enjoy yourself and let nature take its course.'

'But it isn't nature to me,' I said desperately. 'I'm more romantic than you are.'

'Rubbish,' said Marty. She sounded angry. 'You've no idea how romantic I am.'

'All right,' I said wearily, 'forget it. I'm sorry. I've no idea what I'm talking about. But I don't think you appreciate my predicament either.'

'Yes, I do,' said Marty. She sat on my bed, resting her chin on her knees. 'Look,' she said, 'Louis and I are going to give a party. There'll be lots to drink and lots of lovely unattached men. You come along and you'll find your problem gets solved in no time at all.'

'Right now,' I said, 'I don't believe I've got a problem. I go so cold at the thought of all this manoeuvring that I don't believe I could ever want a man again.'

Marty laughed. 'Well, you know better than to take any notice of that. It always come back when you least expect it and wham ! Seriously, you come to our party. It's the easiest solution and you'll enjoy it. But please, please get yourself fixed up first so I don't have to worry about you.'

She gave me the name of her doctor. 'He's sweet. When I went for a check-up I wished I could ask him to test the little gadget personally.'

I shook my head. 'I don't think I could. I always planned to go when I got married.'

'Well, you can tell him you're getting married.'

'It's not him I'm thinking of, it's me. I should feel awful. It's such a personal thing to do for just anyone, someone I haven't even met. I should feel – cheap.'

'Like a whore,' Marty said.

'Yes. Since you mention it.'

'Well, I had to say it for you; it was obvious you'd never spit it out.' Marty rolled on my bed and lay flat, her dark hair spread over the pillow, her face very pale. 'Actually,' she went on, 'that would be the ideal occupation to combine with residential student life. Provided you kept it on a fairly modest scale so as not to attract attention. But I don't suppose I'm the first person to think of that.'

The party was in three weeks' time. After Marty had gone I had a straight talk with myself. Whatever happened, I was not going to allow Marty to launch me on this phase of my life. I had to do it for myself or not at all. I made myself sick with longing by recalling times with Peter in an effort to decide if I was looking for sex or affection. I suppose I wanted both, really, but I was still afraid. How could you tell from a person's face if he was going to write you a letter in a few months' or years' time? But if you did not love him, then you were safe. You could only feel sick at yourself.

I looked at my reflection in the mirror. Was I seriously going to do this thing? I looked quite normal. But how did other people manage? I wonder why there is always this compulsion to seek reassurance from the behaviour of others. It seldom has any relevance to oneself. People are different instead of similar.

On Friday I went to an open dance at another college but first I had several drinks from a bottle I had furtively smuggled into my room. There was no ban on liquor in college but, knowing my own purposes, I felt like an alcoholic or a criminal. On the bus and the tube I had a sense of ridicule. This could not be really happening to me. It was awful the way you could not suddenly be at a place; there were all the prosaic details of the journey to be accomplished first. You sat and looked at the other travellers and handed in your ticket or threw it away. What would they have done if you had suddenly confided in them? We all gamble on not having our privacy invaded. Suppose a strange person came up to me and said, 'I am going to commit suicide.' Would I not feel obliged to stay with him all evening?

I wanted another drink before going in to the dance but I did not dare go in a pub alone. It was not something women could really do. This thought made me smile to myself as I walked round the block. I finally succeeded in calming myself by deciding that I would face this thing in easy stages. Tonight I would do no more than neck unless I met someone who really attracted me. After all, it was five months since anyone had even kissed me. I could not expect myself to plunge in at the deep end. This thought sustained me onto the dance floor.

It was very crowded and I had a variety of partners. One of them seemed quite interested in me but he was red in the face and breathed heavily. I felt that no one else would have him and presently I made an excuse to escape. I had long ago decided I would have to be ruthless. After him I had a lot of Indian partners. Some of them smelt of garlic, which upset me. They were not very good dancers, either, or maybe it was my fault. Our rhythms were different, anyway. West Indians or Africans would probably have been better; they were generally good dancers. But none of them came to ask me.

By the interval I could claim success only in the field of escape. I was tired and the effect of the drinks had nearly worn off, which was depressing. I found a corner seat where I could partly hide. I thought I had fallen asleep and was dreaming when a voice said, 'All alone? Or is your partner fetching you a drink?'

I opened my eyes. He was not very tall, not very broad, but he had blue eyes and regular features and a kind, interested face. He looked normal.

'Yes and no,' I said.

He sat down. 'All alone and no partner. Must be my lucky night. Would you like a cigarette?'

I took one and he lighted it for me.

'My name's Mike Swann. I'm doing postgrad work in Chemistry. All my mates have come along tonight but they came early. I was working so I thought I'd get left high and dry. But here I am. Work late and work fast, it's the only way. Now you tell me your life story.'

I smiled at him and said, 'I'd rather not, I'm trying to forget it.'

'That bad? Well, how about a dance while all the other morons are at the bar? Who are we to scorn Victor Silvester – he's made a lot of money.'

'I'm smoking,' I said.

'I know. But you can tap the ash in my ear. Come on.'

I got up reluctantly and we danced. He held me very close and hummed the tune. Presently he said, 'And what's your name or are you trying to forget that, too?'

'Lois Mitchell.'

'And what are you reading, Lois?'

'English.'

'Where?'

I told him.

'That's one of London's convents, isn't it?' he said.

'Depends how you look at it.' I was beginning to feel depressed. He was only another smart-alec student after all.

'Well, it's all girls, isn't it?'

'Officially, yes.'

My voice must have sounded very bored, for he suddenly stopped dancing in the middle of the floor, stood back and looked hard at me.

'I'm sorry,' he said. 'You really don't want to dance or talk. My mother always said I rode roughshod over people. What would you like to do?'

'If you don't mind,' I said, 'I'd like a drink.'

'Then that's what you shall have.' He glanced towards the bar. 'It's still a bit of a Rugby scrum in here. Shall we go out to a pub? We can get pass-out tickets.'

'All right,' I said.

It was a relief to be outside in the cool air. He had an old black Ford in which we drove to the pub. He told me how much he had paid for it and how long it had taken him to make it go.

'I bore everyone with this story,' he said. 'Don't flatter yourself you're the first. She's called Clementine. I think even if I was a millionaire I'd still have an old car.'

At the pub I had gin and he had beer. I had a faint pang of conscience because he was only a student on a grant, like me. He went on talking about Clementine and then about his family and some of the hitch-hiking trips he and his brother had taken on the continent. His brother was younger than he was and an undergraduate at Oxford. 'The brains of the family,' Mike said cheerfully. He seemed very proud of his brother and talked a lot about him. Then suddenly he stopped and looked at me anxiously.

'Am I boring you to hell?' he asked.

I shook my head. 'I only want to listen. Please go on talking.'

'Okay. But you make it sound like a kind of therapy. Still, who am I to complain? With most girls I can't get two words in.'

We had some more drinks and cigarettes and I began to feel better, even hopeful, though I tried not to be too specific in my own mind. At ten o'clock he looked at his watch and said, 'That dance finishes at eleven-thirty. Want to go back?'

'No,' I said. 'I'd forgotten all about it.'

He leant across and lightly kissed my neck. 'Then what say we go up to Hampstead Heath and look at all the other parked cars?'

I suppose that was my warning and my chance to get out. He was being very fair to me. But I wanted to see how much I could take. The kiss on the neck had not seemed like an insult to Peter's memory. I was curious about myself and it would be a shame to waste the effect of all the gin.

He was not so talkative on the drive but he put the radio on and squeezed my hand when he changed gear. When we got there we found a place to park and sat in silence for a moment. Mike turned off the radio.

'Want to get out and have a stroll?'

'No,' I said, and waited. He turned my face towards him, and kissed me, very gently at first, and then harder, when I made no resistance, sliding his tongue into my mouth. I had never allowed anyone but Peter to kiss me that way and it had seemed sacred to us, though I knew everyone else did it too. But now, though it did not excite me, I thought it just served Peter right. I was sorry I could not find a whole row of men and have them all kiss me like that immediately.

I suppose Mike felt encouraged. I had not moved at all and perhaps my mouth felt slack and welcoming. I was wearing a dress with a low, round neck and his hand slid down my neck to my breast, inside the dress. This did excite me, though I felt slightly sick as well. There was a mixture of pleasure and discomfort I had often known with Peter. Mike was still kissing me. It was funny how men kept that up as if it meant you would let them do anything. It did not affect me at all, though it had with Peter. But his other hand kept moving and that did affect me, in spite of myself. I did not want to stop him; I had a pain now. I was glad when his other hand went to the bottom of my dress and under my skirt. I moved closer to him. I thought it would never reach its destination.

As if he knew he was safe, he stopped kissing my mouth and moved his lips to my neck. I heard myself breathing very hard and fast. I kept my eyes tight shut. I was beginning to feel depraved, like Marty. He was a stranger I had only met two hours ago.

At last his hand was inside my pants. I was terribly excited. I hoped he wasn't disgusted with me. It had been such a long time and he was not repulsive. But then he took his other hand away from my breast. I heard the sound of a zip being pulled and then he took one of my arms from around his neck and tried to place my hand inside his trousers. I felt him, hard and warm, ready for me. I knew what he wanted, and I couldn't do it. He was being very fair and moderate, according to my behaviour, but I felt sick. It was messy, ugly, personal. I would have to love him first. I could not move my hand. And then I drew away with a sharp, sudden movement, right away to the other side of the car and gasped and choked.

He was very angry. 'What the hell do you think you're playing at?' he said. He searched his pockets for cigarettes.

Then he had another search for matches, cursing softly. I had a dreadful pain and I was trying to make a decision.

'Let's get out,' I said urgently. 'It's quite dark. We can go under the trees.'

He looked at me, amazed. 'Are you crazy? What about just now?'

'I can't explain. Come on. It will be all right. Hurry.'

'I haven't got anything with me,' he said.

'I don't care,' I said. I did not recognize myself at all. The five months of nothing had turned me into a ravenous, careless stranger.

We found a place quickly and he came into me at once. It was the most glorious feeling in the world. I suppose the drink helped but I managed not to think of Peter. All I was aware of was my dreadful pain and this was the only thing to make it go away. He was excited and very rough, which was exactly what I wanted. I moved with him at first and then I lay still and pretended he was raping me. I had never imagined I could have an orgasm with someone I hardly knew, but he had to put his hand over my mouth to stop me crying out. His came just after and I felt rich and luxuriated in it. I was satisfied but I wished we could start again. I had never felt so lascivious and I feared it would be the only time in my life.

'My God,' he said, when we were both quiet and less breathless. 'You're a funny one.'

'I know,' I said. 'Does it matter?'

'No,' he said, 'but I'd like to understand you.'

'You've made a good start,' I said.

'You know,' he said presently, 'we took a big risk just now.'

'I know,' I said. 'That should be my line. It's very nice of you to be so concerned.'

'You really don't care, do you?' he said, in a wondering voice. 'Most girls panic like hell.'

'I'll let you into a little secret,' I said, feeling suddenly ridiculously pleased with myself. 'My period just finished.

I'm practically unable. So there. But you could hardly be expected to know that.'

We lay still a little while longer but we were beginning to feel wet and uncomfortable and I was glad when he suggested we should return to the car. He found the matches and we both had cigarettes.

'You're nice,' I said carelessly. I was immensely surprised to find how well and happy I felt, not disgusted or ashamed at all. No wonder Marty had found me old-fashioned. She could feel like this any time. And why should I disapprove of my father? I was no better than he was, was I? Worse probably.

'You're nice, too,' Mike said. 'Do you make a habit of this sort of thing?'

I laughed. 'Does it matter? Afraid you'll catch something?'

'No,' he said, 'but I want to find out what's driving you. You didn't get this way on three gins, and my technique, though fairly adequate, would hardly have got Casanova through life.'

Some of my warmth and pleasure ebbed away. 'Do you have to play psychologist?' I said angrily.

'I'm sorry. I just can't figure you out and I'd like to.'

'Can't you just be satisfied with what you get?'

'Oh, I am. But does that mean we can't talk? Some girls feel hurt if a fellow doesn't talk enough.'

'Not me,' I said. 'I've had enough conversation.'

'Oh, I get it,' he said suddenly, after a pause. 'There's another fellow.'

'Correction,' I said. 'Was. You got your tenses wrong.'

'And he just talked?'

'He talked as well.'

'You made love – you were in love with him?'

'Yes – shut up. You're spoiling everything.'

'I have to know. I can't just drive you back and forget the whole thing. Maybe a lot of fellows would but I can't.'

'Oh, God damn you,' I said, suddenly crying. 'Why d'you

have to spoil everything? Now it's all gone. My lovely feeling's all gone. Why d'you have to bring everything back? Do you go around waking up people with hangovers, too?'

He tried to take hold of my hand but I wouldn't let him. 'I'm sorry,' he said gently. 'But I had the feeling you were using me for a reason and I wanted to know what it was.' He passed me his handkerchief. 'Cheer up. I won't say another word. I get the picture.'

I blew my nose loudly and made dreadful snuffling noises. 'Now I have to tell you,' I said.

'No, you don't,' he said gently.

'Yes, I do. I mean I want to. I went out with him for two years and just before I came to college we started going to bed together and it was all wonderful. We were going to get engaged next year and married when I got my degree. I was so sure nothing could happen to us.' The words came out between enormous sobs and I wondered if he could hear half of what I was saying. I felt more ashamed of crying in front of him than of having intercourse with him. 'This is all your fault,' I went on. 'I hadn't cried once since it happened, not once, do you hear me? That's pretty good, isn't it? And now you have to make me do this.'

He said mildly, 'It's probably just what you need. Why do you have the idea that tears are a bad thing?'

I shook my head. 'I don't know.'

'I think you're in a pretty bad way. It's a pity you didn't get all this over before. When did you split up?'

'Five months ago.' I began to cry again.

'And you haven't had anyone since?'

I shook my head.

'What did you do in the long vac?'

'Nothing.'

'Just stayed in and moped? Weren't your parents worried about you?'

I sat up and stopped crying suddenly. I felt as if I would never want to cry again.

'They're too busy getting divorced,' I said.

'Oh, God,' said Mike. 'You poor kid.'

I felt very calm and remote. 'Would you drive me back to college now, please. It's getting late.'

Mike did not even look at his watch. 'You must have a one o'clock pass if you went to a dance that ended at eleven-thirty. It's early yet.'

'All right, Sherlock Holmes, I have. And I don't want to use it. Now will you take me back?'

'Lois, look here. Why not come back to my flat and we'll have coffee and talk?'

'I told you I don't want to talk and I can make my own coffee.'

'But why?'

I suddenly felt desperately tired. 'Because I don't want to,' I said. 'Why can't everything be uncomplicated and physical? I don't want any more people who talk and tell you things and you tell them things and they pretend they care.'

'It's not like that,' he said.

'Oh yes it is. I know.' I put my fingers together in the darkness but he couldn't see them. 'My father and I were like that and now he's going to marry a girl nineteen years old.'

There was a long pause and I heard him sigh.

'All right,' he said. 'I apologize. I've been trespassing. Bull-headed Mike my friends call me. I'll take you back.'

When we reached college he pulled up outside the building and put a hand on my shoulder.

'May I see you again?'

'No.'

'Please. Just to see how you are.'

'I'd rather not.'

'But why?' He made a helpless gesture. 'Or am I trespassing again?'

'Oh, forget it,' I said. 'It's just the way I feel. The end of an episode.'

'Suppose I want to be more than an episode.'

'Well, suppose you can't.'

'You're very hard,' he said.

'Oh, for God's sake,' I said impatiently, 'people are always telling me that.'

'I'm sorry,' he said. 'I seem to keep saying the wrong thing.'

'Well then, now do you see why it's better to leave it at that?'

'All right,' he said, opening the door for me. 'I won't argue any more. But I may just write to you and you can't stop me.'

I smiled; after all I was really very grateful to him. 'Well,' I said, 'I may just answer.'

ELEVEN

On Sunday Ruth came into my room. She was wearing slacks and looked taller than ever. We greeted each other and she wandered round the room as if she had no purpose in coming, picking up things on my desk and replacing them and staring out of the window.

'Well, nice to see you,' I said, embarrassed. She turned round at once. It was as if I had pressed a button which set her in motion.

'Did Marty ask you to her party?' she enquired.

I nodded.

'Well, there may not be one after all.' She seemed nervously excited as if trying hard to suppress her triumphant agitation.

'What do you mean?' I said, as she obviously wanted to be questioned.

'They've had a quarrel.' She nodded her head and smiled at me.

'A bad one?' I was alarmed.

'I think so. Marty went there for the weekend, you know, but she came back early this morning. I went past her window after breakfast and saw her. I could hardly believe it.' She had lowered her voice and I half expected her to search the room before speaking again. 'She was crying.'

I felt sick. There was an element of indecency about the conversation. Neither of us had any right to intrude on Marty's privacy. I said nothing, hoping to discourage Ruth by my silence. But she continued.

'So I went in,' she said. 'Marty was lying on the bed and I said, "What's the matter?" and she said, "It's Louis, what d'you think?" So I said, "Did you have a fight?" and she said, "Yes," and I said, "Was it very bad?" and she said, "Oh, shut up and get out." So I think it must have been very bad, don't you?'

'I think you just got on her nerves asking questions,' I said.

'But I had to know. It's important.'

'Because of the party?' I jeered, trying to put her off. The image of Marty crying on her bed and being questioned by Ruth really upset me.

Ruth shook her head. 'I think maybe it's over,' she said. Her eyes were very bright, almost glittering.

'What a ghoul you are,' I said furiously.

She smiled. 'You don't understand a thing. I went to see Anne but she wasn't in. She'd know how I feel. But I had to tell someone so I came along here. I think it's serious this time. It's been building up. They've had lots of little quarrels, you know.'

I said, 'I know,' but I felt uneasy.

'She was always so careless,' Ruth said. 'When we shared a room she'd put her letters away and forget to lock the desk sometimes. He wrote to her a lot.'

'You read her letters?'

'I had to. She wouldn't tell me anything – well, only what she wanted me to know, to upset me. She's very cruel, you know.'

I sat there, dumb, looking at her.

'He wrote a lot about the things they did together,' Ruth said. 'Sometimes he called her a tramp and a tart. He said she was cheap. One time after they'd had a row he wrote and told her about another girl and all the things he'd done with her. It was a kind of revenge. I think she burnt that letter, later; it wasn't there when I looked another time. Some of the letters were beautiful – full of French poetry. He's very well read. But I don't think he means half he says. He's funny. Some of the letters were very gloomy. It was rather vague but I think he was talking about suicide. He said he got bad head-aches and he couldn't think.'

'Ruth,' I said, making a big effort, 'I don't want to hear any more. Marty tells us both what she wants us to know and I think it's unforgivable of you to pry.' I was disturbed by the glimpses of the affair that Ruth had given me.

She went on as if she had not heard me. 'He wrote a lot about the other men she'd known. I think they quarrelled a lot about that. He was very jealous, you know.'

'I know,' I said. 'Now will you kindly shut up and get out?'

She looked at me, her eyes wide with surprise and hurt, like a child struck for no reason. 'But I can't talk to anyone else, except Anne, and she's out.'

'Well, you can't talk to me either. Not about your snoop-ing on Marty. And Anne won't want to hear what you've done.'

Ruth looked sulky and disbelieving.

'I think I shall warn Marty about you,' I said.

'Oh, no,' Ruth shook her head but she wasn't scared. She looked powerful. 'You'll upset her. She'd hate to know I've read all those things. Personal things.' She looked at me signi-ficantly. 'You've no idea how personal some of them were. Intimate, really. Yes, that's the word. Marty'll be upset if you tell her.'

I felt real hatred then. 'Get out,' I said. 'You make me sick. Get out before you make the whole room stink.' I could not think of anything bad enough to say and I knew I could not forcibly remove her if she wanted to stay. But she went to the door; her shoulders sagged.

'You've no idea,' she said, 'what it's like not sharing a room with her. I can't sleep. It's so lonely. I sit up half the night sometimes pretending she's going to come in later. One night it was so awful I climbed over the fence and knocked on the window of her room. She let me in and made coffee. That was kind of her, wasn't it?'

I said nothing and she opened the door, slid round it and disappeared. She left it open. I really believe she forgot all about it; it was not just a sort of feeble retaliation for my insults. I was anxious so I went round to Marty's room, but the blinds were drawn and the *Verboten* notice on the door so I could not go in or even knock. But at least she was safe from Ruth. Next I went to Anne's room, but she was not there. I felt so disturbed that I could not be alone. I wanted to be with someone who could share my doubts about Ruth's sanity, but since that was impossible I went to see Jeanne. I found her crouched over *Beowulf*, one finger on the text, another on the Everyman translation.

'Can I help?' I asked.

'Please. I'm getting cross-eyed, going from one to the other. It's good but we can't take it word for word, can we?'

'No, not quite.' I took over the modern version and Jeanne slowly equated it with the text and wrote out her own version in a notebook. She had neat, sloping handwriting. I watched her as she wrote. She was very dark, pretty and excessively feminine. She wore very full or very tight skirts, with fluffy Angora jumpers. She was one of the few girls in college I had never seen wearing slacks.

'You're very industrious for a Sunday morning,' I said.

'Oh, I have to be. John and I went to a dance last night when I should have been doing an essay. If I translate this morning I can do the essay this afternoon.'

'Isn't John coming round today?'

'Not till this evening. We're going to a film.'

'Oh – which one?'

'I don't know. There's nothing we want to see specially, but we decided we shouldn't be alone too much.' She bit her lip. 'It's much harder this term. Sharing a room with Iris helped a lot, though we hated it at the time. Never being sure when she might come in meant we didn't dare go too far.'

'But you don't want to, anyway, do you?'

Jeanne blushed. 'I don't particularly. I mean, I want to wait till we're married. After all, it's not as if we only hold hands. I don't see why we can't go on like this. But John seems to find it hard and that upsets me.'

'Is he pushing you?' I asked.

'Not exactly. He doesn't want me to do anything I'll regret. But he's so sure it will be all right. I'm not. How can I tell which of us knows best? You don't agree with me, I know.'

'Well,' I said, 'seeing how my little romance ended up, I really can't say you're wrong. On the other hand, though, there's Anne.'

'I know,' Jeanne said, 'but how can I be sure I'll be as lucky as Anne?'

'Oh, look here,' I said. 'If you want to be a virgin bride, go ahead and good luck. But let's get your reasons straight. You don't seriously imagine that you and John, engaged to be married, would ruin your whole relationship if you slept together, do you?'

Jeanne looked at me helplessly. 'I don't know. That's what some people say. I know it shouldn't but still. Suppose it did? Suppose it's true what people say about men really wanting you to refuse all the time and wanting to marry virgins and thinking that if you give in before marriage you'll be unfaithful afterwards?'

'My God,' I said, 'you *have* been reading all about it.'

'Well,' said Jeanne simply, 'I worry.'

'In that case,' I said, 'don't ever do it. Not feeling the way you do. It probably *would* ruin everything. You wait.'

'There is something else, too,' Jeanne said. 'I'm afraid of getting pregnant. My sister did, you know, and she had to get married. She's had a lovely little boy but she's not very happy and her husband goes out all the time.'

'Did they intend to get married anyway?' I asked.

Jeanne shook her head. 'I don't know. I don't think so. But we weren't very close, and you can't ask someone a thing like that, not in the circumstances. They weren't engaged – till it happened.'

'It sounds a different set-up to me,' I said, 'but never mind. You stick to your guns. You'd only worry yourself sick.'

'Yes,' Jeanne said. 'Yes, I would.' She sounded relieved. 'But there's another thing I worry about. Suppose, after we're married, I don't like it?'

'Look,' I said. 'Out of my limited experience it gets better and better with practice, like anything else. You need lots of time and patience and the right attitude. It's all in the mind, like the *Goon Show*. Well, a lot of it is, anyway.'

'You look sad,' said Jeanne, watching me. 'I'm sorry. I shouldn't have brought the subject up. But it helps to talk to you. I'm very fond of Iris but I can't talk to her. She's so pure she doesn't even know there's anything to talk about. If a boy kisses her good night she thinks he's fast.'

'He's not only fast, he's brave,' I said. I did not like Iris.

Jeanne giggled. 'Oh, you shouldn't. She's very kind and generous, you know.'

'But only to girls.'

'Oh, Lois.'

'Sorry. Let's get back to *Beowulf*.'

'Yes, we really must. Where were we? "Beowulf spoke, son of Ecgtheow . . ." '

'Where else?' I said and we went on. It was slow work. I had done this part already with Marty. We usually did language work together. She worked much faster than Jeanne. It was unfair that some people should have to work so much harder or longer than other people to achieve the same result. Marty claimed she had merely taught herself to concentrate since she had so little time to spare for work. 'It's easy,' she said; 'anyone can do it.' I felt that by not overworking she had at least preserved her subject as an interest rather than a duty. There was the gloomy tale round college of a girl alleged to have said, when asked why she had chosen to read Mathematics, 'Well, I enjoy everything else.' It was easy to go to university full of the joys of English and lose sight of them in a swamp of hard work or despairing idleness. There was rather more to it, we all soon discovered, than a few favourite poets and novelists who were fun to read.

Jeanne and I tramped on through *Beowulf*. Looking at the translation in my hands I thought, 'I might even enjoy this if I didn't have to learn it.' Jeanne was slow and I flipped through the pages ahead, past the end of the poem. There was Marty's favourite Old English poem *Wulf and Eadwacer*. I looked at it unwillingly; it always depressed me. Typical of Marty to like it so much, I thought.

> Wulf, my Wulf, my yearnings for thee
> Have made me sick, thy rare visits . . .
> A woeful heart and not want of food.

It was not even one of our set texts. But Marty loved it. The first time she had read it she had said, 'Listen. Now this really comes across. It's worth a ton of battles. This could be any woman, any time.'

'A woman not only of her time but for all time,' I said, as this was a piece of criticism so frequent as to have become a standing joke.

Now the poem seemed a bad omen in view of what Ruth had said. I could see Marty lying on her bed as clearly as if I had been there. Was it really a bad quarrel, I wondered? What would Marty do?

> They can easily sunder that which was never joined
>   together
> The song of us two together, the poem ended.

It made me shiver.

'Go on,' said Jeanne, looking up in surprise. 'I've finished. What's the next bit?'

TWELVE

I CONTINUED to make trips to Marty's room all Sunday but she remained incommunicado. Towards night I began to be frightened. Suppose she had done something. I saw the crowded court, the face of the coroner. He was saying, 'And do you mean to say, Miss Mitchell, that you made no attempt to reach your friend all day, when you knew of the desperate state she was in, merely because of a piece of paper stuck on her door?' He would never understand the sacredness of a *Verboten* notice. I should be branded as heartless, selfish, a terrible friend.

I went to see Anne. She was studying, wrapped in a dressing gown, and chain-smoking. I told her what had happened.

'Ruth's probably exaggerating,' she said calmly. 'Wishful thinking and all that. For all we know Louis may have come over and they're making it up right now. Or Marty may have gone out and forgotten to take the notice down. It would be just like her.'

I had to agree that it would. I had cocoa with Anne and we tried to talk of other things, but I could see that she wanted to work so presently I left her. As I wandered down the corridor girls were popping out of bathrooms, hair pinned up, feet shuffling along in flat mules. All supremely important to themselves, I thought, all spending three years of their lives poised between school and work or marriage, or both, in the no-man's land of university life. Time to look round, which we might never have again; a breathing space in which to study books, people, life, ourselves – what we will.

On Monday I was almost cross to see Marty arrive at our nine o'clock lecture. Relief very soon gives way to rage at having been needlessly worried. I suppose I felt a fool. But it was easy to see she had been under some strain. She was very pale and her eyes were puffy, with dark marks under them; more conclusive, however, was the fact that she arrived on time and in full war-paint. Normally she was sloppy and careless about her appearance in college unless Louis was coming over. But today she wore a black dress instead of any old sweater and skirt; her hair was up and beautifully arranged; her eyes were outlined, shadowed, mascara'd; her lipstick was coral pink and shiny. She was even wearing stockings and pale cream, well polished shoes. The ensemble suggested nothing more stridently to me than that she had not slept all night and so had limitless time to prepare.

I said, 'I came to see you yesterday . . .' hoping for information but without much confidence, for Marty had long ago disrupted my cherished notion that friendship involved confiding everything, and immediately.

'I felt unsociable,' she said, with a small smile. 'I did a lot of work, though. Nearly finished my notes for the seminar.'

Then I had a wild hope that she was going to meet Louis after the lecture. That would account for her appearance. But at that moment the lecturer arrived so I could not ask her.

The lecture was about Restoration drama and the lecturer was amusing as well as informative. I took notes, carefully selecting what would be really useful. A vacation reading of my first-year lecture notes had convinced me that I had merely augmented the dustman's load or the winter fuel. In my first frenzy of eagerness and panic I had written down as much as my desperate, slithering pen could produce in the allotted time. Reviewed, it was either patently obvious or totally incomprehensible. Sometimes illegibility made it hard to decide which. Now, in my second year, I was trying to be more selective. Marty said lectures were only a guide to our reading and general approach to books and periods; it was the work we did alone and had dissected at tutorials and seminars that really counted. She wrote hardly anything in lectures and cut quite a few of them, which I was still a little cautious of doing. If I had nowhere else I wanted to go at the time, I felt I might as well attend a lecture, but it was annoying to go and find it a waste of time, when you could have been writing an essay. A lecturer's quality could generally be gauged by the proportion of jaded and busy third-year students in attendance. They turned out in large numbers for the really illuminating; the others they abandoned. First years, on the whole, flocked in faithfully and wrote their arms off. Second years were divided, still making up their minds. Of course, there were a few third years who attended everything, and some prematurely cynical freshers who never appeared at all. Lectures were supposed, on the whole, to be compulsory, but it was only in seminars or small classes for your special subject that you were likely to be missed. Occasionally a lecturer would make a fuss if attendance was very bad or a student particularly slack and then apologies, excuses and a few weeks of reform followed. Mostly, they let it go; doubtless aware, through years of experience, that in the end most people would make a desperate effort and pull through. Moreover, a few rows of meek heads in a lecture room did not necessarily signify retentive brains in action.

We used to argue a lot about the system: whether we wanted more seminars and tutorials and fewer lectures, as it was, we had heard, at Oxford and Cambridge. We thought on the whole that we did; but some of the people who cut their lectures claimed that it was quite hard enough to give in essays on time as it was, without trying to increase output. 'After all we're not just here to work,' they said, 'or we might as well take postal courses and save the government a lot of money.' There still remained the fact, astounding to undergraduates, that most people would pass. The odds were very much in favour of internal students. But among externals the failure rate was high. We were lucky; we had been born at the right time and we were having our chance.

After the lecture Marty asked me to her room to have coffee. On the way I found a letter for me in the 'M' pigeon-hole. The postmark was London area and I did not know the writing. For a full minute it was all a complete mystery to me. Then I knew. Marty was silent as we walked across so I opened the letter and read it. Mike wanted to see me again. He had thought a lot about me, he said. Would I go to a film with him on Saturday or could he come over one afternoon? I could almost see him trying to keep it light and casual, not to start apologizing for Friday night.

When we got to Marty's room it was very, very tidy. Another bad sign. Usually clothes, books and cosmetics were strewn everywhere. I sprawled on the bed while she made coffee, and wrote on file paper telling Mike I would not see him again. It felt good, being able to exclude someone who wanted to stay in my life. Most of the recent traffic had been the other way.

'Can I have an envelope and stamp?' I asked Marty.

'Help yourself. In the desk.'

'Are you going out?' I asked then.

'No. Why?'

'You look so gorgeous.'

Marty laughed, but that didn't mean anything. 'I'm not going anywhere unless you count a tutorial with Cunning-ham.'

'You'll vamp him,' I said brightly.

'He's past it.'

We drank coffee silently. I felt awkward.

'Lois, could I have a cigarette?' Marty asked suddenly.

'Of course.' I fished in my bag. 'I'm so sorry.'

Marty lit up. 'I expect Ruth told you,' she said.

I nodded.

Marty smiled. 'I bet it made her day.'

'It did, in a way. I wanted to wring her neck.'

107

'Why dirty your hands?' Marty said quietly, and then I knew Ruth had not told me everything. But I could not repeat the summary she had given me and ask Marty to fill in the gaps.

'She's a bitch,' Marty said. It was too mild a word for the emotion she obviously felt and I was scared. 'A real bitch,' she repeated.

'Is the party still on?' I asked.

Marty smiled again. 'Oh, yes, I expect so. It's nearly a fortnight away, after all.' But she looked sad and disbelieving. I felt a rush of affection and helplessness as I looked at her and there was nothing I could do for her except go on drinking her coffee and offering her my cigarettes.

On Friday I went to another dance but this time I was trapped by a heavy escort in his thirties who wrapped the car rug round my knees and kissed me solidly for ten minutes. He revolted me physically and I kept my mouth firmly shut and he had to make do with my neck and my closed lips. I seemed not a week but a century away from Mike and Hampstead Heath. But I had made up my mind never to allow myself to be in such desperate need again and so I would have to find partners more frequently, before I really needed them, so that I could remain in command of the situation and able to refuse if necessary.

The following night a dance was held in college. Most of the girls brought their own partners, but I went along anyway. There would probably be some unattached men there, I thought. I had overcome my initial squeamishness over sex with someone other than Peter through sheer hunger; now I wanted to know if I could do it in cold blood. I was afraid to leave it too long in case I lost my nerve and ended up exactly where I had begun.

At our dance (probably overlooked by Marty as too domestic a hunting-ground even for me) I met a lonely male who had come at the invitation of a girl he had met at an intercollegiate dance the week before. She was American, read

English, and was called Barbie. He described her minutely, but she meant nothing to me. She was certainly not in the room and his surprise was quite amusing. 'Never mind,' I said. 'Make do with me.' After a couple of hours dancing and talking I felt the need of a drink. We had no bar so I invited him to my room. The curtains were already drawn and the rest was easy. We had a couple of drinks each – less than I had needed with Mike – sitting close together on the bed. Then he kissed me and we fell backwards. He was really very attractive, but I could feel nothing. He had at least come prepared, which was a comfort and also aroused interesting speculations about Barbie's behaviour last week. He made love very competently, only it was not love and I felt depressed. I also felt immune. He knew it had not been a success and apologized.

'My fault, not yours,' I said, and repeated what I had said to Jeanne. 'It's all in the mind.' I pulled down my skirt and smoothed my hair. We returned to the dance, but I was not sorry to see him go.

On Sunday afternoon I had a shock. I was working in my room when there was a knock on the door. It was Mike. I was speechless with surprise, and also rather angry. I had not expected him to complicate matters by calling on me in spite of my refusal to see him.

'May I come in?' he asked, and came in, as I did not answer.

'I don't brush off easily,' he said.

'So I see.'

'Yes. I want an explanation. Not just a polite letter saying no thanks. I think you owe me that much.'

'I owe you nothing,' I said. I had read about people speaking from between clenched teeth but I had never done it before.

'Oh, I think you do,' he said smoothly. 'You were in a pretty bad way last week and I reckon I did you a big favour.'

I drew back my arm slightly, my pride hurt, longing to strike him. Then somehow I guessed that was what he wanted me to do; he was trying to break me down by insulting me. I tried to reverse the process.

'Quite right,' I said. 'Now I'd like to return it. I don't need any myself right now because I had someone here last night but I'd be more than happy to fix you up if you haven't been so lucky.'

There was a flicker of something across his face, like pain. I had actually hurt him. I waded in for the kill.

'There's the bed,' I said, pointing with one hand. 'A bit hard but better than the ground.'

'All right,' he said. 'You made your point. You really need to hurt someone, don't you? Well, it might as well be me.' The awful thing was, I think, he really did mean it. I went on looking at him and through him, tightening my throat muscles, until he finally turned away. 'Well, you know where I live,' he said, and slammed the door after him. I stood and stared at it. I had done what I wanted to do and yet I had the stupid feeling I had sent away a friend.

THIRTEEN

MARTY and Louis were giving their party to celebrate Louis'
move to a newer, larger flat. It was in a big, crumbling house
and in the hall everything was very dark. Anne and Keith
were invited and we all went over together. Marty had gone
over early that morning and declined all offers of help. As
far as I knew, the quarrel had not yet been made up, though
I still had no idea what it was about. I wished now that I had
not agreed to go to the party.

'I don't like parties where the host and hostess aren't speaking,' I said.

'Who knows?' said Keith. 'They've had all day to make it
up. I'm only worried we'll get there and find them still in
bed and no food or drink ready. "What party?" they'll say
when we walk in.'

Louis greeted us at the door. There were already sounds
of jubilation from within so we were not the first to arrive.
We had certainly tried to come decently late but then so,
presumably, had everyone else.

It was always a surprise to see Louis had just one head. I
had met him a few times before but only briefly as Marty
never wasted time on girls when he was available. But seeing
his effect on Marty and hearing about him from Marty and
Ruth made me build a separate picture of him as a sensual
ogre and a ravening, neurotic beast. Naturally, he could not
be expected to look like a monster.

He looked, in fact, very French (which was something I
always forgot). He was not very tall, but then Marty was
shorter than I was, and he had really black hair and a sallow

skin, currently tanned but always looking slightly in need of a shave even if he had just had one. He had very long eye-lashes, but I never remember noticing the colour of his eyes. I suppose they must have been dark. He was really very attractive, but I could never forget that Anne had once compared him to a handsome monkey. His features were rather monkeyish, except for his mouth, which was beautiful. He had very well-shaped hands, but all his gestures were restrained as if he were trying to prove that he too could behave like a typical English gentleman.

Now he greeted us all with reserved pleasure: no hand kissing, in fact no contact at all. He held a cigarette in one hand and a bottle opener in the other. 'Hullo; please come in. We are delighted to see you all. Marty is in the kitchen; this evening it is a bar. You have each already missed two drinks.' He smiled at us engagingly and some of the things Marty had told me about him floated round my head: impossible to imagine him weeping or beating her head against the wall or changing sex partners with his room-mate. Perhaps Marty had made it all up.

Louis hung our coats in the hall before taking us into the kitchen. It was somehow a shock to see Marty there; for one crazy moment I felt she and Louis were married and the rest was a dream. I looked at her hard, but her face was a party face and revealed nothing. Besides, she was not the sort of friend to shoot meaningful glances at me across a room full of people. She was wearing a straight, gold dress with tiny pleats at the hem that moved with her; her hair was up and elaborately dressed, though if the party was a success it would not last the evening. Her make-up was a work of art and her nails looked lethal.

She gave us all drinks and said, 'After this you help yourselves.' We had all brought bottles and she put them on the table with the others. 'Louis will explain the system to you,' she added without looking at him.

'Oh, yes. All the doors are in the hall which is very convenient,' said Louis. 'Except the dining-room which is here, beside the kitchen.' He pointed and we looked through the doorway at a roomful of people all dancing to French records on the gramophone. 'That is for dancing,' he added unnecessarily. 'There is no carpet.' He returned us to the hall. 'Here is the sitting-room. No dancing here so people can talk.' Couples were already dotted about, some standing, deep in conversation, others deep in armchairs. There was candlelight in both rooms; it was really very pretty.

Louis pointed to the bedroom. 'This is for love,' he said as calmly as if indicating a lavatory and explaining its function. 'There is no bulb in the light. Here, opposite, is the bathroom. Please enjoy yourselves.' He smiled at us and disappeared into the kitchen.

'Well,' said Anne, 'it's certainly a very well organized party.'

'Just Latin frankness,' said Keith. 'They come right out with it, you know. Come to think of it, he put it very delicately.'

'Spare us the alternative versions,' said Anne. 'We can all devise our own.'

'Wonder if there's anyone in there yet?' Keith said thoughtfully.

'Don't let me stand in your way,' I said. 'I want another drink. Do you suppose it would be tactless to go in the kitchen?'

'Go ahead,' said Keith. 'They told us to help ourselves. You won't find them hard at it on the kitchen floor in front of all those people.'

'Don't overdo it, honey,' Anne said. She was worried about my drinking. Usually I appreciated her concern, but tonight it annoyed me. I went into the kitchen and stopped in the doorway. Louis' back was to the door, but Marty was looking at him and I saw her face. 'Please,' she was saying, with urgent humility. I felt horribly intrusive. Then she saw me and propped a smile on her face. I wished myself anywhere but where I was. Louis shrugged silently and turned round. He refilled my glass for me and Marty went suddenly out of the room. I was so upset that I interfered without even the excuse of too much alcohol.

'Be kind to Marty, Louis,' I said, trying to keep my voice light and conversational.

Louis looked at me in surprise, frowning slightly. He gave me my drink and said with perfect courtesy, 'Of course, you may say what you wish, Lois, but you must understand I cannot discuss Marty with you.'

I stared at the floor, deservedly snubbed, yet hating him just the same. It made it even worse that he suddenly appeared overwhelmingly attractive. He waited politely, in case I had anything to add, and then said, 'Excuse me,' and disappeared into the dining-room. I drank my drink in one movement, like people in films. I had never done it before but now I realized how and why they did it. In cases of desperate need it was really quite easy. I refilled my glass and lit a cigarette. I badly wanted to see Anne; she seemed like a buoy of safety to me. I went back in the hall, but she and Keith were not there. I peeped into the sitting-room and saw them both standing next to a tall, broad-shouldered man and a very elegant woman. They were all talking animatedly. Anne saw me and signalled just as I was about to retreat so I had to join them.

Keith introduced me to Mr and Mrs Stone. Mr Stone, it turned out, was one of Keith's professors, and was also supervising Louis' postgraduate work. He and his wife were so deeply and beautifully tanned that they looked like an advertisement for sun-oil.

'Easy to see it didn't rain on your holidays,' I said gaily, my tongue loosened by three drinks.

Mrs Stone laughed. 'We went to Majorca,' she said. 'I can really recommend it. I'd never been before.'

'Looks like I'm the only paleskin on the prairie,' I said.

'Better watch out then,' said Mr Stone. 'You don't want to end up biting the dust.'

I smiled and studied them both, deciding they were nice people. Mrs Stone was tall and large-boned, rather like Ruth in build, but otherwise quite different. She wore a blue-green dress and heaps of blue-green eye shadow to match but no foundation or powder. Her only other make-up was pale, shiny orange lipstick. She had light brown hair, streaked with blonde, arranged in such a casual style that she had obviously come straight from the hairdresser. Her husband was not quite good-looking but very rugged: not a type I usually admire. He had very blue eyes and marvellous teeth. I thought he looked rather American, Hollywood version anyway; not at all a professor of Engineering, except in a film.

They went on talking to Anne and Keith, but went out of their way to include me in the conversation. Just common politeness, I hoped; I did not want to look the waif I felt. Then they saw someone else they knew and excused themselves.

'Fancy Louis inviting them,' said Keith.

Anne shrugged. 'Oh, well, darling, he's not so much in awe of them as you are. They're nice, aren't they? Easy to talk –'

'Damn,' said Keith suddenly. 'I said Mrs Stone. It should be Doctor. How bloody stupid of me.'

'Oh, is she a doctor?' I asked, interested.

'Yes. She's very clever, actually. She's going to America next year on some research project or other. Damn. I hope she didn't notice.'

'Wonder if Louis tried his "this is for love" routine on them when he showed them round?' said Anne.

'Doubt it,' Keith said. 'They've been married ten years or more.'

Anne pouted. With Keith she was occasionally almost

kittenish, a quality she never otherwise displayed. 'Don't be so cynical, darling. One day we'll have been married ten years or more. I don't intend to give up sex in my early thirties even if you do.'

Keith grinned. 'Cheer up, darling. I only meant they can probably wait till they get home.'

'Look,' I said, suddenly desperate and unable to bear it alone any more, 'I'm sorry to change the subject but I just dropped a brick.'

Keith seemed about to make a joke but didn't. They both looked at me seriously. I felt a ridiculous urge to howl. They were such beautiful golden people, full of confidence and strength. They had each other and nothing ever went really wrong for them.

'What did you do, honey?' Anne asked gently because I had stopped.

I swallowed and tried again. 'When I went into the kitchen just now Marty looked as if she was trying to make things up and Louis wouldn't play. She looked so upset – it was awful. I walked right into it. She went out and I – I asked Louis to be nice to her. He very politely told me to mind my own business or words to that effect.'

'Oh, dear,' said Anne.

'I suppose he was quite justified,' I said miserably. 'You don't drink someone's drinks and tell them how to behave at the same time. Not if you've got any sense, anyway. D'you suppose I've made it worse?'

'Oh, no,' said Anne. 'They'll sort it out sometime. It won't do Louis any harm to be given a kick in the pants, however mild. I'd like to give him one myself.'

'Well, I don't agree with you,' Keith said flatly. 'We've got no idea what hell he has to put up with from Marty. He must have a point of view as well, you know. You only hear hers.'

'He makes her miserable,' I said stubbornly.

'And she loves every minute of it,' Keith replied. 'Looks like a perfect union of sadist and masochist to me.'

'It's not as simple as that,' I said, though at one time I had wondered if it might be.

'You women,' said Keith, teasing deliberately. 'You love to make out things are more complicated than they really are.'

'And you men love to give your views on things you don't understand,' said Anne. But her heart wasn't in it. I had got in their way; they did not normally go in for sex warfare, however mild. I smiled at them and excused myself.

In the hall I met Marty coming out of the bathroom. She was wearing rather too much of her favourite scent and the hand she put on my arm was icy cold, though it was quite a warm evening for autumn.

'Are you all right?' I asked, trying not to sound anxious. I wondered if she had been sick.

'Sure, why not? Come with me and meet some people.'

She took me into the dining-room, somewhat more crowded now than when we had arrived. Somehow you never imagine people coming after you at parties.

'We're going to meet Adrienne first,' said Marty. 'You remember, I went to school with her. She's separated from her husband and he's trying to get custody of the baby by proving she's immoral. But the baby's too young to notice, anyway.'

Adrienne was a redhead, her freckles masked by heavy make-up. She wore a huge gold wedding ring and was dressed in a tight black frock. She said, 'Hullo, darling,' to Marty, and looked at me closely. 'Well, aren't you cute?' she said in the way other people comment on the weather.

'Cutest thing I know,' I said. I had already decided I did not like Adrienne. She actually laughed. There was a haze around my eyes as a result of the drinks I had taken. I had not eaten much before I came to the party, either.

'What does Adrienne do?' I whispered to Marty as we moved on. 'Or is that a silly question?'

'Oh, you're quite right,' said Marty, unsmiling. 'But she

117

does some modelling on the side. Actually, she was trained as a shorthand typist.'

'Well, my God,' I said in amazement. 'Her and my mother both.'

Next I met Sheila, a silvery blonde wrapped round a very slim, dark young man called Yves, a friend of Louis. He looked like the prototype of every wolf in creation.

'Next to him Louis looks like Santa Claus,' I whispered, hoping Marty would not be offended.

'Oh, he is,' she said drily, smiling. 'Now over there is Ron. The one kissing that girl. Sheila's engaged to him. I want you to notice him because later on he may ask you where Sheila is and you mustn't tell him even if you know. She'll probably be in bed with Yves. He's been working on her all evening.'

'Ron looks pretty occupied himself,' I said.

'Oh, he's not serious about Maureen; she's just an old flame. But she might just keep him busy for the evening and let Sheila have her chance with Yves. He'd be an education for Sheila. Do her the world of good.' She sounded reminiscent.

It crossed my mind how much Peter would hate all these people and I was not even sure I liked them myself. But I was very fond indeed of Marty. It was as if I had never realized how much until this evening. She seemed more vulnerable than ever as Louis' hostess, at his flat, with his guests. I desperately wanted her to turn to me and say, 'It's all right, you know. We've made it up. Everything's fine.' I was resigned to the fact that I would probably never know what had gone wrong.

'I'm going to introduce you to Tom,' said Marty, 'and if you could keep him out of Adrienne's clutches I'd be grateful.'

'I thought you'd abandoned him,' I said.

'He's a good friend,' said Marty. 'I don't want him eaten alive by Adrienne. He deserves better.'

'Couldn't you team up Adrienne and Yves?' I suggested. 'They sound so alike.'

'Two pros. No good,' said Marty briskly. 'There's Tom over there.'

I looked; he seemed tolerable. Ordinary but pleasant. Obviously Marty had nothing exotic lined up for me this evening. I wondered if it was an entire fabrication that I was to save him from Adrienne. Not that it really mattered.

'I ought to mention,' I said, 'that I already made a start myself in this direction.' I paused, suddenly idiotically embarrassed. 'Two scalps so far.'

'I thought you might,' said Marty. She sounded very remote. 'I didn't really fancy myself as Pandarus, you know.' She introduced me to Tom, squeezed my hand and disappeared into the crowd.

'You haven't got a drink,' said Tom. 'Shall I get you one or would you like to dance?'

'Let's dance,' I said. 'I've had three drinks and I really need a rest before starting again, though it shames me to admit it.'

'Oh, why?' said Tom. 'We all have our limitations.'

To my surprise he was a fantastically good dancer. I had not expected anyone discarded by Marty to be fantastically good at anything. But he made everyone I had ever danced with seem like a fumbling beginner. We danced in silence for quite some time until he said smoothly, as if there had been no gap in the conversation, 'Now my limitations are an inability to stop loving Marty and an obsession with telling people so. Can you bear that, do you think?'

I was so startled that I nearly stopped dancing. It occurred to me that it was a long time since I had heard someone frankly and sincerely use the word love, though I seemed to have been moving through a world of love-substitutes, like tins of instant coffee.

'Yes, I can,' I said. 'In fact I just decided that I like you.' I knew he would not misunderstand me. I could say anything I wanted to say. It was going to be a wonderful party after all. How sensible of Marty to introduce us.

'That's fine,' said Tom. 'Now shall we go on dancing?'

And then I found that my feet had really stopped, after all, without my noticing.

'I always warn people early,' he said, as we moved off again, 'so they can run if they want to. Some do and I don't really blame them. It depends what you're looking for.'

'Right now,' I said. 'Marty is my favourite subject. I'm very worried about her.'

He smiled. 'Oh, yes, this row. It's a bad one, but I think they'll make it up tonight. It's the long-term view that worries me. When Louis goes back to France. Unless something happens to make Marty break with him first she's going to be in a pretty bad way.'

'Do you know what it's all about?' I asked.

He shook his head. 'Probably something quite trivial. The cause is unimportant. It's the actual degree of venom they spit that makes it serious. They are much too alike and basically incompatible. They exhaust one another and they have to separate to recharge.'

He talked calmly and seriously, an expert in his chosen subject. I wondered if he was very unhappy, waiting on the sidelines, a born stretcher-bearer. Or did he derive a certain satisfaction from being so knowledgeable?

When he stopped talking we went on dancing in silence and I realized I would not have to talk for the sake of talking and he would not either. It was a great relief. I felt my body relax and my dancing improve.

After a long time of peace and movement he said, 'Would you like to eat? Then you could start drinking again?'

'Do I look like an alcoholic?'

'No, but inhibited people like us need to drink at parties so that we don't feel superior to everyone else later on.'

This was true but I felt vaguely alarmed.

'Look, I don't know what Marty has told you –'

'She hasn't told me anything except that you're friends and she wanted us to meet.'

'Is this party going to turn into an orgy later on?'

'It's possible. Don't you like orgies?'

'I've never actually attended one,' I said truthfully. 'But right now I feel rather self-conscious about it.'

Tom smiled. 'That proves you're sobering up. Don't worry: there's one thing about an orgy, you can always leave early and nobody will notice.'

We went into the sitting-room and found all sorts of fishy, cheesy and nutty food spread out. There were olives, too, and celery, and garlic-flavoured biscuits. We ate a lot. I began to feel thirsty.

'I'll get you a long drink,' said Tom. 'A special Miles cocktail.'

'Don't be long,' I said. 'You are my refuge and my help.'

He had hardly gone before Marty appeared as if from nowhere.

'Hullo, he's nice, isn't he?' she said.

'Very nice,' I said. 'Has he sworn an oath to go to bed with me?'

'Don't be silly,' she said. 'You don't even have to shake hands if you don't feel like it. He's used to me being neurotic – nothing you do will surprise him.'

'Don't sound so superior,' I said. 'As if you had a monopoly of problems.'

'Oh, God,' she said, 'not you too.'

'Sorry,' I said. 'What happened?'

She shook her head. 'Have you seen Louis?'

'No.'

'Oh, well, stand by for blasting.' And she disappeared again. When Tom returned with the drinks I said, 'I saw Marty on the warpath. Looks like an all-out effort to get him back.'

Tom said, 'It has to be that way. Louis never apologizes.'

We drank. It was lovely but indecipherable.

'What's in this?' I asked.

'Oh, vermouth and things,' he said vaguely. 'It's a happy drink, that's the main thing. As to this party being an orgy,' he went on, again as if there had been no change of subject, 'it isn't really, you know. It's a genuine attempt to please all the people all of the time.'

'I thought that was impossible,' I said.

'So they say. But Louis might just do it.'

'You're very fair to him,' I said. 'Considering.'

'Well,' Tom said, 'I reckon anyone who can hold Marty's interest for so long must have really got something.'

'There might just be a rude answer to that,' I said, flushing slightly.

Tom smiled. 'Oh, there is. But it's not the only answer. I'm afraid I let Marty down on all counts. You see, what she really wants is endless stimulation, mental, physical, whatever, the whole time.'

'I suppose so,' I said slowly. 'That certainly fits in with things she's said. Please don't think I'm being superior but is it something she'll grow out of?'

'Quite probably,' said Tom. 'But that doesn't make it any less urgent a need right now, does it?'

A blast of flamenco from the other room suddenly shot through our conversation. 'That's Marty,' I said, quite certain.

Tom seemed unmoved. Perhaps to him it was like a re-issue of an old film. 'Do you want to watch?'

'I think so.'

A space had been cleared for Marty in the middle of the room. The guests stood round, Anne and Keith among them. Yves had joined Marty and they looked marvellous together. I turned to watch Louis; if Marty had arranged this display for his benefit he would surely show some reaction, although it all seemed very primitive and almost childish to me. Perhaps I had misunderstood and Marty was dancing for the sheer love of it. Louis was smoking a cigarette. His face was expressionless. I looked away again, around the room. Ron and Maureen were nowhere to be seen. Mr Stone was talking to his wife, the doctor. Sheila was looking very disgruntled.

A whole crowd of people who had not been introduced to me were watching the display. To my unskilled eye it appeared very professional.

'There you are,' said Tom. 'Q.E.D.'

'But Louis,' I said. 'No reaction.'

'That's his gimmick.'

Perhaps flamenco music is the most erotic in the world; it seemed so then. Perhaps flamenco dancing is the most sensual ever performed; I thought it was. But at the same time I felt I was witnessing a deliberate set-piece, coldly devised by a desperate woman. As such, I was not even sure if it was impressive or ridiculous.

The dance finally ended, abruptly, as it does, and to my amazement, amid a storm of clapping, Marty and Yves left the room together. I had the foolish idea that they would return to take a bow, as if the curtain had come down and would be raised again. But obviously everyone else knew better. I heard a door close in the hall. People started talking; some laughed. They lit cigarettes, changed the record, started dancing again. Only a few watched Louis. I did. Adrienne was beside him and seemed to be talking to him urgently. It was impossible to tell if he were taking any notice. His face still showed no emotion but his body, dressed in casual party clothes, was completely tense. I wondered what Adrienne was saying. Unobtrusively Tom had fetched me another drink. I drank it hurriedly. He gave me a cigarette but did not take one himself.

'Don't you smoke?' I said, as if it mattered at that particular moment.

'No. I always carried some for Marty and it became a habit.'

I wondered how he could say her name so calmly. 'Tom. What's going to *happen* now?'

He shrugged his shoulders. 'Oh, Louis will retaliate but it's all right. She'll get him back.'

'How do you know?'

'It's the way they work. It's the coldness she had to break through. Once he gets violent, she's won. She's close to him again.'

I felt exhausted. 'Well, it all looks absolutely crazy to me.'

'Not crazy. Just not the way you would behave.'

I kept my eyes on my watch, though I felt embarrassed doing so. Adrienne went on talking to Louis and he went on staring at the door. After about twenty minutes Marty came back alone. Her hair was down. It sprawled defiantly, blatantly, all over her shoulders. Louis moved across to her like an automaton. No one but me took any notice. He slapped her face so hard that her head spun round to one side in almost a half circle, as far as it could go. Marty started to laugh and went on laughing, hysterically. Louis took her by one wrist and disappeared into the bathroom with her. There was the sound of the bolt being shot across and then I heard water running; splashing and gurgling. There was a faint scream, then silence, except for the water.

'You don't suppose he's drowning her?' I said to Tom.

'Don't be silly.'

But I thought he looked rather tense himself now. Just then Anne and Keith came across so I introduced him to them.

'We're going,' said Keith. 'Can we give you a lift?'

'No, thanks,' said Tom. 'How about you, Lois?'

I shook my head, without thinking, bemused.

'Well, we're off,' said Keith. 'We've had enough, as you might say.'

'I'm afraid this party made us feel awfully old,' Anne said. 'Married and middle-aged and all that.'

I smiled. 'I know what you mean.' I felt very tired but not quite prepared to join Anne against Marty even if I disapproved of the evening's performance.

After they had gone, I sat down. My legs felt weak. Yves reappeared and had a consultation with Adrienne; then they left together. Ron reappeared, without Maureen. Sheila fell upon him and you could tell she was nagging him, even across the whole room. I had another cigarette. Half the other one had burnt away in my fingers.

'Do you want to dance?' Tom asked.

'I don't think I could.'

'Do you want another drink?'

'That would be suicidal.'

We sat in silence for a while and I closed my eyes. But I soon opened them again to stop everything spinning round.

'Is it very hot in here?' I asked. 'Or is that just part of my besotted condition?'

'It is very hot,' Tom said, 'but that doesn't let you out completely.'

I laughed and held his hand. It was bony and comforting.

'You're nice,' I said.

'Thanks, that's the story of my life.'

'I'm sorry, would you rather forget it?'

'No, but it's a very ineffectual trademark, I'm afraid.'

The noise in the room mounted. It was hard to hear the water running now. I felt very sorry for Tom.

'Never mind,' I said, 'your turn will come.'

'Do you feel all right?' Tom asked.

'I'm fine,' I said carefully. 'Only I don't like parties. I just decided.'

'Then you mustn't go to any more,' said Tom.

'That's right, I won't.' I leaned against his shoulder. Roars of laughter came from the other side of the room. Somebody was telling a funny story. Presently there were sounds in the hall as if the bathroom door was being opened. The water seemed to have stopped running. No one came into the dining-room, however, so I peered round the kitchen door. Marty, wearing a dressing-gown on which her soaking wet hair was spread out, was trying to pour two drinks, somewhat impeded by the fact that Louis had both arms round her. They were both laughing foolishly, as far as I could see, at nothing at all.

Tom looked too. He was very pale. 'What did I tell you?' he said. 'Old Miles' Almanac triumphs again.'

'Shall we go?' I suggested. I had ominous pains in my back.

'What an excellent idea. I'll get your coat.'

'It's a green one. Do we have to say thank you?' I jerked my head at the kitchen door.

'No, better not disturb them.' He seemed in as great a hurry to leave as I was. We made our way through the hall, ignoring muffled sounds from the bedroom, and the cold air of the night hit us without mercy.

'I'm afraid,' said Tom, 'I forgot to mention I haven't got a car.'

'That's all right,' I said. 'I'll get the tube.'

Tom consulted his watch. 'At half past one in the morning?'

'No. It isn't. It can't be.'

'Well, it is.' He held out his arm to show me.

'So it is.' I sagged against a lamp-post, amazed.

'We should have accepted a lift from your friends. O rather you should.'

'I know,' I said. 'But my mind was on other things. What will you do?'

'Oh, my flat is only ten minutes' walk from here,' he said calmly. 'It's you I'm worried about.'

'Please don't be,' I said politely.

'Well, you've got to sign in or something, haven't you?'

'No,' I said. 'I didn't sign out. I meant to crawl in through my bedroom window. You know, in the classic tradition. Only it's a long walk from here.'

Tom seemed about to sit down on the pavement but I seized his arm. 'Don't. You might never get up again.'

'Well,' he said, 'there are three alternatives. If you can have three alternatives. One, we get a taxi.'

'Expensive,' I said.

'Agreed. Two, we go back and get one of those drunken guests to drive you.'

126

'Risky,' I said.

'Quite so. Three, we walk as best we can to my flat where there is a divan as well as a bed.'

'Start walking,' I said. He seemed the one safe thing in a crazy world and I clung to his hand like a child.

FOURTEEN

WE slept chastely that night and I thought, through the haze of party aftermath, that Tom was exactly the sort of brother Martin should have been. It made me very happy that he knew nothing about me and yet was being so kind. At six, to my shame, I woke him, trying to light the gas for a hot water bottle.

'I'm sorry, are you cold?' he asked drowsily from the couch.

'I have a pain,' I said delicately. Then I thought how ridiculous it was to be coy when I was actually sharing a one-room flat with a comparative stranger. 'My period's starting and I feel awful. Heat always helps me. Trouble is, it's a bit early and I'm not prepared.'

'Top drawer of the dressing-table, Tampax and codeine,' he said. 'Marty left them once. I'll shut my eyes.'

'Tom,' I said, rummaging, 'did Marty actually live with you?'

'For a few weeks,' he said, yawning. 'Till she got bored. She was in a bad way when I met her and she couldn't face going home that vac. Her mother had just remarried and it was going to be one hell of a holy, happy Christmas.'

'Oh, yes, I remember vaguely,' I said. 'Sorry. It's a bit early to start on this.'

'Not at all, my favourite subject, remember? Did you find what you need?'

'Yes, thank you.'

Presently, fortified with warmth and dope and fully protected against the onslaughts of nature, I climbed back into bed. 'I'm glad it's come,' I said confidentially because it seemed only natural that Tom should be interested.

'Did you take a risk?' he asked.

'Not really. Only a very small one. But it was someone I hardly knew. I was in a bad way, too.' Perhaps if I sounded like Marty he would understand. But I did not want him to feel I did this sort of thing carelessly, without effort.

'Don't think about it, it's over,' said Tom surprisingly. 'Go back to sleep.'

And I did, very suddenly, before I could even thank him or apologize for waking him. The next thing I was conscious of was the smell of coffee. Tom was up, dressed in very old, faded trousers and a long, baggy sweater over his shirt.

'How do you feel?' he asked.

'Fine. What time is it?'

'Oh – nearly eleven.'

'I must go to the bathroom.'

'Borrow my dressing-gown. It's on the door.'

When I came back there was grapefruit and toast with butter and marmalade, some on the table, some on a tray.

'Get back in bed,' said Tom. 'This is for you.'

I scrambled in. 'How lovely to be waited on.' I drank nearly all the coffee at once. 'I'm awfully thirsty. I always am after a party.'

Tom refilled my cup. 'Any hangover?'

'A bit. Not really. This is lovely. It's very kind of you.'

'Don't be silly. It's nice to have someone to look after.'

I stayed the whole day. We spent a silent morning with the papers and the wireless, then ate scrambled eggs for lunch. Tom's store cupboard was not very full. In the afternoon we played chess. Peter had taught me and I had forgotten how much I liked it. We had beans on toast for supper and then went to a film. When he left me at college we arranged to go to a dance the following Saturday.

I suppose with Tom I began the sort of life one is meant to lead at university. We discovered a common passion for opera, which I had quelled in myself because Peter did not enjoy it. Tom liked ballet, too, and tried to educate me, though without much success. It seemed too stylized and largely without emotion, at least such as could be communicated to me. I should have been accustomed to it from childhood, I thought. I well remembered afternoons spent listening to Wagner records with my father.

Tom and I went to theatres, too, always in cheap seats as neither of us had much money. I became extremely well-informed as to what was worth seeing in London. Doubtless, it was ridiculous to be at university in the capital and spend your days working or talking to your friends and your weekends in bed with someone who, it turned out, did not want to marry you after all.

I told Tom nothing of importance about myself and he did not ask. Nevertheless, we talked a lot : about him and Marty, about college, about the shows we had seen. I started going to bed with him after about three weeks of friendship. I supposed things would never again move so slowly as they had with Peter during our first year. That part of my life was over. It is one of the hardest lessons, I think, that the clock cannot be turned back.

Bed with Tom was strange. I had no overwhelming desire for it but there seemed no reason to avoid it either. It was neither a failure nor a success. I did not have the dead feeling I had experienced with the American girl's date; neither did I achieve an orgasm anything near the quality of some I had had with Peter or the one with Mike. As my emotions were not involved with Tom I could be quite clinical about the physical aspect. With Peter my feelings had always heightened successes and modified failures. Tom and I just about broke even. We kept each other going. As long as I had Tom I would not have to descend to the desperate state of need in which I had met Mike. I did not want that again. It was humiliating, without love. Even worse was the numbing pointlessness of the encounter in my room on the night of the college dance. I decided I was not really designed for the casual approach. I told Anne about Tom, but not about the others. She understood and seemed quite pleased for me. I played down Tom's obsession with Marty; there must have been few girls who would have listened willingly to all he wanted to say about her. Privately I thought we were like two crippled people helping each other along.

After the party the term ran steadily downhill. Anne celebrated her twenty-first three times; once with her parents, who gave a dance for her; once at a theatre and hotel with Keith; once in college. The college party was a problem. Anne was afraid of inviting people who would spit at each other, but at the same time preferred to give one large party instead of two small ones at which people could be segregated. In the end all passed off well but quietly. Guests were very wary and careful. It was scarcely a sensation as a party but as a social event it went very smoothly. I brought Tom and Marty brought Louis, and Ruth had to go somewhere else, which was really the best way out of Anne's difficulties. Jeanne and John came; he, very attractive but aggressively masculine and followed everywhere by Jeanne's adoring eyes. There were plenty of people from Anne's History department, whom I knew only by sight. Keith made an excellent host and the whole thing ended, with perfect decorum, at eleven.

After meeting Tom I had started working again. I had even started doing a little studying each day, the way I had always intended to. I felt I was living a most orderly life. I did not see very much of Marty as I was now out a lot and she was absorbed in her ecstatic reconciliation. But about a week before the end of term she began to show signs of depression. Louis was going to spend the whole vacation in France with his family.

'Can't you go along?' I asked.

'No. I'm not suitable.' She was neglecting her appearance again : hair straight down, no make-up, dirty jeans and sweater, broken-down flat pumps. 'They don't want to know about me. One day Louis is going to marry the right girl who'll be French and domesticated. Religious, too.' She laughed shortly.

'But you don't want to marry him,' I said, trying to comfort her. 'They aren't really stopping you.'

'It'd be all the same if I did,' she replied morosely.

Then my calm life was punctured, shortly before we went down. There was a letter for me in unfamiliar writing. For a wild moment, before I examined the postmark, I thought it must be from Tom, breaking off with me. Instead I read this:

Dear Lois,

You may be offended at me writing to you but I hope not. I have been wanting to meet you all along but I quite understand you not wanting to meet me. I wouldn't, in your position. The only thing is, David is very anxious for us to meet and he's getting unhappy because we haven't. I know we both want the best for him so if you could see me just once I'd be ever so grateful. Then if you don't want us to meet again I could tell him we just don't get on, as a purely feminine thing. I think it would be all right. Please could you do this? We could meet at a coffee bar or something, there's no need for you to come to the flat again. Any time would suit me. Please come, just this once.

It was signed: 'Philippa Goldberg'.

I showed it to Anne. 'Blackmail,' I said. 'Sheer blackmail. "We both want the best for him." And so bloody understanding. Knowing so much about how I feel, seeing my point of view and all that. He said she was a very understanding person. Well, it certainly looks like it. My God!'

Anne let me rant for a while and then she said, 'All the same, she is in a tricky position. What would you do?'

I said, 'I'm tired of trying to see two sides to every question.'

'I know,' said Anne gently. 'It's just unfortunate that there generally are. You know that really. Don't you think you should see her? You'll have to eventually.'

'You mean at the wedding?' I asked.

'Not necessarily. But some time. It isn't as if you were on your mother's side, like Martin.'

Sometimes, I thought, Anne could be very dense. But she was right. I would have to see her some time if only to stop my father asking me to and looking sad because I didn't. I would have to see her and the sooner the better. It might even be smart to see them together in future; that might at least stop him talking the whole time about how wonderful she was.

So I wrote back, a polite little note, accepting her kind invitation. I had played, late at night, with all manner of savage replies and all sorts of sardonic forms of address on the step-mother theme. I knew I would not use them. We are all brought up to be polite, after all, and life is civilized, not a jungle, so they say.

FIFTEEN

WE met in the station buffet. It was the most unpropitious place I could think of, and besides, I did not want to set out from my mother's house to meet her. I thought of how many times my father must have done that.

She raised her hand when I came in, so presumably there was a likeness, or she had studied photographs, but I would have known her anyway. Sitting alone, at a table with only two chairs (clever of her to find one); brown-haired, pale, dressed in a brown coat with a black fur collar. I wondered if my father had bought it for her. It looked new.

I went over, dumping my suitcase beside the table. She stood up and held out her hand. I longed to ignore it but of course I didn't. We shook hands politely and she said, 'I'll get coffee.'

The first words I had heard her speak. They echoed in my head while she was away. The ash-tray in front of me was full of filter tips. My train had been late, nearly three quarters of an hour.

She had a low voice, but cool, self-possessed. She was attractive, really. I must be fair to her. Not a beauty or wonderfully pretty, but attractive. And she looked quite normal: was she, was this whole meeting, going to be an anticlimax? What had I expected? I didn't know. Hatred had obscured my imagination.

She came back and set the cups on the table before sitting down.

'Thank you for coming,' she said, getting cigarettes out of her bag. 'Will you have one?'

Of course, I did. I longed to make a violent answer and ram them down her throat, but I took one, like a peaceful citizen, and let her light it for me. Then I noticed her hands were shaking and I began to feel better.

She examined her nails for a moment and then looked me full in the face. Her eyes were blue. She had delicate features: Jewish, now I knew, but not heavily so. She wore hardly any make-up. I had spent half an hour in the washroom on the train preparing my face for the occasion.

'Please say something,' she said, 'if it's only that you hate my guts.'

'All right,' I said. 'I do.' And I managed a thin little smile.

She nodded. 'It was very good of you to come.'

Her perfume reached me across the table : glorious, subtle, expensive. I knew it at once, a kind I had always wanted but never bought, and now I never would.

'That's all right,' I said. 'I'm a big-hearted character.'

'I've behaved badly,' she said. 'I had no right to get involved with a married man. But I think it was breaking up already.'

'If it's any comfort to you,' I said, 'my mother thinks so too.'

'It wasn't meant as an excuse,' she said. 'Just a comment. But it isn't any comfort to you, is it?'

'I'm afraid not,' I said. 'But there. I can't expect to have it all my own way, can I?'

And then came the surprise. 'No, you can't,' she said.

Irony is a dangerous weapon, a boomerang. But just as I was thinking this and wondering how to counter, she went on, 'I don't think anyone can. I have gained David and lost my parents. He has gained me and a chance to live as he wants to, but he's lost his wife and son. I just wanted to see if there was any hope of him not losing you, too.'

'I don't think you've got any right to ask me that,' I said. I was very angry.

'No, no rights. But rights don't come into this. We're all

past that stage. Rights were out of it when your parents split up.'

And yet they had both used the word, I thought.

'We are all just people,' she said, 'making mistakes and trying again. It is up to us how well we succeed. There is no question of rights and punishments, all handed over in neat little parcels. You chose what you do and you work hard at it. Maybe, if you are lucky, it comes out right. But there can be no question of taking for granted a smooth passage.' She paused.

'Quite the philosopher, aren't you?' I said.

'I try to make sense,' she said calmly. 'But please say whatever you like if it makes you feel better.'

There is nothing like complete licence for restraining an impulse. 'Thank you,' I said, 'but I think I've probably been as rude as I'm going to be.' I hid my face in the coffee cup and drank. It was railway coffee and tasted of nothing in particular, a nameless drink.

'I love your father very much,' she said quietly. I could feel her watching me. 'And I find that very hard to say to anyone but him. I only want to make him happy. I want to spend my life doing that. But I know perfectly well he won't ever be completely happy. He will always wonder. If I am lucky, he will say to himself, "Yes, I did the right thing." But the question will be there and I must live with it. If you go away from him you could turn the answer into no. Not immediately, perhaps, but one day. I don't know what time will do to us.'

I felt emotion, the last thing I had ever expected or wanted. 'Are you foreign?' I asked, to hide it. 'You sound foreign sometimes.'

'I lived a long time in Israel,' she said. 'And I speak two languages. Sometimes they get mixed up.' She stirred her coffee.

'It's funny,' I said. 'I've wasted a lot of energy hating you.'

'Oh,' she said, 'I've thought and thought about how you

must feel. I tried to think of the best approach. It was awful. I could only do it by putting myself in your shoes and then I felt terrible. I had to stop that or I would never have had the courage to write to you.'

'You probably did the right thing,' I said. 'We had to meet sometime. But you can understand how I didn't want to.'

'Oh, yes. But you see, that's how life is. Complicated, full of taking chances. Next year David and I hope to be married. We want children right away, as soon as possible. But I can't be sure that this will always make him happy. I can only hope and try my best.'

'Presumably he'll have to try, too,' I said.

'Oh, yes. But I can't be responsible for that. I can only do my part.'

She looked very serious and dedicated. I thought my father had probably been very lucky.

'I pray about it sometimes,' she said. 'I think God listens. I don't go to Synagogue any more but I do pray sometimes.'

That made me slightly sick. 'You surprise me.'

'You don't have to be a good person to pray.'

'No,' I said, 'but it's meant to have some effect, isn't it?'

'Yes, it is. But if you meant I should give up your father, what good would that be? He wouldn't go back to your mother now.'

'Pity you didn't start praying a bit sooner.'

She still faced me quite calmly. 'Perhaps I wanted to make myself happy, too. Perhaps I only pray to make myself feel better. I don't think it matters. You are trying to make things so logical. But people aren't like that. You can't take the feelings away.'

'You have very definite views,' I said. 'But I don't believe in God.'

'No,' she said. 'David doesn't either. At least he's not sure. But it doesn't matter. Each person is different.'

'You really don't see any problem, do you?'

'Oh, yes, I do. Haven't I made it clear? Nothing is perfect; there is always a problem. You just do what you can.'

'Yes, I see,' I said.

'I'm sorry. You're tired after your long journey. Everyone tells me I talk too much. But I wanted to explain a little in case I never see you again.'

She said this with the air of one who had been seeing a number of people for the last time.

'Have your parents really cut you off?' I asked, wishing the expression did not sound so Victorian.

'Oh, yes,' she said.

'It seems extraordinary.'

'Not really.' She smiled for the first time. 'You don't know Jewish families. They are devoted but implacable. They might have done it if I had married a Gentile. But this is much worse. I have let them down completely, gone against every principle they ever taught me. I am not their daughter any more.'

'That's hard on you.'

She made a tiny gesture with hands and shoulders, not as definite as a shrug. 'I had a choice. No one forced me to do what I did.'

'You certainly don't bear malice,' I said.

'No . . . well, it's not constructive. I have got so much to do, I can't waste time. I have got to live up to David's vision of happiness.'

'You make it sound very romantic,' I said.

'I'm sorry. Romantic is a dirty word, isn't it? I'm glad I am a painter. It must be very hard for writers. There are so many words they can't use.'

'Surely it's the same in all arts – there are hackneyed elements in everything, aren't there?'

'I suppose so. It seemed more obvious with words. After all, everyone uses them. Not everyone paints or writes music. But perhaps I am too naïve to see it.'

'No,' I said. 'I wouldn't call you naïve.'

'Now you are looking at me as an enemy again.'

'I'm sorry,' I said, surprising myself. 'To tell you the truth, I keep forgetting and then remembering.'

'Yes, I know,' she said. 'You see, that proves my point. It's like the hackneyed words. This is a stereotyped situation. It's corny. It happens all the time in life and to make it worse people read books and articles about it and see it in films. The eternal triangle. The other woman. Middle-aged infatuation. Teenage infatuation. It's a kind of disease. Everyone knows the symptoms and everyone knows the remedy. So what chance is there of a genuine viewpoint? Everyone comes ready to praise and blame in exactly the right proportions. We all sit in cages, like animals in a zoo, with labels underneath. Practically no one can see the people in the situation. They just see the situation because they know it so well. But really it's only people – just people. That's what I'm trying to make you see.'

She paused, breathless, and smiled at me, guilelessly, like a child. 'Oh dear, I do get worked up about this, don't I?'

'Well,' I said, 'you're entitled to.'

'Oh, no, that's rights again. I think I've just got a worked-up character. I get excited about lots of things.'

I took a deep breath and said slowly, 'I can imagine my father being very happy with you.'

She looked abashed. 'That's extremely generous of you. I do appreciate your saying that. But, you know, if it hadn't been me it would have been someone else. I was just lucky.'

I stared at her.

'It's true, you know,' she said. 'You think I am being cynical. But for years your father had been wondering if he could have another sort of life. He wondered so much he destroyed the life he had. Then he had to jump or he would have had nothing.'

'Look,' I said. 'While we're on the subject could we be more specific? I've heard a lot about new lives and feeling alive and so on but I'm not really clear what he was after, ruling out a lot of clichés, that is. My mother, for instance, seems to think he's after his lost youth.'

'Well, he is,' said Philippa. 'In a way.'

I had to smile. 'I should have known that you'd say yes to that. You've been one long surprise.'

We lit fresh cigarettes, mine this time, on the strength of it.

'Well,' she said, 'I can't explain it to you exactly. If I could I'd be very, very clever. We're talking about what people want from their lives, and they don't often know themselves. The words are just a sketch, an approximation. And they're hackneyed, corny. Often they don't get anywhere near. You have to feel it to fill in the difference.'

'Oh, Lawrentian stuff,' I said. 'In the guts and all that.'

'I don't know,' she said vaguely. 'I can only put it like this. When you are young your life is a question mark. You have a number of choices to make. Whether you go to university or art school instead of getting a job is one. Whether you go abroad or stay in England is another. How you earn a living. Which person you marry. The point is, really, what kind of person are you. You don't really know. You keep getting glimpses of yourself as time passes. But each choice you make rules out something else. You could have developed in a different way, perhaps. This has been haunting your father. He made one choice. Now he wants to go back and make another while he has still enough time. In that sense it is his lost youth he wants.'

I said nothing.

'I haven't explained it very well,' she said.

'I think you've made it fairly clear,' I said. 'It's just that I find the whole thing, situation, explanation, everything, terribly confusing.'

'Oh, I know,' she said. 'It is. I wake up sometimes and think, "I'm crazy. This can't be my life. Not really." '

'You, too.'

We smiled at each other.

'Please,' she said urgently, 'please come and see us again before you forget I'm a person, not just the corner of a triangle. That's what you'll do in time, you know.'

'I know.'

'Did it make it worse that we're much the same age?' she asked. 'I thought a lot about that.'

'Yes, I think so,' I said, but now it seemed irrelevant.

'I'll be twenty-one in September,' she said. 'We can't be married before that, even if the divorce comes through. My parents would never give their permission. It seems like a long time to wait. That's silly, isn't it?'

'No,' I said. 'Any time is a long time to wait for something you want.'

We were silent now, exhausted.

'Do you want to go?' she asked presently. 'Are you wondering how to get away?'

'Not like that,' I said, 'but I will have to go. You know?'

'Yes, of course.'

We got up and started to walk out of the station. Outside there was the thin, cold drizzle of an English winter. The town looked drab and sorry for itself.

'The festive season,' I said.

'Yes, I know. It's a shame.'

We walked on, mingling with the Christmas shoppers.

'Look,' I said, 'isn't this your bus-stop?'

'Oh, yes,' she said. 'I would have walked straight past it.'

We stood still and waited but it was a frequent service. A bus came and she got on it. Standing on the platform she waved to me as the bus moved away. And I waved back.

SIXTEEN

MARTIN and I were both postmen that Christmas. We occasionally saw each other on our rounds, heavily muffled and gum-booted, laden with scarves and gloves and oilskins as we squelched our way round town and bordering villages. In fine weather it could be a pleasant job. But at least it was money in our pockets, and it kept us out of the silent, echoing house.

The most notable difference between home and college was the absence of conversation. At college we talked so much; at home conversation was an event. I felt I had to be so careful to avoid mentioning my father and Philippa that conversation with my mother was too tense to be bearable. We confined ourselves to short exchanges about work and food. I remembered the past when we had chattered together for hours about all kinds of feminine things. But now they were all fraught with meaning, evocative of betrayed women and straying men. You could stub your toe on something painful without any warning. Even make-up and fashions, with their underlying purpose of masculine attraction, were suspect. Perhaps I was too sensitive, but then so was she, for I am certain I did not imagine this attitude in her.

Martin was, I think, a great comfort to her. She was pleased to have him home for the entire holiday and they spent many evenings together, sometimes not talking at all, he holding her wool while she wound it. I felt an intruder, conscious of my equivocal position. Who was right? Which side was I on? Or was Philippa right and were we just people making mistakes and trying again? The error might be mine, trying to force events to a pattern. But for years my life had been well shaped and intentional.

Now it was not. Now it was blurred, crowded, empty. I did not seem to have any control over it. I was getting better : I did not think about Peter quite so often; I could picture my father with Philippa without a hot, suffocating pain in my chest. But as for replacing old purpose with new, I had made no headway at all. If Philippa's philosophy was accurate, then I was certainly squandering my youthful faculty of choice.

I had thought a great deal about her since our meeting and been to see them both. My father's joy at this was touching, intense, absurd. It was good to be able to give him such pleasure. We ate a huge meal and played cards. It struck me as funny afterwards. 'And what do you do when you visit your father and his mistress, Miss Mitchell?' – 'We play cards, of course.' But it was good to see them and not have to talk. We drank beer and sat on the floor on cushions, betting halfpennies. I had been afraid their affection would be very obvious and would hurt me, but they hardly glanced at each other all evening and made no attempt at casual contact as people in love often do. I wondered if this was her doing; I could not in all honesty think that my father was naturally so tactful. As it was, their happiness showed only in their voices, though they used no endearments, just each other's names now and then.

I gave them a picture for Christmas and they gave me a hairdrier. It is a bad time of year if you are not religious or a child or there is no one under ten in the household . Neighbours called in, but I could see they were still treating my mother like an emotional invalid and this exhausted her nerves. Their visits annoyed Martin, too, because he felt they were patronizing her. Moreover, they kept telling her and us what a comfort we must be to her.

I wondered what my mother would like to do. Did she, too, dream of another choice? Or had the unkind years made that too hard and unlikely for her? Perhaps working again, living alone, was in fact just such a choice. But I did not really think so. Still, that was not to say that she actually wanted a second marriage. There were so many things I did not know her views on. You lived with someone for so many years but you were conditioned to a certain kind of relationship. You covered one piece of ground with your mother, another with your friends. Was this inevitable, a law of parenthood? If so, then how had my father and I evaded it in the old days: the long, silly talks, the fun, the confidence, the having time for each other out of a schedule of busy years? Perhaps only his job had made it possible, the odd time-table, the erratic way of living. Maybe it was not just a special gift of his as I had always tenderly believed it was. Maybe we were two spasmodic people, incapable of sustained effort, as it was called, meeting here and there, now and then, and occasionally flashing into the warmth I had remembered.

One grey morning after Christmas (there was no snow, of course) a letter came to rescue me from inertia. Marty's writing, black ink, white paper, sloping, messy, angry-looking. I was startled. Marty never wrote letters; a postcard from her was a great concession.

Dearest Lois [she wrote], please invite me to stay. I shall go mad here and they think that anyone who writes as often as Louis must be practically at the altar rails. I'm so bored and now Christmas is over I've really done my duty. Ray has got his fiancée here and all in all it's hell. Can you get me out of it?

I got her out of it. My mother, back at work immediately after the holiday, was pleased for me to have company. Martin, with the prospect of finals in May, was studying quite hard. I wrote back at once and Marty telephoned; two days after her letter she was in the house.

'I've been reading *The Well of Loneliness*,' she announced, throwing a copy at me. 'Rather late in the day, perhaps, but I've always meant to. See what you think.'

I tried it, interested, but gave up before the end, after skipping to see what did happen.

'It's such heavy going,' I complained. 'So much self-pity and steaming emotion.'

Marty laughed. 'You really mean you're basically out of sympathy with the whole set-up.'

'All right, I am.'

'Well, so am I. Don't be defensive about it. You should try a book about male homosexuals, though. I think you'd have far more sympathy with them. Perfectly normal reaction, of course.' She grinned at me. 'Try Mary Renault.'

Time ceased to drag after Marty's arrival. She got the sewing machine out of its retirement, hauled me round the shops on a January sale shopping trip and commenced making clothes for both of us. She had sent my address to France and letters arrived almost daily for her.

'No wonder your mother thought you were practically married,' I said.

She made a face. 'I told her but she wouldn't believe me. He just likes writing letters.'

'Is everything going well?'

'Oh, sure. How can we fight at long distance?'

'Don't some people?'

'Oh, I suppose so. Not our kind of fights, though.'

'You know,' I said, 'I've never understood your kind of fights.'

'Oh, you'd think they were trivial,' she said.

'Funny, that's the last word I'd have thought of.' But then I remembered what Tom had said.

'Well, some of them are. Others –' she paused, screwing up her eyes thoughtfully – 'well, I bet you've never had a man call you filthy names while he was making love to you. Sorry, do I embarrass you?'

I had looked away. 'No, I thought I might embarrass you by staring.'

She ignored that. 'Well, you did ask me, more or less. You

145

see, it's attraction and revulsion the whole time. Sin and redemption. Devil and angel. I blame his Catholic upbringing.'

I looked at her in amazement. 'But they don't all turn out like that.'

'Of course they don't. I just blame it for its effect on someone of Louis' temperament to begin with. Pandering to his fatal weakness. You know, like in Shakespeare, old-fashioned Bradley-type. The fatal flaw.' She giggled. 'The tragic hero.'

'Oh, you're making fun of me,' I said. 'Inventing the whole thing.'

'Rubbish,' said Marty. 'If I could invent things like that I'd make them commercial. How is this coming on?'

'Fine. I've always liked you in red.'

'Well, it's my answer to winter. Hit it with everything you've got before it hits you. I have to make my dress before yours, you understand, because I'm selfish.'

Marty shared my room with me and we had a fire at night. It had been an old childhood treat for me and to have it again made me feel ten years old. We lay in bed and watched the shapes moving on walls and ceiling.

'This takes me back,' I said.

'Where to?'

'Oh – ten, twelve, fourteen. The age of having girlfriends to stay and confiding in them. I can't remember what I confided now but at the time it was terribly important.'

'Lord, yes, wasn't it? How funny, I'd forgotten. And terrible if they told on you. I used to evaluate people by how much I could confide in them.'

'You've changed,' I said.

'Yes, I know. I'm sorry. You'd like a more confidential friend, wouldn't you?'

'It doesn't matter, you're fine,' I said. Darkness and firelight and the small hours still worked the magic of making it easier to say what you meant.

'I do talk about myself a lot,' said Marty. 'Too much, maybe.'

'Yes, but you don't really explain things,' I said. 'It doesn't matter, though.'

'Did you want a sister when you were little?' Marty asked unexpectedly.

'I don't know . . . occasionally, I suppose.'

'Then you didn't really. I did. I used to pretend I had one. She was called Julia. Funny, I think it's a revolting name now. I used to talk to her in the mirror. She was a twin really, you see. She always saw my point of view. I had a very happy childhood.'

'It sounds lonely.'

'No, it wasn't. I had Julia, you see.' She laughed.

'I had Martin,' I said. 'He was very rough. I had to be a tomboy to survive at all. We were very near in age, of course, otherwise he might have ignored me. I was always falling out of trees he dared me to climb and chucking stones into people's green-houses. It was fun.'

'More fun now than then.'

'You're so right. What a pity, though. I hate admitting I wasn't really built for the outdoor life.'

'Much good it would do you now.' Marty lit a cigarette and threw the match in the fire. 'Weren't the days long, though? Each one seemed to go on for weeks and you just played. That "What shall I do today?" feeling.'

'Oh *yes*. I do remember. What did you do on wet days?'

'There weren't any wet days,' Marty said.

'I know. I only remember sunshine, too. But what did you do when you had to stay in?'

'I painted,' said Marty. 'All over the floor. My mother used to put down newspaper first. I enjoyed it. What did you do?'

'We fought,' I said, remembering. 'The house was too small for us. It always ended with me falling off something we'd built or down the stairs or into the bath or something and then I'd cry and Martin would say he was sick of girls.'

147

My God, I thought, maybe that was a bad omen. But he had not mentioned Rick this vacation. I was being ridiculous.

I went to see my father and Philippa again before the last week of the vac, suggesting that Marty might like to come too. I was keen to have her opinion of Philippa.

'No, thanks,' she said. 'Three's company. I'll come on the bus with you, though, and go to the library.'

'Shall I meet you on my way back?' I asked.

'No, don't bother,' she said vaguely. 'I might go to a film or just wander round. I don't know yet.'

By ten o'clock she had not returned. I had been home for hours.

'Where's Marty?' my mother asked.

'Oh, she said she might go to a film.'

An hour went by. Eleven. Then eleven-thirty.

'She ought to be back by now,' said my mother, anxious. 'After all, we are responsible for her.'

'Yes, I know. She'll be along any minute now, I expect.'

We waited. My mother went upstairs to put hot-water bottles in the beds and the phone rang. I jumped at it.

'Hullo, Lois.'

'Where the hell have you been?' I asked furiously, anxiety suddenly dissipated.

'I met someone . . . a boy from Lagos. We met him in Spain with his girl-friend.'

'Does he have a watch?'

'What? Oh. What time is it?' She sounded far away.

'Twenty to twelve.'

'Oh.'

'Is that all you can say? My mother's worried stiff about you.'

'Oh, dear. Lois, can't you tell her I've met an old school-friend and I'll be back tomorrow?'

'No, I cannot. What d'you think this is, an hotel? Look, Marty, she's only gone upstairs. I haven't got long. What are you playing at?'

'I want to spend the night with Sam. I think I've missed the last bus.'

'You mean you hope you have. Well, there's one at ten to twelve.'

Marty sighed. 'Sam's girl-friend has left him,' she said.

'For God's sake … what's that got to do with anything? I can't tell that to my mother, can I? It's hardly an explanation, is it?'

'It is really.'

'Look, if you've got to play comforter you can do it in daylight,' I said rudely.

'Oh, I have. It's not that. It's the nights that are bad. Don't you understand?'

'No. Yes. Look, it's not me, it's my mother. You've got to come back.' Just then my mother came back into the room. 'It's Marty,' I said without covering the mouthpiece. 'Her watch stopped. Look, you can't be far from a bus-stop. Get a move on. You've got about seven minutes. Or the bus station if it's nearer. Ask someone, but hurry.'

'Well done,' said the voice bitterly and the line went dead.

When Marty came in she was charmingly apologetic but announced in the course of her excuses that she had telephoned her mother while in town and felt she ought to return home the next day. 'She's got a cold and my stepfather has his parish; he can't really look after an invalid.'

Alone with her in our room I said furiously, 'Well, I hope you're satisfied. Apart from being rude, what position do you leave me in? Suppose your mother writes or phones? What then?'

'She won't,' said Marty calmly.

'How can you be so sure? You can't.'

'Well, a hundred to one.'

'That's not good enough. I'm carrying the can, remember?'

'Rubbish.' She sat on the bed, pulling off her stockings. 'You acted in good faith. If she does ring up and your mother answers, play dumb. You both think I'm going home. You're as surprised as she is. I'm taking the risk, not you.'

'What about Louis?'

'Well, what about him? D'you suppose he isn't doing something like this? Besides, I know what Sam feels like and people have helped me when I felt like that.'

'I don't care what your excuse is. I meant, what do I do about Louis' letters? He writes to you, in case you'd forgotten.'

'Send them on. I'll give you Sam's address. Oh, and phone number in case of emergency.'

'Emergency.' I laughed.

'There won't be many more letters anyway. It's only a week before we go back.'

'When do you really mean to go back?'

'Oh . . . in about five days. Just in time to pack.'

'You're impossible.'

'Yes.'

'Oh, stop being so meek and agreeing with me.'

'All right. I thought you were cross with me.'

'So I am. Was. Oh, well.' I looked at her, weakened, and we smiled at each other. I sighed. 'You're spoilt. You're an infant.'

'I know. You're quite right.'

'Oh, Marty.'

She spent all the following morning finishing my dress. She made it beautifully. My mother was out at work so after breakfast there were no more awkward questions to answer about trains. I saw Marty onto a bus about three o'clock. To my surprise she hugged me before she left.

SEVENTEEN

EACH new term was the same, I thought. The long drag from the bus-stop with your suitcase, the relief when you saw your trunk in the corridor. Your familiar room, unnaturally bare, awaiting you. The volume of sound in the building increased steadily throughout the day, as more and more people returned. You unpacked, untidily at first, throwing things out, then finding places for them all. Sometimes you began by moving furniture. It was a day when no one need feel any guilt at not studying. People called in on you as they arrived back and you called in on them. The first person in a group to find pans, cups and coffee was highly appreciated. There was always an extra buzz of conversation in the dinner queue on the first night as monotonous, sometimes insincere, questions and answers rocketed to and fro. 'Had a good vac?' –'Marvellous, thanks.'

But things wake up quickly. You must consult your time-table, unpack your books, because lectures begin again the very next day. All the same, it is good to feel that your own life begins again, too, in your own room, with your own friends. You are accustomed to the alternation of term and vacation; you have had this all your life. You chose to go on when you could have rejected it. All your life you have been either dreading or looking forward to the end or the start of something.

January. Almost in the middle of the academic year if you counted. I surveyed my gas allowance and wondered if it would last. Within the allowance, it was refunded to you and often paid your fare home: beyond that you could be seriously out of pocket. Some people smuggled in oil stoves for extra warmth, but this was frowned upon, presumably as dangerous.

I went to ring up Tom. It gave me the feeling of at least having a stake in life, someone to contact outside college. He sounded pleased to hear from me.

'Come round tomorrow,' I said. 'I'll be straight then. It's chaos tonight.'

'I could help you tidy up.'

'No. Come tomorrow when it all looks nice. Come about seven and I'll feed you on my gas-ring.' I was even a little excited, about Tom, of all people. A month of nothing made him seem attractive, not merely kind and lonely.

I wandered across to see Anne. Her room looked blitzed. She and Keith were sitting in the middle of the mess smoking cigarettes.

'Hullo, honey,' she said. 'We're getting married in March.'

I suppose my face expressed absolute astonishment, and then suspicion.

'She's not pregnant,' said Keith, smiling at me. 'At least as far as we know. We got tired of waiting, that's all.'

I sat down on a suitcase. 'What about your parents?'

'They don't know yet.' Anne was chain-smoking. 'We only decided on our way up. Keith came to fetch me and we talked it over. Do you think we're mad?'

'No,' I said, 'but I expect most people will.'

'We're prepared for that,' Keith said. He seemed to exude firmness and decision. 'They can't stop us and that's the main thing.'

'Whatever made you decide?' I asked.

'Marty's party helped,' Anne said surprisingly. 'We felt so out of it, so un-young. So very much of a unit. And for a long time now all this running to and fro, early and late, hoping nobody notices, has been getting us down. It began to seem ridiculous not to be married. And we suddenly asked ourselves why we were waiting.'

'As in the song,' Keith said.

'And there really wasn't any reason. Except that here, unlike America, students nearly always do wait to get married till they finish college.'

'And money, of course,' I said.

Keith laughed. 'Well, there, of course, you have us. We'll be damned hard up, but we reckon it's worth it. We're just sick of the whole business dragging on and on.'

'My parents helped a lot,' said Anne reflectively. 'It was more Homes and Gardens than ever this vac. Christmas in the country. And Barbara is positively insufferable. She's practically engaged to someone who's so frightfully, frightfully county it just isn't true. I don't fit in any more and I get so irritable and put my foot in everything.' She paused and took a deep breath. 'Well, that's a synopsis, anyway. Details following.'

'Yes, but there aren't any really,' Keith said. 'We're just sick of waiting. Four years already and two more will make six. Well, the hell with it. I reckon we'll study better if we're living together. We're worn out with all this racketing around.'

'Hardly a reason you can put across though,' I said.

'It doesn't matter. We've waited long enough and that's that.'

They smiled at each other confidently.

'We'll show 'em,' said Keith.

'Will it be tough?' I asked them.

'Rugged.'

'But you *are* engaged.'

'Yes, but I think they've always hoped it might fall through. And they're sure to think we'll have a baby and I can't prove we won't.'

'You could try,' I said.

We all laughed.

'You'll have to move fast,' I said, thinking it over. 'You've got two months.'

'I know,' Anne said, 'but if people are going to hate a thing anyway why drag it out? We'll tell them next weekend and then I'll see the Principal.'

'She'll be charmed,' I said.

'Yes, but there's nothing she can do. It has been known before.'

We thought of two students who had been married when we came and who graduated last summer. One had got an upper second, the other a lower second and a baby.

'The thing is, I gather,' Anne said, 'not so much the work and kids as not to die of starvation before finals.'

'Well, I'm pretty near that already,' said Keith. He got up, stretching. 'Let's go out for a meal and leave all this mess.'

'Well, of course, you eat like an ox.' Anne looked at him affectionately.

'What do you know about oxen and their eating habits?'

They laughed and held hands.

'Why don't you come with us, Lois?' Keith asked. He was obviously sincere, but in a way this made it worse and more impossible than ever to accept; they had so much they did not mind sparing me one of their evenings.

'No, thanks,' I said lightly. 'Busy. I've got Tom coming tomorrow and I want to see Marty tonight.'

They stayed and chatted for a few more minutes but were patently anxious to be off and I excused myself so they could go. I went across to Marty's room, but she was not there. Her trunks had arrived and a suitcase lay on the bed disgorging clothes, but there was no sign of the owner. She had not even left a note, though she must have known I would come. Gone to Louis, I supposed, like a homing pigeon. Or a cat on the tiles. But I knew it was only envy that made me think like that about her. I think I had felt more restless since meeting Philippa, someone with real purpose in her life.

I heard a footstep in the doorway and turned round. Ruth was there, smiling at me.

'Doesn't waste much time, does she?'

I shrugged my shoulders.

'Do you think they'll catch her one day?' She sounded genuinely interested as in an academic problem.

'Who?' I said, purposely dense. But I felt guilty. Once I had had no quarrel with Ruth. Now I always seemed obliged to fight with her over Marty.

'The authorities.'

She made it sound like life in 1984.

'I don't know. Get someone in the Maths department to work out the odds.'

She still stood there, despite my rudeness, looking friendly and homeless. 'Would you like some coffee?' she said.

There seemed no point in refusing so I said, 'All right. Thank you.'

Her room was very tidy and conventional, with none of the individual touches Marty had imposed on the room they had shared.

'Did you have a good vac?' she asked.

'Fine. How about you?'

'Oh, it was all right. I had a letter from Marty just before Christmas.' Her face brightened. 'She was bored. I expect she wrote to everyone.'

There was nothing I could say to that.

'Did you see her at all?' Ruth asked.

'For a few days,' I said reluctantly, not wanting to hurt her for no reason.

'She was bored because Louis was in France,' Ruth said confidently.

'That's right.'

'But I expect she had someone else while he was away, didn't she?'

I felt irritated. 'Yes, since you ask.'

Ruth smiled. 'I knew she would. I thought about her a lot in the vac.'

That was no surprise. I drank my coffee and lit a cigarette

but Ruth's next remark nearly made me choke myself. I could never have foreseen it.

'Do you think she'll go to hell?' Ruth asked casually.

I looked at her in blank astonishment and said, 'What?'

'Marty,' said Ruth.

'Will Marty go to hell?' I murmured.

'Yes. I've been wondering. Do you think she will?'

'I don't believe in hell,' I said. But I felt this was almost an irrelevant answer.

'I think she will,' said Ruth. 'I've been reading a book about it. She's in mortal sin.'

'What on earth are you talking about?'

'A book one of the Catholics lent me,' Ruth said cheerfully. 'It was very interesting. Marty is in mortal sin and if she doesn't repent before she dies she'll go to hell.'

'But Marty isn't a Catholic,' I said, perplexed, and then wondered: the dead father, the convent school; some promise half-fulfilled, perhaps?

'I don't think that matters. She's leading an immoral life.'

'Perhaps she doesn't think it's immoral.'

'Oh. Well, that might make a difference.' She seemed a little disappointed. I could not really imagine the word immoral holding much significance for Marty as applied to her life, but Ruth was clearly keen on the idea of Marty in hell. I wondered what had brought this on and again I had the uneasy feeling that something should have been done about Ruth and some responsible person ought to supervise her before she became any worse.

'I must go,' I said. 'I haven't finished unpacking. Thank you for the coffee.' I stood up.

'You always run away,' Ruth said accurately. I was taken aback so made no reply but walked to the door. She stopped me, saying, 'Lois.'

'What now?' I kept my back turned to her defensively.

'I could have saved her, you know. I wasn't asking for very much.'

My neck prickled coldly. Ruth sighed. 'Sometimes I thought there really was a chance,' she said.

I went out.

When Tom arrived at seven the next day I was disproportionately glad to see him. But I even had to hide some of my delight for fear it embarrassed him. After all, he had explained his position to me very clearly before we began.

I had cooked spaghetti and a good meat sauce. He said it was nice to see me and had I had a good vac and we started to eat. He seemed hungry; I always suspected he starved himself when he was alone. We had wine with the meal, not very potent, but warming and pleasant. We felt too relaxed afterwards to play chess or cards. Tom helped me clear away.

'How's Marty?' he said.

He had done well, I thought, not to ask before.

'She was all right in the vac. I haven't seen her yet this term. She cut her lectures today.'

'She must have had a lonely month of it,' Tom said.

My God, I thought irritably, how the sympathy flowed for her. Perhaps the solution was to introduce Tom to Ruth. I didn't answer. Tom put some records on the gramophone and stretched out on my bed. He patted the empty space (such as it was) beside him.

'Coming, darling?'

I wondered what the word meant. Anne and Keith used it, Peter and I had thought it expressed everything we wanted to say. From Tom it probably meant: 'I need you, hurry up. I want to be saved.' I resented it wildly, idiotically, but I wanted to be saved, too, so I lay down on the bed. Perhaps after all, there would be a miracle.

Tom kissed me and stroked my hair. For some reason I couldn't unhook my mind and I started thinking how calm and friendly his hands were, like those of someone used to animals. There now, good dog, not going to hurt you, nothing to worry about. I tried to respond but I thought at the time that it was no good if you had to try, and immediately another section of my mind contradicted and told me that concentration was of the essence. Round and round I went while Tom made all the banal physical adjustments to clothing necessary. We seldom undressed now, unless we were spending a whole night together, which was not often. I think I had once said I preferred it that way. Tom did not take very long about making love or whatever you called it, nor on the other hand was he quick and brutal like people in some magazines. He was not particularly anything. I thought there was a great resemblance between sex and food and Tom was certainly plain cooking, nothing fancy. At his best, a good square meal; otherwise usually a decent snack that kept you going for a while, anyway. But God help you if you wanted more than meat and two veg., indifferently cooked.

My mind drifted off on a performance-rating system. One must give due importance to orgasm, of course, but not forget timing, preparation, aftermath, emotion, and nebulous extras. You could use food all the way. At one extreme – what? Egg and chips, beans on toast, rice pudding; at the other caviar, chicken, champagne. It was up to you. One girl's high was another's low, presumably. You took your pick of what made you sick. I could even make up an advertising jingle about it.

Tom had stopped. Cessation of activity made my brain jerk back into reality. I tried to smile at him.

'Are you all right?'

I wished he would not always ask me this, and so promptly. I nodded; it was easier than answering.

He lay on his back, and sighed. I lit a cigarette. We adjusted our clothing again. I wished I were asleep and could remain so for a long time.

'You're not,' he said suddenly, like a policeman catching a suspect out on a detail.

'I'm fine,' I said. I did not want to discuss it.

He shifted position. 'It's my fault. I'm not very good. I know it; Marty always said so.'

That was all I needed. I wanted to scream: 'You're a rotten psychologist anyway,' but then I felt a wave of pity for him so I said, 'That was unkind of her.'

'She was right,' he said flatly.

'But she needn't have said it. It can't have helped.'

'No. I don't know what I was like before that, but I think I got worse afterwards.'

'I'm not surprised.'

'I think she meant it to put me off, really, when she didn't need me any more.'

Again I was impressed by the humility aroused in Marty's devotees. He did not sound at all offended.

'How very unpleasant,' I said.

'Not really. I think I have weak urges, anyway, compared to her.'

Now it was comic, ridiculous, as well as pathetic. He spoke so seriously. 'She's a connoisseur, really. It means so much more to her.'

'Marty Walsh, her life and work,' I said.

'Lois, what's the matter?' He sounded surprised, for the first time.

'Do you ever pretend I'm her?' I asked roughly.

He hesitated, before answering, 'Sometimes.'

'Well, that's nice.' I got up violently and went to the mirror to tidy myself; repair my face and comb my hair.

To give him his due he did not wriggle or apologize or make excuses. He said simply, 'Haven't you ever pretended I was someone else?'

Of course I had, quite often to begin with; until I discovered it didn't work very well and later on I thought it was bad for me, anyway, retarding my recovery, so I tried to avoid it.

'So she did tell you about me,' I said.

'No. She didn't have to. I'd be a fool not to know there was someone. I thought we'd get on so well, being in the same boat.'

159

'You were a great help,' I said. I was feeling unreasonably furious that it was not even possible to quarrel with him. Instead we had to end up handing bouquets to each other.

'Can't we go on like that?' he asked.

'I don't know,' I said wearily. 'I suppose so.'

'Till you meet someone else,' he added, 'I mean. Or even after, if you like.'

He talked in clichés, I decided. I played the conversation over. Was it because he did not read enough or was he simply uncritical of what he read?

'What about you?' I said. 'Aren't you ever going to meet someone else?'

'I don't know.' He sounded surprised. 'I certainly hope so.'

'Well, I suppose it's something that you're not vowing eternal fidelity.'

'Lois, what's the matter? I've upset you.'

I brushed my hair till my head hurt.

'I want to help you. That's what friends are supposed to do.'

'Oh, shut up.'

He was silent. Then the guilt took over. He was kind and well meaning; he had warned me in the beginning of how it would be. I had accepted, and now I was blaming him. I had nothing to gain by insulting him and without him I could expect to return to a dismal round of pick-ups. I enjoyed our outings together and the fact that he was always there when I needed him. Was I kicking away my sticks before I could really manage without them?

'I'm sorry,' I said, without looking round. 'I'm being silly and I'm in a bad mood.'

'That's all right,' he said, quite calmly. 'Forget it.' And I remembered how Marty had said that he was used to her tantrums, or something like that, and nothing I could do would surprise him.

EIGHTEEN

SINCE we were not sufficiently involved to have a relationship to patch up, we were able to resume where we had left off last term, as if we had never made a bad start to this one. Tom never referred to the scene I had made and when we were together it was really as if it had never happened, the way people always say it will be but it never is if the people are in love with each other. It may be even better after whatever-it-is, but some impression has been made.

No impression was made on us. We continued our tour of theatres, films, art galleries and cheap restaurants. Sometimes I felt like a visitor to Britain on an economy guided tour. Only when I was alone did I remember sometimes what I had said and how I had felt that day. I was not sure I really understood myself.

Once we went to the Old Vic and I was able to show off as they did one of our set plays. I argued textural criticism with Tom who thought the Arden edition was a lot of nonsense anyway as Shakespeare probably dashed the things off without a second look. As I had often inclined to this view I was arguing to some extent against myself, always a salutary if uncomfortable experience. At least I was thinking and talking about something I was supposed to be studying but which was so often relegated to the background. Tom argued logically and politely, without heat. When we had exhausted the Arden Shakespeares we moved on to religion. He had no formal church adherence but he was sure about God and life after death and wanted me to believe too. So I told him specially about Ruth and Marty and hell.

At college I tried to work fairly steadily again. There was a kind of satisfaction in keeping my translation up to date or turning in a good essay. But I suppose my chief interest at this time was in Anne's wedding. The Principal was coldly sceptical about the wisdom of Anne's plans, and in communication with her mother who was violently opposed to the wedding. Anne's parents had never heard anything so crazy, they said, and would do everything they could to stop it, though of course Anne had obviously timed it carefully and, being over twenty-one, she could please herself and do just what she liked, no matter how it upset them, and very likely would as she'd been quite heartless since meeting Keith and it was probably all his idea anyway; he couldn't wait to get her away from her family and drag her down to his own level, and when they had both failed their degrees and were living on a pittance with a growing family to support, they needn't expect any help from Anne's parents.

The arguments ran mainly on these lines with various assorted extras thrown in. Keith went to see Anne's parents every weekend for another instalment; at first Anne went too until she decided she could not stand the strain. Then a stream of letters arrived from home for her. She opened the first and was so upset that I had to open the others for her and vet them. If it was particularly bad I would say, 'The mixture as before. Do you want it?' and Anne would shiver a little and say, 'I don't think so.' If the tone of it was reasonably calm I said, 'It's all right; you can read it,' and she took it and read in silence, her mouth screwed up like someone tasting a lemon.

At night in her room or mine we talked endlessly around the subject. Once when she had said, 'It's awful. Much worse than I expected,' three or four times I said tentatively, 'Have you thought about postponing the wedding?'

She shook her head. 'No. It's tempting to give in for a peaceful life again, but I can't. We promised each other, Keith and I. We can't go back; it would break us. And can you

imagine what the vacs would be like at home after all this?'
She went on shaking her head sadly. 'No. It's hopeless.'

'Poor Anne.'

She sighed and leaned back in her chair. 'It's awfully depressing,' she said. 'And I'm not doing any work.'

We had indeed got into a bad routine. Talking too far into the night meant we were tired the next day and either slept late or went to bed in the afternoons, a thing neither of us had made a habit of before. Then somehow Anne caught a bad cold which lingered. She was smoking too much and this did not help. She became very thin and coughed and coughed everywhere she went. When she went to bed she often could not sleep but lay awake coughing and thinking. I teased her that she was going into a decline like a Victorian lady.

Keith was angry and blamed her parents for her state of health. This did not enhance his visits to them. Moreover, time was running low.

'What will you do, Anne,' I asked, 'if they don't come round?'

'Keith's arranging a register office wedding for the day after we go down,' Anne said.

She was very pale. I said, 'Do you feel all right?'

She smiled. 'Yes. I'm just more filial than I thought. I hate upsetting them. I know it will be worth it in the end but right now I feel awful.'

'Do you want to give up?'

'Not really. But nearly, if you can see the difference. I suppose I just wish it could be happy and normal, the way it is for other people.'

'I wonder if it is,' I said. 'I dare say weddings cause more trouble than we realize. There's probably nearly always some kind of argument beforehand about something. It's that sort of subject. There's so much involved. How about Keith's parents? How do they feel?' I was always forgetting them but they lived in Yorkshire and Anne and Keith had visited them a few times.

'Oh, they're all for it,' Anne said. 'But I feel it's only because mine aren't. They're furious that my parents don't think their Keith is good enough for me after they managed to send him to grammar school and university. But his father keeps saying to me, "You will see that he works, won't you, lass?" so I think they're afraid I'll be a distraction. They're desperately keen for him to get his degree. Of course he will – it's only a question of what sort of degree, but they don't see it like that. And they don't fancy the register office at all. They'd like us to be married up there in the parish church, but I feel that'd be adding insult to injury. On the other hand, to be fair to Keith, why not?'

Poor Anne, I thought. It was the first time anything had really hit her. But it would not last long.

'You've only got three weeks,' I said.

'Yes.' She sighed. 'If something doesn't happen soon . . .'

Of course, something did. Anne's luck had not run out; it was merely hiding. A week later her parents capitulated and after a few frosty evenings of discussion the big thaw commenced. The imminent date before the registrar had proved too much for them. Anne and Keith agreed to postpone the wedding till April since it was impossible to prepare food, clothes and invitations in such a short time. Anne invited one of the dons, the only one who had supported her plan, and various people from her history department.

'Do you want to bring Tom?' she asked me.

'I'd rather come alone,' I said.

Anne had wept with relief when her parents gave way; now the rehabilitation process began. She looked dreadful and we pumped vitamins into her and made her eat second helpings of everything. Keith was triumphant but still furious at what he called the unnecessary fuss and the suffering it had caused Anne. All through he had been immensely protective towards her. This was only as it should be, but it made me feel bitterly envious and I was ashamed.

'Should I ask Marty and Louis?' Anne wanted to know.

'I suppose you could.'

Lists were all over Anne's room and she was in a fever of preparation. As it turned out, Marty refused. Louis was spending Easter with his family and she preferred not to come alone.

'I'll be there,' I said to her. 'We could give each other moral support.'

'You're hardly an escort.'

Anne and Keith had found a flat and were busy decorating it. Some of us went over occasionally to help them and Keith's friends did too. They had had to pay a premium before they could have the flat and were buying furniture for it, all with money Anne's grandmother had left her a year or two before.

'When we move in we'll be broke,' Anne said, 'but it doesn't matter.' She was beginning to look radiant, the way brides should. I wondered how much of the money she and Keith were spending they would have spent anyway, and how much was going to impress on her parents that they were not living in a slum.

Term ended and I went home. Anne's wedding punctuated the vac for me and gave it some point, somewhere to focus my attention. The church was small and full; there seemed to be several hundred guests, most of them friends of Anne's parents. She herself looked like the leading model from a magazine's bridal issue. Her parents had bought her a trousseau such as I only expected to see in a film. Keith's parents were there and treading very warily indeed. Politeness was the order of the day. Anne's parents were both so charming that I wanted to rub my eyes as if I had been asleep. How could these be the same people who had been involved in the sordid screaming match of a few weeks ago?

I chatted to Anne's History professor and later to Keith's Mr Stone.

'So you're in favour of the wedding,' I said. 'I know you must be or they wouldn't have asked you.'

He smiled. 'Why not? When young people have really made up their minds it's a good thing for them to be married. They feel settled, work better.'

'Anne's parents are afraid she'll have a baby before finals,' I said. I had had several glasses of champagne.

'She's a sensible girl,' Mr Stone said. 'I'm willing to trust her common sense and good judgement. You know, she's married a very bright young man. He might even manage to get a first.' He jerked his head towards a corner of the room. 'My wife's over there trying to pacify parents. It must be tough having children.'

'Oh. Haven't you any?' I was surprised. I had imagined him to be a family man when I first met him, and Keith had mentioned ten years of marriage which made me take children for granted.

'No. No, we haven't.'

I looked and saw Dr Stone, elegant as ever, trying to draw parents and in-laws together.

The reception was held at Anne's parents' home. This, too, was so huge and gracious that it seemed to belong to some film set. No doubt my horizons were too limited from years in a four up, two down semi. And there were, of course, many people far richer than this. For a moment I thought of Peter and wondered how his parents would have compared with Anne's.

Anne and Keith were slowly making their way round, having a few words with everyone. When my turn came Anne said, 'D'you think everything's going all right?'

'It's perfect and you look wonderful,' I said, truthful though unoriginal.

Anne smiled. 'I don't think anyone would know there'd been any trouble, do you?' she said.

'You have a right good tuck in,' said Keith, winking at me. Then, changing voices, 'Actually, I'm being just too respectable today. I thought it was the least I could do till I get her home. Then it's collars off and braces showing.'

'I'm eating and drinking like a fiend,' Anne said. 'Not very bridal but there it is.'

Keith held her hand. 'Well, she doesn't know when she'll get the next lot,' he said.

Later on I met Barbara. She was a thinner, shorter and somehow shinier version of Anne, very pretty but with a spun glass finish. She chatted pleasantly enough but used her left hand a lot in the conversation. I could not blame her; I had never seen a diamond so huge. That was where the upper classes scored. They could get away with anything; I would never, for instance, suppose the stone to be a fake. I had not imagined I could be so class-conscious, but Anne's family, the occasion, the whole set-up made me feel acutely bourgeois. The fiancé was a surprise: rather small, with brown hair verging on red, and glasses. The glasses gave me a shock but the voice was exactly as cultured as I had expected. I looked at them both and found it terribly hard to imagine them in bed together, the game I sometimes played when I was alone at a party. 'We're getting married in September,' Barbara said. She made it sound the most aristocratic month in the whole year.

Nevertheless, it was an anticlimax to be at home again after Anne's wedding. I kept thinking of her and Keith together. They had had their bout of trouble, all two months of it; now I could see no reason why everything should not again be smooth for them indefinitely. But I took pleasure all the same in telling Philippa about the wedding because I knew how anxious she was to be married.

'They're very lucky,' she said after listening attentively.

'Yes, aren't they?' I said. But I could not really touch her. She was sure of my father's adoration and poured forth her love in answer. I watched them together and wondered when I would have someone for myself again.

I went to a few dances as a weak experiment but after a little petting in bushes and dark alleys I panicked and retreated. Tom, I thought bitterly, could afford to laugh at me, only he was too kind to do so.

Martin was working as never before, as if he had just invented the idea of cramming. Terror had set in. I watched with a feeling of unreality. It was a year until my turn and I could hardly see myself working so densely. But it is always hard to see how work is done, the separate minutes of study of which it is composed, and so in self-defence you imagine you will never do it. As you get nearer, too, the target dwindles, as it must, for sanity's sake.

One afternoon, though, the phone rang and a girl's voice asked for Martin. The shock this gave me made me realize how I had consigned my brother to one fixed category. He went downstairs in considerable haste to take the call. The following evening he abandoned his books and went out. I was sure beyond doubt that he had gone to meet her, though I had no evidence. She could have been phoning to pass on a message, ask for an address, anything. My mother had gone to the theatre with some people from her office and I was alone in the house. About eight-thirty the door bell rang and I found on the step an untidy, dark-haired young man, complete with haversack.

'Good evening,' he said apologetically. 'I am so sorry to disturb you but could I have a word with Martin?'

I knew him at once, though I had never seen a photograph. He had a shy manner and an extraordinarily appealing smile. 'You're Rick, aren't you?' I said.

'That's right.' He seemed pleased I knew and I felt awful at what I had to tell him.

'I'm afraid Martin's out,' I said. 'I'm frightfully sorry but I don't know where he's gone.'

His face closed down, as if curtains were drawn or shutters moved into place. I had read about light going out of people's faces but never seen it before. Absurd to think that because things have become clichés they no longer happen to anyone.

'I'm sorry to have troubled you,' he said eventually, and

began to shift back into position the haversack he had half taken off.

I felt so anxious to help him that I said foolishly, 'Would you like to come in and wait? Maybe he'll be back soon,' though Martin had said as he went out that I was not to wait up for him.

'No,' he said, and managed the lovely smile again. 'It doesn't matter. Thank you very much.' And he went away down the path, without looking round again. I watched till he was out of sight, but there was nothing I could do. I felt quite awful and when I could no longer see him I went inside and brooded about the incident. I had such conflicting, ridiculous feelings that I hardly knew myself. Why was I so sure that Rick had guessed where Martin was? I thought he had looked like someone suddenly under sentence of death. When my mother came in we had cocoa and chatted for a few minutes about nothing. I told her Martin had gone out and she was not worried, only pleased because he had been working so hard. Presently we went to bed but I lay awake smoking, feeling vicious, until I heard Martin come in. Then I went along to his room. He was whistling softly to himself as he undressed.

'Glad you're so happy,' I said, and when he stared at me in astonishment I told him what had happened.

'Oh well,' he said, turning his back on me. 'He knows what he can do.' His voice was hard, with just a faint undercurrent of emotion.

'Oh, that's great. I'm proud of you. Congratulations,' I said.

'Go away, Lois, you don't understand.'

'That's right, take the easy way out, pull up the ladder.'

'Damn it, shut up, will you? You don't know what the hell you're talking about.' He was literally shaking with anger.

I could not explain myself. Previously, I had worried about Martin and longed for him to be normal, as people called it.

Now I felt I had seen real human misery for two minutes and it was such a shock, like films of Belsen. I still wanted Martin to be normal but I felt convinced he had started to achieve this in some brutal, thoughtless way, like a man slashing someone else's main artery to stop them from picking his pocket. Why not a simple sock on the jaw? At least, this was something near in words to how I felt. It was really inexpressible and very painful, a black, choking mass of feeling. And so, in a typically feminine, utterly illogical way, for the first time in my life I hated my brother.

NINETEEN

I COULD not work out any sensible connection in my mind, but from that day onwards I began to think compulsively about Mike Swann. I had the wild idea that if I saw him and told him about the incident he would understand without my trying to explain it to him. It was dreadful that the world should be full of people who loved and were betrayed, whatever the excuse. I felt panic-stricken, as if I ought to run somewhere away from something. The days dragged and Martin and I did not speak. He was out a lot, not working any more. How glad I was to pack my trunks and two days later to follow them to the station. I felt the house was contaminated.

There was no one to see me off at the station as my mother was at work, but I did not mind. The train could not go fast enough for me and it was hard to keep my mind on a book, though I tried to read, hoping to accelerate time. When I finally reached college I washed and changed immediately and began an intensive search for Mike's one and only letter. I was immensely relieved that I was not a person who threw away letters, though I did try to keep them tidy. I knew, therefore, that it must be somewhere.

Eventually I found it, with others in a shoe-box in my wardrobe. I set out at once, the letter in my bag, folded so that the address was instantly visible when I opened the bag. There was a transport conspiracy against me and I just missed buses and tubes. When I found the house it was small and ordinary, semi-detached. A comfortable-looking woman of about sixty opened the door to me.

'Mr Swann?' I said. 'Is he in? Could I see him, please?'

She shook her head slowly. 'He's gone, dear. Went at Easter, he did.'

I knew only too well what my face expressed. Why had it never occurred to me that he might have moved? Why had I only remembered his saying, 'Well, you know where I live,' and assumed he would be there until I chose to call on him? For now it became very clear to me that subconsciously I had always intended to do so. As it happened, I had missed him by only two weeks.

The woman was staring at me. I made an effort. 'Do you know where he went? Did he leave an address?'

'No, dear. He just packed his bags and went. He paid his rent, of course. He was ever such a good tenant, very quiet.'

She seemed to have quite a motherly affection for him. I stared at the ground and said nothing.

'Was it important, dear?' she asked next, just a shade of impatience in her voice, wanting to close the door, no doubt.

I followed the pattern; there was nothing else for me to do. 'No; it doesn't matter. Thank you very much. Sorry to have troubled you.' She had closed the door before I reached the gate.

I walked for a long time without noticing where I was going. At first there was just blind disappointment, then I tried to reason with myself. I had acted on impulse. I had met Mike only twice, both times in rather tense situations. I was probably chasing a symbol, not a real man. I could have no knowledge of his true character from our brief acquaintance, therefore the whole thing, the urge to find him, the disappointment, were fabrications of my brain. It was likely that I had romanticized every detail that I remembered. He had suddenly turned into my saviour, my future. The idea could not be based on any known fact.

So I told myself as I walked, aimlessly but fast, along street after street. I repeated and repeated my own rationalization, but it had very little effect. The truth remained, that he had, however briefly, been interested in me myself.

I found I was a little more receptive to the idea that he had probably long ago found someone else. I would be mad to believe he had not. Maybe it was a blessing that I had not found him; suppose he had been with her, how would I have explained the reason for my visit? I could not even fully explain it to myself. Nevertheless, my London had suddenly become an unfriendly place where you could lose someone important and never find him again. I could not even remember which college he had attended and I dared not go to Senate House and ask them to trace him through the entire university, even assuming this to be possible. I could give no adequate reason for such a thing. Besides, the urge was evaporating and only the disappointment remained, together with a new kind of fright. Suppose I had found him and he had not remembered me. Come to that, not every detail of his face was still vivid in my mind. Suppose we had stared at each other without recognition, saying, 'I'm sorry, I don't quite . . .'

By now I was utterly dispirited and got on the first bus I saw. After a succession of short rides on various buses, presumably more or less out of my way, I hit on a familiar route and arrived back at college in time for supper. I was at the end of the queue and sat with people I did not know, who all chattered gaily to each other. It reminded me of how life went on and people were bright and jolly. Afterwards I went straight back to my room and thought how strange it was to have Anne no longer in college. When there was a knock on my door I got quite a shock. I had almost convinced myself that I was alone in a world of strangers. Self-pity is always ludicrous in retrospect.

'Hullo,' said Marty, 'may I come in?'

She was wearing narrow velvet pants, ignoring as usual the Principal's request that slacks should not be worn to evening meals in hall, and a long loose blouse over them. Her hair was down but well brushed and shining.

'Hullo,' I said, staring at her. 'Why aren't you with Louis?' I was very surprised to see her.

She came in, closed the door and climbed on the bed where she curled up, resting her chin on her knees and wrapping her arms round her legs.

'He's got flu,' she announced. 'I rang up and this deathly voice answered. He doesn't want to see anyone.' She giggled. 'He thinks it's the end of the world.'

'Don't you see yourself as Florence Nightingale then?'

'Not me. I hate illness and I'm bad at coping with it. I don't like people round me when I'm ill.'

'Well, it's nice to see you,' I said, feeling faint warmth creeping back into my brain.

'Good.' She smiled at me. 'Actually, I've got a message for you. Tom rang up.'

'Oh.' I remembered then that I should have phoned him as usual as soon as I arrived. 'Oh, well, a thrill for him when you answered.'

'That's right. But he said, will you ring him back?'

'Oh. Well, not tonight. I don't feel like Tom, even on the phone.'

Marty rolled over and laughed, hair splashing over the bedspread. 'How well I know that feeling. So the time has come, has it? Good. Who is he?'

'Oh God,' I said. 'Hell. Damn it all.'

'Sod it,' Marty supplied helpfully.

'Yes. Thank you. Etc., etc. There isn't anyone. I feel as if I've been to a cremation.'

Marty waited, silent but enquiring. I told her, as best I could, the events of the past few days.

'Poor you,' said Marty, comfortingly off-hand. 'But do stop saying you don't understand. You've had enough stooging around. You want to be in love again. If that isn't normal I don't know what is.'

'I want to be happy,' I said. 'Everybody should be. I just decided I hate seeing people miserable, including me. Especially me.'

'God, I wish I could do finals in life, love and sex,' said

174

Marty. 'A psychological exposé of the feminine mind and heart by an experienced amateur. My God. It's a far cry from the Development of the Language and Literary Criticism. Look –' And she sat up again. 'This stuff about being happy is all very well. Fine if you can make it. But the only really important thing is to be alive.'

Again that word, I thought.

'Happy or unhappy,' she went on, 'it doesn't really make much difference so long as something is going on and you're involved.'

I said, 'Look, I understand your point of view; it's the old excitement philosophy. It's fine for you but I'm sure I always wanted to be happy the way Anne did. It worked out for her. She's safe and happy and married. That was all I wanted.'

'That was a long time ago,' Marty said quietly.

'Well, I envy Anne,' I insisted.

'I don't. I'm not at all ready to be married. But she is, I agree. It will suit her very well. Maybe she's more grown up than I am. It doesn't matter. When I'm tired of the way I live I'll give it up.'

'You make it sound easy,' I said.

'Well . . .' Marty waved her arms in the air. 'I just do what I want to do. But even that can get quite complicated.'

'You've got a lot more energy than I have,' I said. 'I can get tired just discussing it with you.'

She laughed. 'Let's make some coffee; it'll wake you up.'

'I haven't finished unpacking.'

'Well, I have. Come over to my room and I'll make the coffee.'

I went. 'How tidy you are,' I exclaimed as we went in.

'Yes, Ruth came and helped me.'

'Oh, Ruth.' My depression deepened. 'Marty, I think Ruth's been very odd since last term, maybe sooner. She's terribly inconsequential when you talk to her and she's getting morbid. She read a book on religion and decided you were going to hell.'

Marty smiled. 'I know. She told me.'

'Oh, did she? What did you say?'

'I told her that if there is such a place it will probably suit me very well.'

'And?'

'And nothing. She said I shouldn't joke about it and I said balls and we finished unpacking in silence.'

'Ever get the feeling she's drifting away from you?' I asked, and we burst out laughing.

'That's better,' Marty said. 'Now you're more yourself. Just a minute, I'll put a notice on the door. There. Now have some coffee and a cigarette.'

'All the same, though,' I went on, 'she is in a funny state.'

'It's sublimation,' said Marty. 'Simple.'

'Perhaps too simple?' I suggested.

'Rubbish. Don't let education warp your mind. It's one of the risks we run here, you know – making everything more complex than it really is. We're so trained to look for hidden meanings. Of course it's sublimation. She'll probably end up taking the veil and the best of luck to her. Lots of queers find religion a great comfort.'

'Aren't you being rather brutal?'

'Look, I can only behave according to the way I feel. I don't believe suffering is the worst thing that can happen to someone. Nothingness is. Detachment. Unfeeling, as Orwell might call it.'

'I see,' I said. 'I wonder if you're right. I'm sure Anne wouldn't say so and I always thought I agreed with her.'

'Times change and people with them,' Marty said. 'Pardon me for not being a great, original mind. I might have agreed with Anne once, though.'

'Really?'

'Well, almost. It's hard to remember now, but I think so.'

I thought, concentrated. 'Marty, you've met a lot of people. How d'you meet them?'

Marty ground out one cigarette and lit another. 'Well, I

don't join fretwork and cookery classes like in women's magazines advice columns.'

'Surprise, surprise.'

'Let's see. Louis I met at a party –'

'Given by?'

'Adrienne.'

'Who knew him how?'

'He was a friend of her husband.'

'Who met him where?'

'In Paris.'

'I see. Go on.'

'You mean where did I meet the others?'

'That's right.'

'Well, Yves was a friend of Louis. Jerry shared a room with Louis. Tom and I met at a dance – you must have noticed what a good dancer he is. Sam turned up in a library and Ramon was in a café.'

'And Ray?'

'Oh. In a sweet-shop, of all places.'

I had a feeling from the tone of her voice that I should not have asked this, so I said hurriedly, 'I know Jerry shared a room with Louis, but that doesn't tell me how you met him.'

'We were both trying to find a taxi in the rain.'

I was silent.

'Well, that was an abortive conversation,' said Marty cheerfully.

'I'm sorry. I don't know why I suddenly wondered.'

'Well, you don't have to have a reason. Have some more coffee.'

'I think I just feel in a funny mood,' I said.

'It's the end of something,' said Marty. 'You always do.'

I stayed with her the rest of the evening and all through the next day, clinging for support. Our lectures threw up a lot of new books and the day after I said I would go to Foyle's to get some of them. I felt restless, cooped up in the building.

It was a fine April day, not warm but bright. I enjoyed the ride into town. It had rained in the morning and everything looked washed and new. I had still not telephoned Tom and I kept pushing the thought to the back of my mind. At least it was an outing, I told myself, and I could browse around. I might not even buy anything, but now was the time, while my grant lay untouched. And their second-hand department was very good.

I remember it all so well. Afterwards you hold your breath and frighten yourself with contemplation of the thin strands of coincidence. I think I had vague, suppressed ideas that I might run into Mike Swann if I turned up casually at enough student-frequented places sufficiently often. Crazy, in a university that size. But I went.

I had been there for about half an hour, I suppose, and I was really enjoying myself with the smell and feel of books and all the rich freedom of dipping into them with no one to disturb me. But my subconscious must have been alert because when a voice said, 'Hullo,' I wheeled round, certain, and was sharply disappointed to see Mr Stone behind me. That proved I had not remembered voices, at any rate.

'Oh, hullo,' I said.

'Sorry, did I startle you?'

'No. Well, a bit. I was miles away, I'm afraid.'

He smiled. 'Oh, please don't be apologetic. It's really rather ill-mannered to speak in a book-shop; like a church or a doctor's waiting-room.'

'Not at all. I'm glad you did.' I had no idea what to say. 'But I know what you mean.'

'Good. Shall we resume our holy silence?'

'Yes. If you like. By all means.' I felt absurdly wrong-footed.

We went on looking at books. He seemed immediately absorbed again but my powers of concentration had departed. I felt ridiculously aware of the size of him; he looked strong, unacademic, wrong almost, in Foyle's. Buying guns or fishing tackle, perhaps; the sort of person I had always previously ignored, even despised.

After we had spent about ten or fifteen minutes like that he suddenly turned to me, smiling, and said, 'How is your friend Mrs Lindsay?'

It was a shock to hear Anne's married name. 'Oh, she's fine. I'm going to see them on Sunday.' I had seen Anne after lectures but her happiness was so obvious that I found it hard to talk to her.

'Did they have a honeymoon?'

'No, they went straight to the flat; they were so glad to have their own home at last they couldn't wait to get at it.' There at least, I thought, they had pleased themselves.

'It's nice for them,' said Mr Stone. 'I remember how we felt. A long time ago now but you don't forget. Matter of fact, I'm at a loose end today. I saw my wife off to the States yesterday and I'm feeling very sorry for myself.'

'You and me both,' I said, I don't know why.

'Oh, why?' He looked at me tolerantly, only mildly interested, I imagine, but polite.

'I went to look someone up and they'd moved.' I was surprised to hear myself telling so much of the truth.

'Had he?' Mr Stone was smiling at me and I felt myself – shame of them all – actually blushing.

'It was just a silly impulse,' I said hastily. 'I'd only met him once, last October.'

'Oh, well, we all have our silly impulses. I think it's a pity not to act on them sometimes. Anyway, I'm sure our lonely state deserves a coffee. Would you like one?'

I suppose I hesitated, because he said quickly, 'Or are you in a hurry to get somewhere?'

'Oh. No. No, I'm not.'

'And you're not allergic to coffee?'

'No.'

'Good. That's fine then. Are you ready?'

'Yes.'

'We haven't bought anything, either of us,' he said.

'Poor old Foyle's.'

'Never mind, I expect they're used to it. They still look very prosperous.'

We walked together through the shop and out into Charing Cross Road. I wondered, mildly frantic, if my face and hair looked all right. Women always think like that even with men who don't matter. It seems so important to look desirable, if possible to everyone; it lowers self-esteem if you don't, and confidence evaporates.

We walked for a while and he talked about his wife and her career and what a wonderful chance it was for her.

'When will you see her again?' I asked.

'I'm probably going over there for the long vac.'

'Please tell her sometime how much I admire her – I think she's terrifically elegant.'

He seemed pleased. 'Thank you. I will. I think she's rather lovely myself.'

We had coffee at an Espresso place where half of it was froth but it had a pleasant taste. I stirred in sugar carefully so as not to disturb the froth which I ate slowly with a spoon. He watched me and said finally, 'You can have mine as well if you like.'

'Oh, dear, am I disgusting you?'

'Not at all. I don't enjoy froth, that's all, and I was wondering how I could decently dispose of it.'

When mine was finished I scooped his off the top of his cup, watched by the woman behind the counter.

'You didn't really want coffee,' I said. 'You were just being kind.'

'Not at all. I shall enjoy what's left. And I never do things just to be kind.'

'Don't you really?'

'No. I think it's patronizing and horrible.'

'Why?'

'I don't like to see human beings in such an unequal relationship.'

'That's interesting.' I went on with the froth. 'Only one is brought up with the idea of kindness as a virtue.'

'One is brought up with all kinds of ideas but one has to sort the false from the true as one grows up; and now do you think we could drop the *one*? It always struck me as a singularly useless pronoun.'

I was delighted. 'By all means. But you're not being fair, you shouldn't know about Engineering and English.'

'It's hardly knowing about English to spot a pronoun, is it? I don't suppose I could tell Alfred from Aelfric.'

'Oh, what a horrible piece of one-upmanship.'

'I'm sorry. Is it really? I had a sister who was so mad on the stuff she went round the house spouting it and I never really found out what was well known and what obscure. Excuse me. Would you like a cigarette?'

'Yes, please.' He had caught me at the moment of thinking: 'Dare I take out my own or will that be rude?' We both had cigarettes and he finished his coffee, but I kept some of mine although it was getting cold, because I wanted an excuse not to go.

We smoked in silence and I felt no desperate urge to make conversation until he said, 'Do you find all that stuff – translation and so on – fairly easy or not?'

I shrugged. 'Well, we use cribs and try to sort them out and improve on them. It's hard work alone, but mostly I think we work in pairs. I do mine with Marty, when she's there. Do you remember her? The girl who did the flamenco dance at Louis' party last autumn.'

'Oh yes.' He looked amused. 'That's a delicate way of putting it; I do congratulate you. Louis' girl-friend. You know, at times I wonder if that young woman isn't rather more than Louis needs.'

'Do you? Well, of course, I see it from the other angle.'

'Yes, of course. Forgive me. I only meant I hope they don't come to grief somewhere along the line.'

'I don't think Marty cares about grief so long as she feels alive, and I nearly quote,' I said.

He raised his eyebrows. 'Is that what they call living for kicks?'

'I don't know; I'm not really with it.'

We smiled at each other.

'Finished?' he asked.

I stared doubtfully at the pool in the bottom of my cup.

'Would you like some more?'

'Please. That's nice of you.'

'Well, I would like some more. But only on the same terms, that you dispose of my froth.'

I listened to the noise the machine made and then Mr Stone was back with the two cups. 'Mr Stone,' I said, 'how well do you know Louis?'

'Not very well. He's very reserved. A nice enough young man, I'd say; maybe a bit neurotic. His work is usually good.'

'How funny.'

'What?'

'The different ways people see people.'

He laughed. 'Oh well, there you really have hit on a fundamental mystery. Go on.'

'Well, I've only met Louis a few times and it was always such an anticlimax after what I'd heard and the effect he had on Marty. It's just one crisis after another, you know.'

'I rather gathered it was something of the sort.'

'I'm sure they must enjoy it. But it's the normal surface that's so incongruous.'

'And therefore fascinating.'

'Yes.'

There was a pause and then Mr Stone said, 'What are your plans when you leave college?'

I shook my head. 'Nil, at the moment.'

'Oh, well, there's plenty of time yet,' he said encouragingly.

But I thought: 'Only four more terms including this one and I haven't been happy for a year. Everyone else grabs and seizes something.' The coffee cup blurred.

I heard Mr Stone saying, 'Would you like another cigarette?' and I nodded, not speaking.

He gave me one and lit it, saying, 'Finish your coffee and we'll get out of here.'

I shook my head.

'I'd like to take you for a drive if I may.'

I dragged hard on the cigarette and blew my nose, ashamed of myself. 'Thank you,' I managed. 'I'd like that.'

'Good, then that's settled. I'm afraid it's a bit of a walk to the car; parking is getting more and more of a nightmare in town.'

I don't remember where we drove but it was somewhere bright and shiny, out of town, amid the April weather. He drove well and not too fast and I looked about me and we did not talk for a long time. I kept wanting to say how kind he was and remembering he probably wouldn't like it.

'I got all my lectures over this morning,' he said. 'How about you?'

'I'm missing one now,' I told him.

'Oh dear, my bad influence. But I don't think you'd concentrate.'

'I know I wouldn't.'

We drove on and talked about travel and how you could get into a dream-like state when you went anywhere new so that it seemed pointless to go back.

'D'you ever feel unreal?' I asked.

'Quite often. But not as often as I used to.'

'I suppose that means you grow out of it.'

'I don't know what it means. Please don't be so angry.'

'I'm sorry.'

'And you don't have to apologize. Just stop being angry if you can. Or tell me what's wrong. Has someone been pushing you around?'

'Nothing so active.'

'Is it the young man who's bothering you? The one who wasn't there?'

'I don't know. I thought about it a lot. But I don't think I'm heart-broken. Listen.' And to prove my point I quoted for him:

> As I was going up the stair
> I met a man who wasn't there.
> He wasn't there again today
> I wish that he would go away.

I watched and saw him smile. 'Very funny,' he said, 'but it has its serious side. This young man, if you only met him once, must have represented something pretty important.'

'Yes,' I said roughly, 'he was genuinely interested in me. Positively anxious about my welfare. And I gave him the boot.'

It was a relief to speak, but as soon as it was out I wished I had not said it.

'Did you have a reason?' Mr Stone asked calmly.

'Well, I must have had.'

'I don't know. Perhaps.'

'Would I do a thing like that for no reason?'

'You might. I don't know you well enough to say. What was your reason?'

I sighed and said ungraciously, 'Must we?'

'I think so.'

And that, of course, was what I wanted to hear.

'I was tired of being kicked. My feelings were hurt – my pride, I suppose. You know how self-centred we young people are. I wanted to kick someone myself for a change.'

'I know the feeling.'

'Do you?'

'Yes. It's not so rare but it's very nasty. Who had been kicking you?'

'Oh, I wish I had put it some other way. Look, Mr Stone, you don't have to listen to all this.'

'I want to listen. And you might as well call me Matthew. Now I must make a confession: I can't remember your name.'

'Lois Mitchell.'

'Well, Lois, who had been hurting you?'

'Now you sound like a social worker.'

'Oh, that's not a bad thing to be, but I'm not and I'd rather you weren't unpleasant about it.'

I lit one of my own cigarettes then, hurriedly, feeling terribly snubbed.

'Now tell me what happened,' said Matthew calmly, as if I had never been rude at all.

I tried not to swallow, selecting my words carefully. 'Well, it started last April. My parents separated and my boy-friend got tired of me. All in a fortnight. They all wrote letters, you see – it was quite monotonous really. I'd always ... got on very well with my father, so I was on his side, but my mother told me he was going to marry a girl about my age as soon as he got his divorce. I met her; she was very nice, terribly in love with him and eager to start having children and so on. He was getting a whole new life. She tried to make out he still needed me. She was very considerate. The awful part was she was very likeable and sort of ... gentle. She said life was just people making mistakes and trying again. But she was in there with it, doing something. I was outside and I didn't have anyone, I wasn't doing anything. He couldn't stop talking about her and how marvellous she was. He was mad for me to see it just as he did. I don't know how different it might have been if I'd still had Peter. We were going to get engaged this year and married when I left college.'

'How long did you know him?'

'Two years.'

'And how long were you having a love affair?'

'Nearly a year. You're very understanding.'

'Not particularly. But I'm not a fool. How about your mother in all this?'

'Oh . . .' I paused and thought. 'I felt sorry for her. Poor old thing left high and dry. It was so easy for my father . . . But I couldn't really, well, love her.'

'No, I see that. Are you an only child, Lois?'

'No, I've got a brother.'

'Older or younger?'

'A year older.'

'How did he react to all this?'

'Well, he was on my mother's side. I know this sounds mathematical, but after they separated there didn't seem much point in keeping up pretence or being decently evasive.'

'No, of course not. Go on.'

'Well, he's at Cambridge in his final year. He hasn't been near my father since it happened. I think he's been quite a comfort to my mother while he was there but he seemed to get a sort of thing about a boy at his college, used to be furious if I asked questions. Then he met this girl and it all stopped, only the boy came to see him while he was out and I was alone. I felt so sad . . . I can't explain, but it was so awful, so callous. I wanted to kill Martin, I really did. I thought he was only thinking of himself and that's what I'd been doing and everyone else and that's when I remembered Mike. Only it was too late.'

'How did you first meet Mike?'

I felt my face and neck grow hot. 'I'm sorry, Mr Stone, Matthew, I've gone embarrassed. It's very silly.'

It was worse than silly. Remembering how I met Mike had reminded me of a lot more, and moreover of what had not happened since last term.

'He was your first lover after you lost your boy-friend, was he?'

'That's right. It was a sort of one-night-stand. I was desperate —'

'Well, there's no need to sound so ashamed. What was it — April to October? For a normal young woman you managed pretty well. I couldn't have got through April and I don't mind admitting it.'

'Everyone makes excuses for men, though. They say it's different.'

'Well, I don't agree. And neither does Claire – my wife. She'd tell you if she were here. You can only judge by yourself and your friends anyway. Have you been crawling around feeling abnormal?'

'I don't know . . . sometimes.'

'Well, cut that out for a start. What happened after this Mike?'

'Oh, another pick-up – a dead loss.'

'Don't use words like that, you're trying to cheapen yourself. Cut out the guilt and castigation. You and Mike got on well together?'

'Yes.'

'And the other fellow was no good?'

'That's right. But I was in a funny mood –'

'There you go again, blaming yourself. Stop it, will you? That's how people give themselves complexes. What harm will it do him now if you blame him?'

'None.' I smiled against my will.

'Good. Then blame him. Silly young fool, incompetent idiot, of course it was his fault. Go on, say it.'

But I was laughing too much.

'All right,' Matthew said. 'What happened next?'

I watched his hands on the driving-wheel, wishing they could touch me.

'Oh, I met someone else.'

'Good or bad?'

'Indifferent.'

'Oh, dear.'

'No, I'm being unfair. I knew what I was taking on, and later I changed my mind.'

'Stop going round in circles, Lois.'

'All right. You're being very tough with me.'

'Time someone was. Much more comforting than sogginess.'

'Yes, it is.'

'Don't think I can't be soggy, though. Go on about this fellow. What's his name?'

'Tom. He's an old flame of Marty's and still carrying a torch for her. He's a wonderful dancer, though. Actually, he was very kind to me –'

'There you are.'

'Yes, but he was a great help and I needed someone. It wasn't the kindness that got me down, just the constant reference to Marty. But I knew it would be like that so it's really my fault not his –'

'There you go again. You must stop this. Are you a masochist or something?'

'I don't think so. Not more than most women, anyway.'

'Well, you soon will be if you go on like this. Has this thing been dragging on since last autumn?'

'Yes.'

'Do you want to end it?'

I sighed. 'It's getting on my nerves but quite honestly, Mr – Matthew, since we're being so frank, I can't afford to. The alternative is worse.'

I was still watching his hands on the wheel and they seemed to be gripping it extraordinarily hard.

'You poor little devil,' he said. 'God, it's unfair. And all because that little rat of a boy dropped you in the first place.'

'He couldn't help changing his mind,' I said peaceably, feeling calmer.

'Yes, you're quite right, he couldn't and I'm being soggy.'

I was amused. 'Is that your special word?'

'Yes, it's – yes. Look here, Lois, we'll have to turn back, I think, it's getting on, but shall we have a meal on the way? Will you dine with me?'

'Thank you. I'd love to.'

188

We stopped at a roadhouse. I don't even remember what we ate except that I enjoyed it. Over the meal he looked hard at me with the very blue eyes and said, 'I don't want you to regret a word you've said to me.'

'I won't.'

'Regrets are always a waste of time. I want you to feel free to say anything to me. I really do understand. And people have silly habits of being ashamed of getting close to each other and saying things.'

'Yes, I know.'

'Of course you do.'

The tan had faded quite a lot from his face and more lines showed, so that he looked altogether older. He gave me his phone number on a piece of paper.

'Ring me any time you feel like a chat,' he said.

'Thank you. I will.'

'I mean it.'

'I know.' I smiled.

'Just remember I'm there and I'm a friend. You can get lost in this town and feel there's nobody.'

'Yes, you can.'

'Are your friends good?'

'Yes, they're very good.'

'When they're not too busy, you mean.'

'Yes. But I was the same before I got disengaged, as it were.'

He nodded.

On the drive back we talked about his student days and how the life was unchanged for students now: cheap meals and digs, or board and residence in hall; work skimped, then rushed or laboured through all night; friends, talking, always talking and argument about people, sex, religion, even politics; above all probably a sense of freedom and adventure. A pause in your life; a space no one could deprive you of, in which you could experiment. He had seen it all once as I saw it now.

He insisted on dropping me on the doorsteps of college and I could not explain why this was inconvenient. I waited a while and then walked down to the bus-stop. I went straight to Tom's flat without any doubt that he would be there. He was very pleased to see me and without many words we went to bed. I had probably never been so eager since he had known me and he was hungry too after weeks of separation, but it was no better or worse than usual for me except for the few moments when I did, I really did, pretend (remembering not to be ashamed or to despise myself) that he was Matthew.

TWENTY

'HOW are things with your parents, Anne?'

Anne smiled. 'Oh, much better. Fine. They came to dinner last week. It was so nice to see them. Before the wedding we were all so busy it was hard to tell if things were really better or not.'

Lucky Anne. Everything was coming right for her, of course, just as it should be.

'How's married life?' Stupid question, but everyone asked it.

'Wonderful. Only wish we'd got married earlier. It's so relaxing. No more rushing and hiding. Such a relief. And time to bother about extras, like food and clothes and so on. And much less sex-obsessed, I think, because it's there for the taking, any time.'

Well, that put the rest of us in our place.

'Sorry to sound off like that,' Anne added, 'but it is rather my favourite subject at the moment. I've been so lucky and I know it. Lucky to meet Keith in the first place, of course.'

Now, was that for my benefit?

'What made you fall in love with Keith, Anne?'

Anne would know, of course. She had the answer to everything. It was only other people who weren't sure, didn't know, fumbled for words that were only an approximation to what they dimly felt.

She was smiling. 'Oh – he was fun. And attractive. But mainly I think it was because he listened and understood. He knew what I meant. I could say anything to him. And then, when he loved me, that was a big reason for loving him.

That's why I don't really believe in unrequited love. It's so different it ought to have another name, anyway.'

There was no help to be had from Anne. But I was being more unfair to her than ever, bitterly annotating our conversation in my head. Anne, the girl with too much, who lived happily ever after.

We chatted on about other things. Anne was dress-making and trying out new recipes from her new cookery book. Keith was working hard in the next room, cramming. It was not long now, two months, less. Anne was not working so hard but in her final year she would. Keith would get a job in the summer so they would not be hard up for very long; they only had to manage for a little while, short enough to be amusing, a challenge.

You need a strong constitution to visit happy, newly-married friends. Or a sense of superiority.

Matthew seemed far away, a dream. When I got back to college I telephoned him to make sure he was real. His telephone voice was good, more exciting than his voice face to face. To prove I could talk about someone other than myself I told him all about Anne and Keith and their nice flat and how happy they were. He seemed interested. Then I said, 'Do you think I could come round and see you for half an hour? I'm rather fed up.'

There was a second of hesitation, the kind that spells doom and you always know though you won't admit it to yourself.

'Well – the fact is, Lois, I've got some people here. I'm sorry – look, if you'd like to come out for a drink a bit later on? Or tomorrow morning for coffee?'

'No, thank you.'

'Now don't be hurt. I just can't get away right now.'

'No, thank you. And it doesn't matter, friend,' I said, and hung up.

Somebody wrote that suffering does not improve the character. I'd like to meet him. I've often wondered what was done to him that made him finally notice this fact about himself.

On Monday Marty was not at our first lecture. I went along to her room. She was sitting on the bed, just staring in front of her. There were pages of a letter spread out all over the bed. For one appalling moment I thought that Louis had written, breaking off their association, and Tom and I would have to find some way of coping with the unpredictable, ensuing mess.

'Whatever's happened?'

Her face was quite white: no make-up, no colour, no expression and her hair just hung and lay where it fell. For the first time I caught a glimpse of her as a small old woman and I was frightened.

'Nothing much. Just a letter from my mother with all the details of Ray's wedding. He must have got her pregnant, it wasn't to be till the summer. He must have got her pregnant at Christmas.' She laughed. 'It's funny, really, isn't it? And trust my mother to write me all about it.'

'Marty, I'm so sorry, can I do anything?'

'Just leave me. This is all about nothing, you know, I'm just burying my dead, and burying them and burying them,' and she suddenly fell over onto the bed and lay there shaking but with no sound emerging. I thought with the long black hair she looked like Antigone in a production I'd seen. Antigone scratching at the earth to cover her brother's corpse.

I went back to my room, and thought that Marty was the most solitary person I had ever met. It did not matter, really, whether she made her own unhappiness or not, whether she was self-dramatizing, masochistic, or neurotic. When things hit her, whatever the cause, she was alone.

Perhaps we were all alone. I sat down and tried to reason. I had feared this before, years ago, before I had met Peter. But my father's presence had seemed to contradict the idea, the way he understood the trivial adolescent fervours I chose to confide in him. Then there had been Peter and we were a team, shielded against all malice. When you had someone on your side, the idea of aloneness was ridiculous. But when you hadn't it was convincing. This was the big fear, the vast cavern beneath the feet; this was the reason why everyone ran and scurried so, searching and grabbing. This was why people wrote poetry about islands, and the difficulty of communication, of closeness ... John Donne, Matthew Arnold, others I could not remember. This was why people jumped into impossible marriages, pointless love affairs, because they were afraid to wait, to go on, in case they never found what they needed. They took something rather than wait and gamble on everything, or nothing.

But suppose all closeness was an illusion. After all, you spent more time with yourself than with anyone else. Joke. But life was really one long conversation inside your head, occasionally interrupted. Only you really knew. You encouraged yourself and made allowances. You could never get into someone else's head to see if it functioned in the same way. We were each a prisoner of one personality. There was even no way of knowing if the words you used meant what you meant when they were heard. And civilization and language were so old that there were probably no new thoughts to be thought about anything.

On Tuesday there was a letter from Matthew.

Dear Lois, I would like to see you for a drink and a chat on Tuesday evening. I shall be at your tube station by eight if I don't hear from you. Matthew.

Very brief, no apologies or concessions. I wanted to ignore it, but more than that I wanted to see him. I was alone in college; Anne at home with Keith, Marty, looking serene and polished, gone to visit a convalescent Louis, Jeanne entertaining John with another couple as chaperons. So I went.

The car was already waiting when I arrived so I got in and said, 'Hullo.'

'Hullo,' said Matthew, and drove off. 'Glad you could make it.'

'Are you?' I said.

'Well, of course. I wouldn't have asked you if I hadn't wanted to see you.'

There was a silence until I said, 'Aren't you going to mention the phone call?'

'What's the point? I'd rather forget it. You were unreasonable and I was tactless. Can you make a profitable discussion out of that?'

'I suppose not.'

'Well, at any rate, now do you believe I don't go in for being kind?'

I grinned. 'I certainly do.'

'Good. That's something.'

At the pub I had Martini and Matthew had Scotch.

'Where did you learn to drink?' he asked.

'Learn?'

'Well, you know what you like and obviously enjoy it. I should say you have a fair capacity, but we shall find out. Who initiated you?'

'Oh. My father. One of those hard-drinking reporters you see in films, the kind people say don't exist. We drank together socially in his spare moments. My mother didn't like it. And I think he also had the idea that if I was used to it I'd be less likely to be taken advantage of by some unscrupulous chap I didn't really fancy.'

He smiled. I watched his hands as they held his glass and I felt my body stir.

'Cigarette?' he asked suddenly, taking them out, and we both had one.

'And did your father teach you to smoke too?' he asked.

'No, that was girls at school. When my mother found out she said I could do it openly and my consumption dropped quite a lot.'

'Very sensible of her.'

'Yes, it was. It went up again, of course, with Peter and college and all that.'

'Yes, of course, it would.'

A pause. Then, 'Matthew, why are you bothering with me?' I had not meant to ask but I was quite glad when it was out.

He smiled; defensively, I thought. 'That's a funny question.'

'No, it isn't.' Why did he make me argumentative, stubborn?

'Well, I find you interesting and I enjoy talking and listening and I think we're both lonely.'

'What about your friends?'

'Well, what about them?'

'You've got them; why do you need me?'

'My dear girl, I never said I needed you.' He raised his voice slightly. 'I enjoy your company and I think you need more than that boy-friend of yours; someone, that is, not necessarily me, only I happened to come along.'

'Yes, I see.' I kept my voice light. 'You're quite right. Could I have another drink?'

'I'm so sorry.'

We had two more each and talked about whether I could make a career in journalism and how his wife had always known she wanted to be a doctor. He dropped me at the bottom of the road leading to college, after holding my hand in both his and kissing me on the forehead; I suppose to make me feel like a child. Only I didn't feel like a child. I shivered somewhere far down inside me, while keeping outwardly still, and there was a wave of heat in my chest. He said, 'Look after yourself,' and drove away and I went back to college and lay awake, planning and hoping.

After that I didn't see him for about a fortnight but I telephoned often. I got into the habit of phoning late at night and there was the radio in the background with soft, late-night music. He would tell me about the work he was doing, deliberately technical so I could not understand and I would pretend to, which amused us both. He had a cat and I wanted to hear all about it, every time. I wanted to see it, too. It was easier for me to phone him than the other way round because that involved messages and people coming to fetch me. Besides, I was supposed to be the one in need. I wondered if he thought he was doing something mildly dangerous or if he never considered it at all. He was thirty-five. I asked him once. Did that make him very different from me inside? I had no way of knowing. All prisoners of our personalities . . .

But although I did not see him often I thought about him nearly all the time, the way you always do to sustain a relationship with someone who is away a lot. I had not thought about one person continuously in this way for a long time.

At the end of the fortnight he took me to a French film in town. We argued about whether it was true to life or too analytical, full of false notes. Strange how enjoyable these pointless conversations are: they only hinge upon different views of life, after all – yours, the author's, the film director's.

He dropped me at the tube station that night after just patting my cheek, which enraged me. I had said there was no need to drive right up to college and he didn't argue. I suppose it was then I started adding things up and noticing his caution. Dropping me at tubes, at the end of the road, not getting out of the car, never coming into college. Of course, it would not do; he was known in the university. A married lecturer and a girl student, on friendly visiting terms. It would never do. All the same he had said, 'I couldn't have got through April myself and I don't mind admitting it.' A joke, to be consoling, quite impersonal? Or what? I wondered on what basis he and his wife organized their separation, and I could not ask. I wondered why they had no children.

I asked about that one evening, after four drinks, when I felt less sensitive about his feelings.

'Claire had several miscarriages,' he said. 'Finally we decided not to try any more, for a few years, anyway. It's such a depressing business. They couldn't find any medical reason for it and Claire felt she could only get cheerful again if she concentrated on work for a while.'

'I see; it was rude of me to ask.'

'A little,' he said frankly, in a way I now almost took for granted, 'but it's the sort of thing you always wonder about people, especially when you're young.'

'Another snide reference to my youth,' I said, having noted them all. He looked at me.

'Well, you *are* young,' he said.

'Don't you know enough about young people to know they don't like being reminded of their youth?'

'I'm sorry,' he said, 'but I thought you were old enough not to mind. After all, you are nearly twenty.'

We laughed at that and I said immediately afterwards, 'Can I see your pussy-cat tonight?'

His face went cloudy.

'Please,' I said. 'I think you're being awfully mean. I'm pussy-cat starved. There's only one at college and it's a fat, old cross thing that scratches me when I pick it up.'

He got up then for a packet of cigarettes and when he came back his face was clear and he smiled at me. 'All right,' he said. 'Come on.'

We drove to Bloomsbury where he had a house and a sort of tiny garden.

'Romantic,' I said, to tease him.

'No, just near our work.'

'University-land,' I said. 'Like Disney-land. Where all the good children play.'

He looked at me in surprise as he opened the door. 'Whatever are you talking about? You were on gin tonight. Doesn't it agree with you?'

'It does,' I said. 'It does agree with me. It agrees with me beautifully.'

'Well,' Matthew said, 'never was a question more thoroughly answered, and in the negative.'

There was a soft thud as something landed beside us.

'There she is,' he said.

'Where did she come from?'

She was small and neat, tabby to the last hair, with pale, huge greenish eyes and long whiskers. She rolled herself round Matthew's legs, somehow managing to do it with immense dignity.

'She's Claire's, really,' he said, 'but she's making do with me.'

'May I pick her up or will she hate it?'

'She'll love it, she's very affectionate. And even if she didn't she'd only sulk, not scratch. She's very polite, a real lady.'

I picked her up and held her securely, one hand under her back feet, the other stroking her head while her front paws rested on my shoulder. I always held cats in this position; it seemed to suit them and me.

'She sits a lot on the hall stand,' said Matthew. 'That's why you couldn't see her when you came in. She gets hidden by the coats.'

After what seemed like a moment of hesitation he led me into the sitting-room, which was quite large. I had expected something more sophisticated. There was a rust carpet and a black settee and two dark green armchairs. The curtains were a light grey, silky stuff and all the paint was white. The furniture, though fairly modern, looked comfortable rather than smart.

'This is nice,' I said. 'You don't know how good it is to be in a house and a home instead of a room or a flat.'

'Is it?' he asked, smiling, looking at the cat rather than me. 'Good. I'm going to make some coffee.'

'I don't want any,' I said.

'Maybe not, but you need it. We both do.' He vanished and I talked to the cat, putting my face close to hers.

'You don't, do you, pet? You don't want any coffee, little pussy-cat, and what's more you won't get any, so how about that?' and so on, the way some women talk to babies. She looked me full in the face with her cool eyes, and for a moment we touched noses.

Matthew came back at last with the percolator and two mugs. 'Do you mind using these?'

'Not a bit. Can I help?'

He disappeared again and returned with sugar, milk and spoons. 'There you are. No, you can't help. I did bring milk but I think we should have it black.'

I looked at him. He was sitting beside me on the couch and putting things on the coffee table. I felt so conscious of his physical nearness that I wanted to yell aloud. I put the cat down and she strolled off across the carpet, stopping to stretch and arch her back.

'Do you really think we're drunk?' I said. 'Surely not. You can't.'

'Not drunk, no,' he said, pouring out coffee. 'Just a little high.'

'Well, I enjoy being high,' I protested. 'Why do I have to spoil it all by drinking coffee?'

'You don't,' he said evenly, 'but I do.'

'Why?' I could hear my voice becoming petulant and childish.

'Because otherwise I might do something indiscreet, like the young men your father wanted to protect you from.'

'I wouldn't mind,' I said in a low voice. It was mean of him to mention my father at that moment but I ignored it.

'I know that,' he said, and drank.

I stared at the carpet. 'Is it so obvious?'

'Didn't you mean it to be?'

I was silent.

'There's no need to be ashamed,' he said. 'It's a perfectly natural reaction. Only the time has come to call a halt and think. I'm very much at fault for letting things drift, shall we say, this far. But you're a very attractive girl who happened to appeal to me and I thought, rather smugly, I could cope.

I also had more altruistic motives which you've heard about *ad nauseam*, so I won't bother repeating those. I made a rash comment on the problems of sexual abstinence, which has probably lingered in your mind. Well, I meant it, but there are various solutions to these problems, particularly for men, as you probably realize.'

'Yes,' I said in a muffled voice, 'you're being very delicate.'

'Well,' he went on, 'I felt I should explain at this point that while I'm very much attracted to you and enjoy our discussions, I am primarily a man who loves his wife, who happens to be very lovely and very intelligent and stimulating and exciting.'

'Thank you for the lesson.'

'I'm sorry – did I sound pompous? It had to be said.'

'Is she also understanding?'

'What do you mean?'

'Now you're play-acting with me. Does she ... condone, that's the word, your affairs with other women?'

There was a pause and I felt I had struck oil.

'And when exactly did we establish that I have affairs with other women?'

'Well, don't you?'

We looked at each other, openly, for the first time since the conversation began.

'Never when Claire is at home,' he said. 'Normally one-night-stands or casual, meaningless, physical relationships with people who understand the position. I never get emotionally involved.'

'And what does she do?'

Again there was a pause until he said, 'Quite probably the same thing; I have never asked. We've had various separations owing to work, holidays, illness of relatives and so on. We always admitted that physical fidelity might crack after a certain unspecified length of time.'

I bowed my head. 'All very clinical.'

'We don't like to drift into things, either of us. We like to know exactly where we are. And we know we belong together, whatever happens when we're apart.'

The cat climbed onto the window-sill and settled down behind the stiff, silver-grey curtains, curling her tail around her paws.

I said, watching her, 'Have you just given me my marching orders?' and was surprised at the newly desolate feeling.

Matthew said, 'No. I've just explained how it will be if you stay. You'll maybe get hurt. You certainly won't get a fair deal.'

'I don't mind getting hurt again,' I said and realized that it was true.

He took my hands in both his and I trembled all over. He smiled.

'I've only been to Tom once this term,' I said.

'That was foolish.'

'I know.'

Our faces were nearer together but he made one last effort. 'Lois, if you stay around a man in my situation long enough you get what you ask for. Be very sure you really want it.'

'Oh, I do, I do.'

'You want more than that.'

'I can't have it, I know that. It doesn't matter. I've thought of nothing but you since we met.'

He kissed me then, at last, and there was flooding fire and colliding tongues and a crazy feeling of home-coming. He ran his hands all over me and I pitched headlong into his arms. Minutes passed as we lay on the couch, embracing and exploring. The warmth and the excitement mounted for both of us, and for me also a stirring of emotion that was only just familiar but infinitely welcome. Then came the jarring interruption: first only in words, his voice in my ear saying, 'Do you have anything with you?' and I shook my head and heard Marty all over again.

'Don't you?' I said stupidly, though I think I would have happily lain kissing and caressing much longer.

'No.' He held me a moment longer, then he sat up and took a deep breath; it was ages before he let it out in a heavy sigh. 'When we use anything Claire is the one.' Mentioning her name seemed to calm him; he lit a cigarette. 'Want one?'

I shook my head, horrified at the anticlimax, and yet somehow still happy at the mere fact of having been close to him.

'I'm sorry, Lois,' he said in his ordinary voice. 'Shows I don't make a habit of this, though, or I'd have emergency stocks. I'm very sorry. Getting this far isn't very good for either of us.'

'I think I'll have some coffee,' I said, shaken.

'Of course.' He poured it out for me. 'Look here, this may be all for the best, give us more time to think. We're not past the point of no return.'

'How eager you are.'

'Now stop that. You know perfectly well what I mean. And I'm not taking chances with you.'

The next day I went to Marty's doctor.

TWENTY-ONE

THERE were six weeks of term left and during that time Matthew made love to me only eight times and I fell in love with him. There could not be any whole nights together; he could not come to my room and he would not let me stay at his house. I minded this very much.

He had a much better body than any man I had ever known and I derived enormous pleasure from watching him dress and undress. He had immense vitality, too, and cared about my satisfaction and I tried hard to pretend this was all I cared about. But I wanted to make him happy. I watched anxiously to see if this time was better than last time; valued the moments afterwards when he was quiet and grateful. I often thought how much more he would have given to his wife and I knew this was right and what I had to expect. I had agreed to accept it. I hoped I did not give away too much when I kissed him or stroked his body; I was afraid that he might decide I was becoming too involved and end the affair in my own best interests.

We had four meetings, I think, when we just had a drink or saw a film and he held my hand, so I suppose we met twelve times in all the six weeks. I was in fact seeing him approximately twice a week which for someone in his position was a generous allowance. It felt so much less. I phoned him two or three times a week as well which was probably an imposition but he never complained and was usually free to talk. I did not argue any more but rang off at once if he was busy.

I wanted to cook for him but he never let me. In fact he

seemed reluctant about allowing me in the kitchen even to make coffee. It was a lovely kitchen, full of modern equipment but with wooden surfaces, not white enamel or steel. I suppose he felt it was sacred to her. We never went to bed in their bedroom, either, always in the guest-room or the sitting-room. I preferred the guest-room; I felt like a tart downstairs and I think he realized, as after a few times we gave up using the sitting-room except for talk and coffee. I developed a mild obsession about their bedroom, remembering Moravia's *Woman of Rome* and how she and her lover go to bed in the grand bedroom of his employer and she bathes in the splendid bathroom. Something like that; I may be embroidering.

I thought Matthew was very frugal about our affair but could say nothing; you don't criticize the crumbs the rich man drops from his table for you.

It was a lonely six weeks because I could not talk to anyone about him. At least I did not feel it was safe to do so. Anne and Marty both knew him through Keith and Louis and might possibly recognize the situation if I discussed it with them. So I said to Marty who guessed, of course, that there was someone, that, 'Yes, there is someone,' and 'No, I'd rather not talk about it.'

Tom came over one night, about three weeks after it had begun. I'd been neglecting him badly; I'd met him twice, I think, and then only for a drink – oh, and once we went to a dance.

'There is someone else, isn't there?' he said, after meandering round my room for a bit.

'Yes, there is. I've been meaning to say something only I never got round to it.'

'It's all right, I understand. I'm glad for you. Are you happy?'

'Yes and no. You know how it is.'

He peered at me. 'You look different. That's how I guessed. But you don't look happy exactly.'

'Did you look happy when you had Marty all to yourself?'

'I don't suppose so. But then I knew it couldn't last.'

'Snap,' I said.

He was silent for a long time after that and patted my hand. Finally he said, 'Never mind. Enjoy it while you can. And if you ever want to look me up again, later on, please do.'

It was nice of him. I said, 'Thank you, Tom. I'm afraid it's out of the question now, the way I feel –'

'Oh, I understand that,' he said hurriedly.

'– but you're very kind and I do appreciate it. And I'm sorry about the times I bit your head off.'

'Oh, but I didn't mind,' he said.

'I know, but it's still rude and bad of me, even if I had written permission.'

He stayed to supper. I think we both felt enormous friendliness and relaxation. At the same time I was conscious of the dregs of guilt.

'Tom, I do hope you'll meet someone soon and forget about Marty. You can't spend your life picking up casualties like me.'

'I know.'

'Is it getting any better at all?'

'Oh, yes, I think so, really.' He was eating ravenously as always. 'There are some days when I don't think about her at all.'

I gave up. He was hopeless. We cleared away the dishes and played chess until ten o'clock.

The last time Matthew and I were together was five days before the end of term. We lay side by side, hot and exhausted, on the narrow guest-room bed and I stared at the ceiling, picturing him on his way to America. His flight was scheduled for three days after we went down.

He held my hand and kissed it and suddenly the whole thing was too much for me. I tried hard to keep my voice steady as I said, 'Please, Matthew, lie on top of me again and kiss me.'

He did so without speaking and I clung to him tightly, feeling how warm and strong he was and thinking wildly, 'Now why don't they drop one of their bombs and it wouldn't matter.'

Only it would have mattered very much to him, in bed with the wrong woman and longing to be with Claire. I remembered this a moment afterwards and let go of him, saying, 'Well, I suppose we'd better get up,' to save him the trouble of wondering when and how to say it without hurting my feelings. He kissed my shoulder and said, 'Fraid so,' rolling off me and off the bed.

I turned over to hide my face and said casually, 'Do we meet again before you go?'

He did not hesitate. 'I don't think so. I've got a lot of things to do.'

'Meaning you want to have a decent interval.' This time it slipped out and shocked me, too.

'I wish you wouldn't say things like that, Lois.'

He always used my name, or nothing at all. No phoney endearments. I think I'd have given a lot for one hefty, dishonest 'Darling.'

'Sorry,' I said humbly. 'I'm a bitch.'

'Now stop that.' He was dressing, quickly and methodically; I could hear his movements and the rustle of garments. I pulled up the bedclothes over me. There is no point in exposing yourself to a satiated male unless he loves you. It can even be humiliating to prove how very uninteresting your body has become.

'I'll go and make some coffee,' Matthew said. He went downstairs and I got up slowly and put on my clothes. I straightened the bed and opened the window and went to the lavatory and repaired my face and combed my hair. Then I went downstairs to drink coffee before he drove me back to college.

TWENTY-TWO

THERE was still the problem of the summer to be overcome. Two or three days before the end of term I was packing in my room when Anne called in.

'How nice not to be a part of all that,' she said first, observing the mess on the floor.

'Yes. You're lucky.'

Anne cleared a space on the bed and sat down. 'Cigarette?'

'No, thanks. I'm too busy to enjoy it.'

Anne lit one for herself. 'Cheap brand,' she said cheerfully. 'How are the mighty fallen. Actually, it's all in a worthy cause and this is it. How do you fancy spending the summer in Italy?'

'How do you mean?'

'With us. You and Tom if possible.'

Of course she still thought it was Tom and I could hardly correct her.

'Look, I'll tell you our plan,' she went on, 'and you can say what you think. We are going to sublet our flat for three months. One month we spend in a furnished room, both working and living on toast to save as much as possible. Then we take off for Italy where we rent a villa and just sit on the beach and drink wine and eat spaghetti till the end of September.'

'Sounds glorious,' I said.

'Well,' Anne said, 'we regard this as our last chance. Keith could get a proper job right away but he'll never have another long vac in his life. Next year he'll be working anyway, so my holiday will be no use to me. Even if I take up teaching I'll never get more than six weeks at a stretch again and Keith'll probably start with a fortnight working up to a month.'

'Oh yes, you're quite right,' I said.

'Well, then will you? I must be honest, not only do we want your company, your cash would help too. If you two come we can all stay two months. If not, we may only manage for one, for all our big talk. If Marty and Louis liked to come we could almost live in luxury.'

'They're going to Greece this year,' I said.

'Oh, are they? Oh, well, it might have been a bit much. Look, I've worked it all out on paper; here you are. Estimate of budget split four ways. I think it's possible.'

It was funny to see Anne so preoccupied with money.

'Don't you have to pay in advance?' I asked.

'Not till nearly the end of July. We're very lucky but it's the friend of a friend and they've given us first refusal till July first and our word is our bond till the twenty-eighth.'

'That's very good. They're not so friendly you can have it for nothing?'

'Not that friendly.' Anne laughed. 'Do come. It'd be so nice, apart from being a help. I mean, we could advertise for anyone, just to help out with funds, but we really want friends we know are compatible.'

'I'll talk to Tom,' I said. 'I would like to come, really.' The more I thought about it, the more it resembled salvation. Only Tom remained as a possible obstacle. And I could not go alone to spoil Anne and Keith's holiday and make them feel sorry for me the whole time, the lonesome third. Besides, I could not contribute enough cash.

I abandoned my packing, suddenly tired, and sat down on a suitcase. Anne gave me a cigarette.

'Now for less pleasant matters,' she said.

Immediately I felt she must have found out.

'It's Ruth,' she said.

'Ruth?' I was hysterical with relief. 'We can't take her as well, surely?'

Anne laughed. 'Don't even make jokes like that. No, it's just that she waylaid me today and asked me in for coffee. We had a long chat – or rather I had a long listen. I should think my ears stood up and wagged practically. Did you have any idea she's almost a Roman Catholic?'

I took a deep breath. 'Has it gone as far as that? The last time she mentioned religion she'd latched on to the idea of Marty in hell, which seemed to give her a certain amount of satisfaction, to say the least.'

'Oh well, it's gone much further than that. I heard all about the precious blood redeeming sinners and how Christ died for us, though especially for Marty and Ruth, I felt, and how she might yet save Marty's soul by prayer and mortification, oh, and lots more, but those were the main points. Not that I care if she does become a Catholic or anything else for that matter, but I do think she's getting hold of it from the wrong end. I think it satisfies some morbid instinct. I'm not at all sure the Catholics themselves would encourage her if they could see into her head.'

'Marty said it was sublimation,' I said.

'I expect she's right. Does she see much of Ruth these days?'

'I don't know.'

'I wonder if it would help or make things worse. Has Ruth in fact given Marty up in her mind, gone beyond her?'

We talked the subject to exhaustion and then dropped it, without having reached any conclusion. When Anne had gone I went to ring up Tom to tell him about her idea.

'Sounds marvellous,' he said.

'Yes.'

'You don't sound keen.'

'Oh, I am in a way. It's just that, well, I am very involved with someone –'

'And you don't want to be away from him.'

'No, it's not that. We can't be together anyway. It's just that, being so involved, I shall rather want to keep my distance, if you don't mind.'

'Oh, I see,' he said at once. 'Yes, of course.' There was no emotion in his voice.

'I may be wrong,' I said, 'but that's how I feel at the moment and it's only fair to warn you.'

'That's all right,' said Tom. 'And if you change your mind under the hot Italian sun you just tell me.'

I laughed. 'All right. But don't count on it.'

'No, I won't. But I'd still like to go. There are other considerations . . .'

'Yes, of course. Good. I'll tell Anne then.'

How polite we were and what good friends. I phoned my mother to get her official blessing.

'I want to spend August and September in Italy with Anne and Keith,' I said, after the preliminary greetings. It was not a very good line and we had to shout rather. 'Is that all right? I'd be home all July, working.'

'I suppose so.' She sounded doubtful. 'Are they the ones who got married?'

'Yes.'

'Oh. Well, I suppose it's all right if you really want to.'

'I do. It's our last chance of a long vac abroad and I've never been, my own fault, I know.'

'Yes, I see. All right then. Oh, Lois —'

'Yes?'

'Don't go.'

'I wasn't.'

'No, well, it's just that Martin may be getting engaged this summer.'

'What?'

'Yes, it's sudden, isn't it? Her name's Pat and I think it began in the holidays. She's going to come and stay here anyway and he seems very serious about her.'

'When?'

'What?'

'When is she coming to stay?'

'Oh, July or August. I don't really know yet. It depends on her parents. He met her at college, you know, so I expect they have plenty in common.'

The pips went.

'Mother, I'm sorry, I've no more change. See you on Friday.' I hung up. So Martin at least had saved himself.

I got a job as a waitress for July and hoped that tales of tips which I had heard were not too exaggerated. At the end of my first day I went to see my father and Philippa.

They were pleased. 'Come in, have some coffee, how nice to see you,' and so on, they said.

I sat down and let them wait on me, told them about my job.

'Well, how are things with you?' my father asked presently. 'You look better than the last time I saw you.'

'Yes,' I said. 'I'm having an affair with a married man.'

They were both speechless. My father stared at me; Philippa looked first at me and then, quickly, at him.

'He's on his way to America right now,' I said. 'To spend three months with his wife. He really loves her, of course. I'm just a kind of private convenience.' I laughed. 'This time, you see, it's the wife who's going to win.'

'Lois, you poor baby,' said my father dramatically, 'what have I done?'

'Of course, they're only in their thirties,' I went on. 'She's too young for the scrap-heap yet. Maybe I should call back in ten years. Only then I'll be too old, won't I? Can't win either way, can I? But he'll win. Whatever happens, he'll be all right. Only I love him, that's the joke. I love him. I love him.'

I heard my voice screaming louder and louder, coming from somewhere far off, like an amplifier in a dance hall and then there was my father's hand on my face as he hit me and I heard Philippa say, 'David,' in an authoritative voice and her arms went round me.

I cried and cried, for nearly half an hour, wallowing in it, unable to stop once I had really begun. My father stroked my hair and then he went away somewhere and I went on crying while Philippa held me.

Eventually it was all over and there were the dreary mechanics of mopping-up and nose-blowing and the embarrassment of facing each other again.

'I apologize,' I said. 'I was very rude. I don't know why –'

And Philippa, as I might have known, said, 'It's all right, I understand.'

And my father stroked my hair again and said, 'Forget it.'

I kept away from them for the rest of July, not, with the hours I worked, that there was very much time for visiting, anyway. A week before I was due to leave for Italy Martin arrived, with Pat. They had been holidaying with her parents; at least, so they said. Judging from her appearance, I thought cattily, it was probably true. She was indeterminate. Pale brown hair and blue eyes, pale pink skin, plumpish, ordinary figure, clothes and make-up providing no unfair advantages. No doubt she made Martin feel very safe indeed.

Martin seemed genuinely surprised that I found so little to say to her. I watched instead my mother, trying gallantly to be pleased for Martin and to accept this person who was going to take him away for ever. I caught a real glimpse of parental agony and tried to transfer it: in her position how would I feel?

Martin discussed his results. He'd been sure he had done badly but Pat, of course, had known he'd done well and (surprise, surprise) Pat was right. I felt like clapping.

And so it came to August. I returned to London, met Tom, and we set off with Anne and Keith. Holidays are usually anticlimaxes in one way or another, enjoyable mostly in retrospect or imagination, but this one seemed blessed by the gods. Perhaps because it was Anne's holiday it was so ordained. But the sun shone and the sky and sea were blue and we ate, drank and slept, and nearby there was a beach so unfrequented we called it ours; in short, there were no flaws, no grit in the eye or pains in the stomach; everything flowed past in warmth and enchantment and there was peace, so much peace, which I sank down into, and no emotion, of course, but none, so that I became drugged, refreshed, intoxicated, unconscious. Not a holiday you enjoyed, nothing so coarse, but a cure, a restoration: a limbo of the heart.

TWENTY-THREE

And just as well, considering what the autumn term had in store for us. We arrived back at college full of energy and Anne came in with me to go on a tour of her friends, informing them of Keith's first, which he insisted was entirely due to her wifely inspiration. I made straight for my room, superficially tired by travel. When I opened the door I saw Marty.

'Well, hullo,' I said, really glad to see her. 'What a surprise to have you waiting for me. Did you have a good time in Greece?' I shut the door behind me and dropped my suitcase.

'It's a beautiful place,' she said, and added, all in a rush, 'Oh, I *am* glad to see you.'

I was alarmed; she sounded so intense. 'What's the matter? You haven't had another fight, have you?'

She actually laughed, more or less. 'Oh, no. We're on the best of speaking terms. Only we have just the one topic of conversation, you see.'

We stared at each other.

'He says, "Has it?" and I say, "No." Or he says "It can't be," and I say "It is".'

She paused again for a moment, her eyes bright with fright. 'Lois, I'm pregnant, and I'm going to have an abortion.'

It's always hard to remember what you really felt at moments of emotion such as this. I know I had a surge of compassion and anger, mixed with ignoble relief that this thing had not happened to me, and a stronger sensation of incredulity that it had happened at all to anyone and to Marty in particular.

I rushed over to her and said, 'No, darling. Oh, no. No.

I'm so sorry.' I rocked her in my arms and she felt thin and quite tense. She did not cry or hold on to me or anything but just sat there and let herself be rocked. Her hair felt silky against my face. I said, 'Darling, you can't be sure yet, it's probably just a false alarm. 'I knew then that Marty – moody, preoccupied, uncommunicative, was more than a friend; she was the sister I had never had or the other self I had never become and I loved her and wanted to protect her and take a knife to anyone who tried to hurt her. 'How late is it?' I asked, trying to keep my voice calm.

'Twelve days.'

'Well, you've done a lot of travelling; that could account for it.'

'Not for twelve days.'

'It's possible.' I wanted so much to convince us both.

'Not for me. I've always done a lot of travelling and I've never been more than five days late. Never ever.' Her voice slipped from emphasis to hysteria and I realized that for her the border between them was extremely narrow.

'But you're always so careful,' I said, trying another approach. 'It can't be.'

'Well, this time I wasn't, and it is,' she said, getting up and starting to walk up and down. I noticed that she was wearing a blue-grey cotton frock I had not seen before, probably made specially for her holiday.

'I'll make some coffee,' I said. 'Have a cigarette and we'll talk about it. Or not, whatever you like.'

'Oh, we must talk,' she said in a dreary voice. 'I've run out of cigarettes. About an hour ago but I didn't want to move once I got here.'

'Poor love, how long were you waiting? I *am* sorry.'

'It's not your fault. I'm not really sure. You can work it out, I suppose : twelve cigarettes in a chain at ten minutes each and an hour with none . . . three hours.'

'Oh, God, I am sorry.' I gave her my packet. 'I've got plenty, have them all if you like.'

She lit one immediately. 'Pity you can't have an abortion with nicotine poisoning. Dead easy.'

'Marty, you're not serious about this abortion? If it has happened, I mean, and we can't be sure it has.'

'I don't really think I have an alternative. You haven't been doing your sums, have you? The happy event would be some time the end of May, beginning of June. Don't we have a date with finals early in June?'

'Yes, I know. There is that.'

'Is that all you can say? My God, maybe it never occurred to you but I came here to get a degree, not to have a baby by Louis, of all people. And for Christ's sake don't start telling me it's murder or I'll cut my throat and do the nice doctor out of his fee.' She made a frightful strangling noise as if she were choking. 'God, you don't think I'm doing this for fun, do you? Do you think I *want* to or something? For one thing, I'm dead scared I may die.'

'I know, I know. I was just frightened for you.'

'You can join the club.'

'All right.' I sat down, not feeling I could leave her even to fetch water to make coffee. 'Let's tackle it the other way. You're twelve days late and you've been careless. How careless?'

She shook her head vaguely. 'Oh, absolutely. I just took a chance.'

'Oh, Marty, but why?'

'Haven't you ever been in a situation where it just wasn't possible to say, "Excuse me for a moment," and pick up where you left off?' She looked at me almost angrily.

I bowed my head. 'I know what you mean.'

'I don't think you do. You're picturing some hot, passionate scene. Well, it wasn't like that. We had a row, a goddam blistering one about almost nothing and we weren't speaking or touching or anything for four days. We just went to bed at night and turned our backs. Of course I wasn't prepared, nothing was further from my mind, and you know Louis never apologizes, so it was up to me to sort it out. Only this time he did. He woke me up at three in the morning to apologize. So what do you do with a present like that?' She was almost crying and I knew it was useless to reason with her.

'I know,' I said.

After a moment's silence she shrugged her shoulders and said briskly. 'Oh, well, that's what you get for being senti-mental. I've taken chances before and they all worked out. But they weren't sentimental ones.'

I could not see, logically, that there could be any physical difference, but there obviously was in her mind.

'Where is Louis now?' I asked.

'At the flat. I sent him away. He's ringing up helpful friends.'

'What do you mean, you've sent him away?'

'Well, there was no point in his hanging about here, having the same enthralling conversation over and over.'

'Marty?'

'What?'

'Can I ask – is there a chance of your marrying him? Even for a short while –'

'Marrying Louis?'

'You wouldn't consider it?'

'And get divorced afterwards? Look, Louis' family is Catholic, you know.'

'But if you married in a registrar office they wouldn't recog-nize the marriage anyway, would they?' I said desperately.

'Lois, that's logic. They don't feel like that. You obviously can't imagine it, but I know. It would be their son involved in a pagan shot-gun wedding with a tramp, and a squalid divorce case later on. It would be a nightmare. Anyway,' she ended wearily, 'I wouldn't marry Louis if he were an orphan.'

'No?'

'I couldn't. And I know he couldn't. It would be just awful. My parents would have to know, too.'

'Yes, of course.'

'Can you imagine their reaction? Can you imagine the look on that parson's face? Oh, they'd be wonderful. So forgiving. So shocked. What would they do, I wonder? Adopt it? Have someone else adopt it? Keep me and it together at home with them? Well, they're not going to know. And anyway, Louis hasn't suggested marriage. He knows it wouldn't work.' She put her face in her hands. 'Oh, God, it's such a mess; I can't believe it's happening to me.'

No, I thought; that really was the crux of the whole thing. I could not believe it either.

'Look, honey,' I said, 'can I leave you a moment to get some water so I can make coffee? I think we need some. I'll run all the way.'

Marty did not smile. 'Yes, please,' she said.

When I came back with the water she said, 'You will stay with me, won't you?'

'Of course I will.' I lit a cigarette.

'I don't want to be alone. I get so frightened, not knowing what they're going to do to me. I can't think about anything else.'

'Oh, Marty.' I was really alarmed for her. 'Do you really have to?'

'Yes, I really have to.' She turned on me. 'And I'd rather not play games pretending I don't. The sooner I get used to the idea the better.'

'I suppose it might just come overnight.' But I was becoming imbued with her hopelessness.

'It won't. I haven't any signs at all. It's all set for a nice long holiday. Funny, really, to think how I used to suffer and curse it – my God, I'd pay money for a good stiff pain right now.'

I bit my lip. 'Yes, I know. You poor love. Isn't there anything we can do?'

Marty laughed briefly. 'Well, you could try chucking me downstairs. I don't suppose the dons would notice.'

'Well, *some* form of violent exercise might help ...'

'Oh, Lois, it's only in films that babies pop out conveniently like that. Not that I haven't been jumping about like a yoyo, I must admit. Anyway, it's not really a baby yet, it's pin-head cells, and later on it's a fish and all kinds of things, isn't that right?'

'That's right.'

'Well, I suggest we pin up a notice to that effect, just to make sure we remember.'

'Oh, Marty –'

'You see, I'm not being logical. I'd take any amount of pills to dissolve it and get it out. I'd have any injection in my arm or leg or anywhere *normal* to get rid of it and I wouldn't feel the least bit awful. But they'll have to do something inside me – in here.' She sat down suddenly and folded her arms tight across her pelvis. 'Lois, I'm vulnerable in there. I know what it feels like, I've pushed things in often enough. It's so soft and helpless and I'm going to pay them to push things in and make it bleed.' She put her hand over her mouth with a faint sob. 'Going to be sick,' she muttered and rushed from the room.

When she came back the coffee was ready. 'Can you face it?' I asked.

'Oh, yes, I'd like some. I'm all right now. Actually I think that was more nerves than pregnancy, believe it or not. Black, please, and lots of sugar for once.'

We drank slowly, in silence. I looked at the familiar room and wondered if I might yet wake up.

'Well,' she said presently, 'Greece is one place I shan't be revisiting in a hurry. Pity, too. It's a glorious spot. How was your holiday?'

'Oh, fine. Marty, why didn't you write?'

'There didn't seem any point. Why worry three people instead of two?'

'As a friend, that's all,' I said.

'Don't worry. You'll have done more than your share by the time this is over – if you stay with me, that is.'

'Of course I'm staying with you.'

'I wouldn't blame you if you didn't, it'll be nasty. No, that's a lie; I would blame you but quite unfairly.'

'Not unfairly at all. That's what friends are for.'

'Yes. My God, can you see it? "Do you know who your real friends are? Invite them all to your next abortion and find out." '

I held her cold hand in mine. 'Marty, aren't there some pills you can try? You always hear of people trying pills.'

'Yes, you do, don't you? Actually, I feel full up to here with them. We came back four days ago, you know.'

'Oh, I see.'

'Anyway, I don't think you can get hold of things that really work. Otherwise everyone would, wouldn't they? I've certainly sampled a few products.'

'And no effect?'

'Other than a few thousand trips to the lavatory, no.'

'What about gin and hot-baths? You always read about that.'

'I can't face the hot bath, somehow; I just want cold ones all the time. But I've tried oceans of gin, more for oblivion than miscarriage, though.'

'Isn't it worth trying?'

'I suppose in theory anything is but I just can't be bothered; I'm so sure that for me it's got to be the ultimate deterrent, as you might say.' She laughed. 'I can just see it. The crafty little man with his instrument, whatever it is, saying "Now this won't hurt." Like dentists.'

'Oh, don't, Marty.'

'No, I'm not helping myself, am I?'

We were silent again. Somewhere, faintly, in the main building the bell rang for supper.

'Can you face eating, honey?'

'Yes.' She got up. 'I'm ever so fit. I bet I'd have a madly healthy pregnancy. I'm probably ideally designed for it. Just one of Nature's ironic jokes.'

At the door she caught hold of my arm. 'You won't tell anyone, will you? Not anyone at all. Not yet.'

TWENTY-FOUR

AFTER that the nightmare never left us. Every morning I woke up to remember it, to identify the black brooding shape that hovered above our heads or sat on my chest, heavy and dead-smelling as a bag of coal.

'It makes a change from dreading finals, anyway,' Marty said.

As the days passed we tacitly abandoned hope. Marty was not awaiting a late period; she was pregnant. She had been right all the time. The thing which happened to other people, which provided material for statistics and articles in the papers, had happened to her and I was going to stay with her until it was over.

She could not bear to be alone at night, so sometimes I camped in her room and sometimes she camped in mine. I had to fight down a ridiculous urge to insist on her having the bed every time. I caught myself fetching and carrying for her... Absurd, reflex action.

I found it very hard not being able to discuss it with anyone else. In fact, this convinced me that there is a fundamental need in women to talk over important matters with someone other than the person involved, and that this is not the act of disloyalty that men often think it is. But I couldn't so I didn't. Louis came sometimes to report on his progress but he didn't stay very long, though I always left them alone together. He and I only exchanged what are called conventional greetings; I can't imagine what you say in these circumstances to someone other than a personal friend and evidently he didn't know either. So we made no reference to it at all. I did consider launching a savage attack one day when I thought how lightly he was getting off compared to Marty, but I abandoned the idea. It might upset her; there was no telling how she really felt about him, in spite of all she had said. It could certainly serve no useful purpose at this stage: they had both been careless, the damage was done, and he had not run away; he was doing his best to get Marty out of it according to the way they had chosen. My job was to stay with Marty, not to make judgements.

I heard nothing from Matthew, who must have been back in London but doubtless not yet frustrated enough to get in touch with me. I did not contact him, mainly because I was terrified of letting something slip. I knew logically he would do nothing even if I did, but emotionally I classed him with authority, as a temporary threat. As far as is possible with the person you love, I put him out of my mind. What I badly wanted, really longed for, was someone who loved me, who would share my anxiety so that I could better help Marty with hers.

She tried very hard to put her mind to work as a form of escape but it was not very successful and I had to manufacture an essay for her, copying her style as best I could, and choosing another subject for myself to avoid complications. Routine translations I did for her and in a seminar we were lucky; she was not asked a question. Every lecture I went to she attended also and I went to nearly everything because I thought it would occupy us and leave less time to fill with talk or silence. Even with enforced abstinence at lectures and meals Marty smoked about thirty-five cigarettes a day. I got through about twenty myself, instead of my usual ten or twelve. I felt grateful that we were both so heavily tanned from the summer; it gave a façade of health and well-being. I dreaded anyone saying to me or especially Marty, 'What's up? You look a bit off.'

Evenings were difficult to cater for. We went to a lot of films and I checked as far as possible to make sure they were free from all reference to pregnancy, babies, miscarriage or abortion. It took a bit of doing and it's amazing how many of them were not. We saw a lot of films we would not have gone near in the old days. I developed an insane regard for the past as a trouble-free time of peace and yearned for it, nostalgically. Once I queued for hours outside Covent Garden because Marty wanted to see *Swan Lake*. By some fluke we got seats, returns, more than we could really afford but it seemed a minor consideration. She was so pleased. 'It's so white and clean,' she said. I looked at her once during the performance and the tears were pouring down her cheeks.

About half-way through October we started seeing people who would help us. Apparently we had to pass from contact to contact and be screened in case we were police agents involved in undercover work aiming at the exposure of these persecuted public benefactors. It made me feel hysterical till I was almost at the stage of looking round to find the hidden film cameras. Louis' original contact was at his college, of course, and knew someone who had recently made use of these facilities. She vouched for us, but we still had to be checked and this meant some highly ambiguous conversations in which we explained our predicament, and various medical men proclaimed their integrity. I found it all very confusing but Marty said we were making progress. She was slightly better now that we were actually doing something. When we reached our final contact there arose the question of money. Forty pounds were required. It sounded dangerously cheap to me but Marty assured me that in unsterilized zones you could go a lot cheaper than that. She suddenly appeared to develop an almost professional interest in the subject. Louis provided twenty and this was the best he could do. Marty and I raised ten each, and we were all set. November the fifth, by some ghastly mischance, was the date fixed and Marty quoted the old rhyme. 'I bet we will remember it, too,' she said.

At this point she sprang a surprise. I had not thought beyond the ordeal itself but one night Marty said suddenly, 'Where am I going to go afterwards?'

'Oh. I suppose we can't stay here.'

'Well, it's a bit public if anything goes wrong. Suppose I scream or haemorrhage? And go to hospital in an ambulance from college? I might as well put a notice on the board. Come to think of it, we should have had a collecting-box in the hall for the money. We could have put a notice underneath: "Pay up; it might have been you." No, I want to be somewhere safe. Will you ask Anne for me?'

I was stupefied, though I suppose I should have thought of it. 'Anne?'

'Yes. They've got a self-contained flat. We could both get official leave of absence and be quite safe.'

'You don't mind her knowing?'

'Not any more. I've thought about it a lot, all the places I could go, I mean. Adrienne would have me, only she's just had an abortion herself, a nice, plushy Harley Street one for a hundred and fifty guineas to prevent mental illness. It's a cosy little joke to her. I haven't told her anything. Tom would put me up but I couldn't do that to him.'

I hesitated and said, 'You don't want to be with Louis?'

'Christ, no.' Then she softened and said, 'Poor Louis. I'm so sorry for him.'

'Sorry for him?'

'Yes. He can't do anything to help. No man should ever be in that position.'

I took a deep breath and said. 'All right then. I'll ask Anne. Do you mind if I go alone?'

Marty shook her head. 'I don't want to face her, anyway, unless she's agreed. I know she's not a real friend of mine but I think she will. I do like her, you know. I should feel ever so much better about everything in her flat.'

I went to see Anne on a lectureless afternoon, having telephoned to make sure she was in. I wanted to see her entirely alone, even without Keith. I left Marty fully supplied with coffee and books and cigarettes, lying in her bed. She wasn't feeling too good: tired, funny. I had the wild hope that she was going to miscarry naturally before November the fifth but I knew really that she wouldn't. On my way to Anne's I looked at the scenery and the weather (of course, it had to be a wonderfully bright October) and thought, well, this ought to cure me of my romantic attachment to London, based on nothing more solid than freedom and two terms of happiness with Peter and one with Matthew. As I travelled to Anne's flat it seemed quite mad that red London buses should be running normally and people walking along the streets.

When I told Anne I watched her face and saw it change swiftly from shock to compassion.

'Of course. You didn't think I'd refuse, surely?'

'No, I suppose not. You're sure Keith won't mind?'

'He'll say just the same. Oh, Lois, I wish you could have told me before.'

'Marty wouldn't let me tell anyone,' I said.

'No . . . I see that. But I wish we could have known, just to share it. I know we couldn't have done anything.'

'Oh, Anne . . .' It was my first chance to give way and I felt weak. 'I wish she didn't have to.'

'I know, so do I. But I think she's right, really,' said Anne.

'Do you?'

'Well, I see her point. She can't marry Louis if it wouldn't work out, and there are her parents and his parents and everyone at college and her degree, most of all.'

'Yes, I know, there's all that.'

'Well, unless you're just against all abortions on principle, you must admit she has a pretty solid case for one, if you're trying to justify it, that is.'

I shook my head. 'I don't know what I'm trying to do. I think I'm just plain scared. Oh, Anne, suppose anything happens to her. She doesn't sleep at all well, she sort of mutters to herself; I can't hear much, just the odd word here and there, but it frightens me.' I shivered.

'I think we need a drink,' Anne said, rising.

'It's only three o'clock.'

'That's right. Whisky suit you? We just got paid.'

I took it gratefully. 'Anne, what if something does happen to her?'

'It won't. She goes straight to hospital at the first sign of anything dangerous.'

My teeth actually rattled on the glass as I tried to drink from it. 'They're not very nice to you in these cases. The girl who got us this contact said to stay out if you possibly can, because they get rough if they suspect at all.'

'Better than dying.'

'Anne.'

'Honey, I'm sorry but it's what we're both thinking. It's better said.'

'I suppose so.'

'Please believe I'm not being callous. I'm as worried as you are. I'm only trying to be practical, I think we need to be. We can't talk Marty out of it so we can only believe she's doing the right thing for her, and get her through it.'

'What would you do, Anne, if it were you – in her position?'

Anne hesitated. 'I don't know, I really don't. The same, probably.'

'Would you? Would you really?'

'I don't know. How do any of us know what we'd do till we get in the situation?'

'I'm surprised you said that. I thought you'd have the answer to everything,' I said, wondering.

Anne looked surprised, even a little disappointed. 'Do you still have that idea after two years and sharing a room with me?'

I felt ashamed. 'I'm sorry. It was a silly remark. I just thought you'd be sure, one way or the other.'

'Well, I'm not,' said Anne. 'Are you?'

'No.'

'Well, then. We're not in the situation and we don't know. Marty is and she's made up her mind. I think we have to settle for that.'

'Yes, I know. You *are* right. Anne —'

'What?'

'I just hope she's all right afterwards, really all right, I mean.'

Strangely, Anne shivered now. 'Yes. So do I.'

'She'll be very grateful she can come,' I said.

Anne said, 'Please give her my love. I'll call in tomorrow.'

When I got back to college I found Marty still on the bed, being sick into a metal waste-paper bin. I held her head till it was over and fetched her some tissues and a glass of water.

'Do you feel all right?' I asked eventually.

She lay back exhausted. 'Yes. Thank you very much. I've had a most entertaining afternoon. What did Anne say?'

'You're very welcome and she sends her love. What happened while I was away?' I sat on the edge of the bed and held her hand.

'Well, Tom came.'

'Oh.' I was relieved.

'Wait,' said Marty. 'He half suspected, so I told him. Can you guess what he did?'

'No,' I said, but I wasn't trying.

'He asked me to marry him. Practically implored me. It was most embarrassing, actually. Towards the end of it Ruth came in and she guessed, somehow. I swear she's got a sixth sense about me. Anyway, she launched her tirade about murder and mortal sin, only she had Tom to reckon with and he turned into a veritable tiger. Bawled her out in all directions; it was fantastic. Complete rout. She retreated, threatening to pray for my immortal soul, so I suppose I got off lightly, really, only it seemed to affect my inside, hence the pretty little scene when you came in.'

'Oh, Marty,' I said, 'honey. I am so sorry. Why ever didn't I put *Verboten* on the door before I went out?'

Marty shivered. 'Well, I didn't think of it, either. Perhaps it's only associated with happier days. You know, right now I can't believe things will ever be normal again.'

When I went to my room for Ryvita and Bovril, as Marty didn't feel equal to college supper, I found a note in my door. 'Dear Lois, please phone me, I have talked frankly with Marty, Tom.' It was exactly like him. I went wearily to phone, thinking, 'Dear Tom, with all your good intentions, there is no time or place for any of this.'

'I got your note,' I said. 'Very discreet.'

'Lois, you've got to talk to her,' he said rapidly. 'Persuade her. Do something.'

'It's no good, Tom.'

'Did she tell you everything?'

'Yes, she told me.'

'Well, you must talk her out of it, make her see it my way, if I can't. Damn it, Lois, she'll listen to you.'

'She won't listen to anyone, Tom, honestly. She wants her degree more than anything – oh, I know she's never admitted it before, but I believe her – and she's made up her mind to this; she doesn't want to reopen the issue, it's bad enough as it is.'

'D'you think I don't know that? I want to help her.'

'I don't think you can, not the way you want to, anyway.'

There was a pause and a choking sound as if Tom was crying.

'Please accept her decision,' I said, to give him time. 'She's really thought it over carefully. She's very unhappy and the only thing we can do is get her through it. I just hope Ruth won't talk.'

'She won't,' said Tom in a muffled voice. 'I'd kill her. I told her a lot more when I got her outside, that Marty didn't hear. She knows I'll kill her if she talks.'

It did not sound like an empty threat at all.

TWENTY-FIVE

THE day came. We had both slept badly and by five o'clock we were wide awake. Marty raised herself on her elbows and looked down at me.

'Hullo,' she said. 'It's D-day.'

'Yes.'

'Maybe we should say A-day.' She lay back in bed with a sigh.

I said nothing, wondering however we were going to get through all the hours of the day beforehand.

'You've been wonderful,' Marty said presently.

'It's nothing. I wish there'd been more for me to do.'

College was so still and quiet. It was too early even for the usual early risers, the chapel-goers, the crammers. We spoke in low voices.

'Lois, I don't really think I'm going to die.'

'Of course you're not,' I said vehemently.

'But if anything does happen – I don't want them to know it was Louis.'

'Oh, Marty –'

'I really mean it. I'm serious, Lois. He's hardly been here this term, anyway, and no one need know he was in Greece. I told my mother I was going to Greece with Adrienne, and she'll cover for me automatically. You can tell them I broke off with Louis last term and I wouldn't make it up this term when he asked me, because of what happened in Greece. That's all you know, if they ask you. Not who it was or how it happened or anything. Have you got it clear?'

'Yes.'

'I want to get everything settled now,' she went on, 'in case I'm not thinking too well later on. It's so easy to sound sentimental and Dickensian – I don't want that, but I do want to be tidy.'

This new aspect of Marty was almost unbearable to me.

'They mustn't know about Louis,' she said again. 'They'd never understand how it was and I won't have my life dissected by a lot of cruds. Please promise.'

'I promise.'

'Thank you.' She sighed heavily. 'You're marvellous. Look, I bet I live to be eighty, really I do, but just supposing – well, my mother'll take everything so you'd better grab any books you want before she swoops.'

'Oh, Marty, please.'

'I'm not being morbid on purpose, honestly. It's just what to do if the bomb falls. Highly improbable but silly to ignore the possibility. Only we have better odds, I'm sure. It's important about the books. I want you to have anything you can use because they'll only go in a glass case; my mother doesn't read. And don't let her get her paws on any books Louis gave me – take those out for a start. They're mostly French ones and they're all written in, so you'll know. It's very important. You didn't know how dedicated I am, did you?'

'No.'

'Well, I love my books. My second favourite subject – oh, God. Lois?'

'Yes, darling.'

'Please burn all my letters. I'm such a fool. I've always kept everything. Just burn the lot. Wish they had grates in this place but you can use the waste bin, the one I was sick in. That should be all right. There's rather a lot, though.'

'I'll find every one.'

'Oh, bless you. Have I been too bloody Victorian like those awful *Little Women*? One girl made her will, didn't she? I always thought she was a pompous little beast and I don't want to be like that. I haven't, have I?'

'No, honey, not a bit.'

'Oh, good. That's all right then. And I haven't any money so there's no problem there. Only three things for you to remember. No, there is another thing.'

'What is it?'

'Well, again I say, I know everything's going to be all right but just in case – I mean, that's why I've said all this, to cover every possibility before it's out of my hands. Not to be morbid or upset you.'

'Yes, I know.'

'Well, just you remember how lucky I've been. I've had a marvellous life.'

She sounded as if she really meant it and when I looked up to see her face I saw that she had suddenly fallen asleep.

She slept until ten when Louis arrived with a spray of flowers. He stayed about twenty minutes and Marty said nothing about the visit afterwards, so I could not ask her. She got up and dressed and packed her suitcase with all the things she would need for the weekend. We drew the curtains and stared at the overcast day.

'It looks like rain,' I said.

'Of course it does. It's November the fifth.'

We looked at each other. I think at that moment I could have panicked and I was terrified that I was going to let Marty down.

'It's all right,' she said, quite calmly. 'I'm going dead inside. Numb. It's much better.'

By the late post there was a letter for me from Matthew asking to see me that evening. A few months ago I could not have imagined any circumstances in which I would ignore a summons from him but I knew I was going to ignore this one.

'No lunch for me,' said Marty so I went in alone and sat

opposite Jeanne who was very excited about her parents' forthcoming visit that weekend. They were going to the theatre with her and John and taking them out to dinner afterwards. She talked about it almost constantly, which saved me from making conversation. I did not feel much like eating either but I did my best because I thought I might need it.

When I got back to Marty it was five to one. She was sitting on the bed, her suitcase beside her, and looking out of the window. She had Louis' flowers on her coat.

'It's starting to rain,' she said.

I looked, and it was.

'Good thing I didn't have my hair done,' she said. 'I thought about it, you know, as a morale raiser but in the end I decided to leave it till afterwards. I'd only mess it up being in bed all weekend.'

There was a moment's silence and we both stared through the window.

'We really should be going now,' I said.

'I know,' Marty said, but she did not move. We looked at the rain slowly thickening and descending on our well-tended college garden.

'Funny,' she said and we went out together.

We took the tube into town and waited at the prescribed tube station until a complete stranger came up to us with every appearance of recognition, and we followed her a long way to an innocent-looking block of flats and went in by separate doors as instructed. We met upstairs and she let us into one of the flats where a man in a white coat made polite and soothing noises and we handed over the money. It seemed to me that everything was happening much too fast and there was a lot more to say if only I could think of it, but I only had time to hug Marty before they took her away from me and the waiting began.

The waiting was the worst time of all so far.

When Marty eventually came back and they helped her on

with her coat I felt so weak I could hardly stand. I was drained of emotion; I felt that I had swum, sunk and surfaced a few thousand times in some prehistoric quicksand. All incredulity had vanished and everything was just too real. My knees shook and I had scarcely the strength to stub out my current cigarette.

'Come along, dear,' said the nurse. 'You've got to look after your friend.'

'It's all right, Lois,' Marty said. I noticed that she had made up her face with great care.

The doctor shook hands with her. 'I've given her the pills and instructions. You'll see to that, won't you? She won't be feeling very grand. And don't get in touch with us, of course, not that there's any reason you should want to.'

They both looked so normal, ordinary. Just friendly, busy, professional people doing their job. It was only another piece of evidence that we all wore masks. What else did I expect?

The nurse said good-bye to us after explaining how everything should go and how we would know whether Marty needed to go to hospital. Of course she wouldn't but if she did we must both remember not to give anything away and of course we did understand that, didn't we? We said yes of course, and left.

Outside it was still raining.

'Well,' Marty said. 'So far so good.'

'Are you really all right?'

'At the moment.'

I hesitated and then said, 'Was it very bad?'

She appeared to consider her answer. 'Nasty, I'd say, but hygienic. I think we're in luck.'

'I'm going to get a taxi.'

Marty grabbed hold of me. 'Don't be crazy, it'll cost pounds from here. It's not far to the tube.'

I gave in. 'All right. But we're having one at the other end and don't argue.'

In the tube we stared in front of us speechlessly in the

traditional way. It was such an ordinary journey that my sense of unreality began to return. Had we really done this thing? I looked at Marty once. Nothing about her suggested anything unusual, except perhaps the unnaturally tight set of her mouth.

When we got out of the tube I found a taxi and we subsided into it. Marty huddled in a corner of the seat, the flowers still pinned to her coat, rather crushed.

'I think I'd like a cigarette,' she said.

'Yes, of course.' I lit cigarettes for both of us.

'You know,' she said, 'you're the only real girl-friend I've ever had. I never liked girls very much.'

I squeezed her hand but she took it away quite soon so I guessed that she did not want to be touched.

'It's good that we're going to Anne's, isn't it?' she said presently. And then, 'Oh dear, I do hope I'm going to be good this weekend.'

I said, 'Of course you are. And it doesn't matter if you aren't.'

'Yes, it does. You've all been so good to me, I don't want to let you down.'

When we reached the flat Anne was wonderfully calm and welcoming. She had borrowed a camp bed to put near the couch and turned her sitting-room into a bedroom for us.

'This is your room,' she said. 'Keith and I will keep out of your way, unless you want us around.'

'I'm so grateful, Anne,' said Marty.

'Just take care of yourself and get well,' Anne said.

When Keith came in he said, 'Hullo, love, how are you?' and Marty smiled at him and said, 'I'm fine.'

'Well, you have a good rest,' Keith said.

'May I ring up Louis?' Marty asked. 'Just to tell him stage one is over.'

'Of course – in the dining-room.'

'How is she really?' they asked me as the door closed.

'I don't know. I suppose – as well as can be expected. I'm so glad you're both here. I think I'd go mad alone. It's all so fantastic.'

'She looks very shocked to me,' Anne said.

'Well, I suppose that's not surprising.'

Marty could not eat but we all made some attempt at supper and afterwards we put Marty to bed. She did not want to play cards or listen to music or do anything distracting.

'It's stopped raining,' she said suddenly. 'I *am* glad.'

We stared at her.

'It's bonfire night,' she reminded us.

It began that night, while the fireworks exploded outside. We had all gone to bed very early and I had been asleep. Sobbing woke me up. I leaned across to Marty and she grabbed my hand and hung on till I thought she would break it. She kept saying, 'Oh God, oh God, oh God,' and then, 'This is the really degrading part.'

'Don't be ridiculous.'

'I'm glad it's dark. You won't put the light on, will you?'

'Of course I won't if you don't want it.'

'They say it's worse than having a baby,' she said.

'Don't think about that.'

There was a pause and then the sobbing started again. In between she kept saying in a muffled voice, 'I'm not going to die. I'm going to get over this. I'm going to get over it.'

'Of course you are,' I said.

She was threshing about in all directions and sweating dreadfully. Now all I remember is an endless night and declining day of animal pain and pills and mopping up. I wish I did not remember anything about it at all. I have tried hard to forget. I remember thinking at the time, 'I'll never be this close to anyone else again. In all my life everything else will be an anticlimax.'

She was better on Saturday and much better on Sunday. We were all having breakfast and she was drinking coffee when she suddenly said, 'It's over, isn't it?' Then, as if she lacked co-ordination, she simply dropped the cup and burst into tears.

When it was over she was quite calm. 'Will you ring up Louis and tell him I'm all right,' she said.

'Don't you . . .'

'No, I don't want to speak to him.'

I couldn't face it either so Keith did it for us. And that was that.

TWENTY-SIX

MARTY made what they called a good recovery. She went to her own doctor for a check-up and he said she had been very lucky. He asked her to see him again in a few weeks' time.

I did not telephone Matthew for nearly a week after we returned to college. I was so exhausted that I felt I would not be able to talk to him without revealing what had happened. I slept heavily and had dreams about Marty in which everything had yet to be done. In the midst of this came an invitation to their wedding from my father and Philippa, enclosed in a letter. I wrote back, saying I had flu.

Marty was very quiet. She sat in her room most of the time, did a minimum of work, and mostly seemed to smoke cigarettes and stare in front of her. She moved listlessly and hardly talked at all. Anne said it was a natural reaction and actually I felt much the same. All vitality had been used up and the drama was over. Now it was something that had happened in the past, and we were the people it had happened to.

Louis came to see Marty once that week. Afterwards she said to me, 'I wonder if it will ever be the same again.'

I did not know what to say.

'It seems so dead to me,' she said, 'but he seems to feel just the same. He keeps talking about next month when we can make love again.'

'You are sticking to doctor's orders then?'

'Oh yes.' She smiled. 'It's not difficult for me, anyway. I'm glad to have an excuse for not finding out.'

'Finding out what?'

'If it can ever be the same again.'

I phoned Matthew on Thursday and he sounded glad to hear from me.

'I'm sorry about last week,' I said, 'but I went away for the weekend and I haven't been very well since I got back.'

'I'm sorry to hear that,' he said. 'I wondered what had happened. When am I going to see you?'

'Do you want to?'

He seemed surprised. 'I haven't seen you since June.'

'I know, but you've been busy. How was America? Did you have a wonderful time?'

'Yes.'

'And your wife was pleased to see you?'

'Yes.'

'Well, that's fine then.'

There was a pause.

'Lois, has something happened?'

'No, Matthew, nothing.'

'Well, am I going to see you?'

I laughed. 'You sound quite keen. It's a nice change, I must say, though I suppose it's just nature taking its course.'

'All right, I deserve that.'

'I'm sorry, Matthew, I'm tired.'

'All right, Lois, I can understand. Will you meet me for a drink? Shall I pick you up at college?'

I wished I could appreciate this as I would have done in the summer, but it seemed to be happening to someone else.

'All right, Matthew.'

'Tonight?'

'Oh no, I'm not well enough, honestly. Next week.'

'When?'

'Oh, I don't know. Say Tuesday.'

'All right. Tuesday at eight.'

'Yes. I'm sorry. I'm full of aspirin and stuff.'

'Don't worry. Just look after yourself.' He rang off.

I felt better, less reluctant, when I saw him; I had forgotten just how attractive he was. I think part of the attraction was that he looked so fit and well and powerful whereas most of the men I had met since Peter had been ordinarily thin and short and pale.

'It's nice to see you again,' he said. 'I've missed you.'

That gave me a funny feeling. 'Have you?'

'Yes, I have. I must be greedy, I suppose, in fact I know I am.'

'Oh well, it's a small vice,' I said.

He stared at me. 'You are in a funny mood tonight.'

I agreed. 'Yes, I am. Can I have a tomato juice?'

'On the wagon as well?'

'If you like.'

He got me the drink and whisky for himself.

I said, 'Matthew, what are you aiming at?'

'Aiming at?'

'Yes. Is this just a drink and a chat or are you aiming at bed?'

To give him his due he went on looking straight at me, but maybe he was relying on the hypnotic effect of the very blue eyes. 'That depends on you.'

'Well, I haven't come prepared,' I said, 'so you may as well abandon hope since you can't enter here.'

'All right,' he said. 'As you wish.'

I went on as if I had been wound up. 'Don't you ever think you're behaving rather shabbily towards Claire?'

He raised his eyebrow. 'I don't think that has anything to do with you.'

'Oh, but it has. I had to listen to your recital of all her virtues. I think I have a right to mention her name. I want to make sure that such a paragon doesn't get a dirty deal.'

'Well, you can put your mind at rest,' he said, with just a hint of anger. 'I've a fair idea she's doing much the same herself in the States.'

'But you didn't know that last term,' I said.

'No, I didn't. And I had a mildly guilty conscience, as you may have noticed.'

'But that didn't stop you.'

'No, but – No, it didn't.'

'Oh – you mean I threw myself at you so it wasn't your fault?'

'No, I don't mean that exactly. But I think you encouraged me.'

'Oh, you're quite right, I did.'

He sighed and said, 'Lois, are you trying to say we're finished?'

'Oh, no, not particularly.'

'Then what exactly is the point of this conversation?'

I played with my empty glass. 'I don't know, quite. I'm just curious. I want to learn about people. Why they do what they do. How they really feel. After all, we come to university partly to broaden our minds, don't we? I've learnt a lot already but I don't want to waste any opportunities. There's not a lot of time left.'

'Well?'

'I'd like to know what sort of a relationship you and Claire have, for a start.'

He frowned. 'How do you describe a relationship?'

'Some people can.'

'Well, it's just normal. I mean, whatever you do yourself seems normal to you, doesn't it?'

'Does it?'

'Well, it does to me. But women are a lot more devious than men, aren't they? Usually, anyway.'

'Meaning Claire isn't?'

'Well, she is a scientist. That helps, I think.'

'Oh, are we going to have a good old-fashioned arts versus science argument?'

'I hope not. You asked me a question and I tried to answer it. It's no use getting annoyed with the answer.'

'No, of course not. How sensible you are. You make it all so simple.'

Matthew sighed and said, 'Lois, I wish you'd tell me what's happened. It's obviously had an effect on you.'

I said, 'Well, I'm sorry but I can't. It's entirely feminine and illogical and irrelevant and I don't understand it myself.'

There was a long pause.

'Shall I run you back?' he asked finally.

'No, I'd like to go home with you.'

'But you said –'

'Well, I was lying. In my devious feminine way. There now.'

'I wish you'd stop being so angry,' he said.

'Yes, so do I. Maybe I will quite soon.'

In the car he kissed me and I knew from my reaction that body and mind had diverged again.

'Can you stay the night?' he asked.

'No, I'd rather not.'

'But last term I thought you wanted to.'

'Yes, I did. But time marches on.'

I suppose logically it should have been a failure. But it wasn't. It was better, if anything, although beforehand I was inexplicably frightened.

'You're very talented,' I said afterwards.

'You're quite an able performer yourself.' He was relaxed and happy, thinking everything was all right. He rolled over and kissed my shoulder. 'Lois, let's just enjoy what we have. Let's not fight.'

'All right,' I said. I felt cold all over. But then it is a chilling experience to fall suddenly out of love with someone.

Of course, human nature being as inconsistent as it is, I did not remain in such a securely detached position for the rest of the term. Sometimes a little emotion crept back, and I almost hoped it would stay. It never did. I longed for a fresh start but at the same time I thought, 'We may as well drift on like this, it's my last year, why not? He'll only get someone else if it isn't me and I need something.' We still had lots of talks, too, and discussed life after death and the modern novel and all sorts of educational matters. I also went to a lot of dances with Tom; he came to see Marty every day but she would never go out with him. She hardly saw Louis at all; she had told him not to come. 'He only gets frustrated,' she said, 'and I get bored.' I was afraid for her, though Tom, of course, thought this was the ideal way out. He had always been convinced that she should abandon Louis before he abandoned her. I wished then that I understood Louis but I could hardly go to see him and say, 'Tell me all about yourself.'

Marty went to few lectures but she sat in her room and read the entire works of Fielding. Then she moved on to Dickens and Thackeray. She was always there, in the same chair, with two piles of books, one increasing, one decreasing, on the floor beside her. I did a fair amount of work, too, on things I enjoyed: poetry and modern novels, and made notes I hoped I could revise from. It was a full, uneventful life. We hardly talked at all. I felt our friendship was recharging itself on silence and absence after all we had drawn from it.

Just before the end of term, though, when we were packing, she came into my room and said, 'Well, now for it, I suppose.'

'Louis?' I said.

'Yes. I'm officially fit for action. Only I don't want to.'

'Well then, don't. You don't have to, whatever he says.'

'Oh, I'm not doing it for him. I've got to do it for myself. I've got to find out if it still works. You know, I'm terrified I may not react any more; maybe something went wrong with that.'

'Oh, no, Marty.'

'Well, that's how I feel. That I may have lost it for ever,

with anyone. The other thing is, I'm scared of Louis' body. It seems to have death in it. God, that's corny, isn't it? But I feel it.'

'Then don't go back to him.'

'Oh, I must. Because I'm frightened. That's something I've got to beat. Only it's not exciting any more, to be with him. We've got nothing to say. We don't argue any more. I don't feel anything except pity.'

'Pity?'

'Yes, of course. He couldn't do anything after he got the money and the address. He was absolutely helpless. I had to go through it alone – oh, I'm not forgetting all you did, truly –'

'I know,' I said.

'But it happened to me alone. He couldn't save me. We both started it, but I had to finish it alone. That was all wrong.'

'Aren't you making up something that was sheer biology?' I suggested.

'No, I can't explain. He couldn't do anything.'

'But you wouldn't let him be there.'

'He should have been someone else,' she said.

'Oh, Marty.'

'Well, this was something our relationship didn't cater for. It was too much for us. I think it's destroyed what we had.'

On the last day of term she came in and said, 'I was right, you see. Full marks for perspicacity.'

'Are you sure? You haven't given it very long.'

'I don't need to.' She shuddered. 'I knew at once, but he insisted we go on. He tried everything. He's so pathetic. I should never have seen him like that, it's indecent. October started it and this is the end.'

'I'm very sorry,' I said.

She said slowly, 'Yes. It's a pity. Only now I have to find

out if this is just something that happens with Louis, or if I'm really finished.'

I went home and prepared for Christmas. There were only my mother and I, as Martin was staying with Pat and her parents. I hoped there would be lots of lovely clean snow.

TWENTY-SEVEN

Two terms to go. Finals were beginning to assume reality as something that would actually happen to us. Anne was working hard, spending nearly all of each day in the library. Marty and I looked at our thirty-odd Old and Middle English texts and started to revise our translations, taking turns with the originals and reading the modern versions aloud. It was slow work and we had a tight schedule. I used to see lines of print in my head even after we had stopped. We sorted out the nine papers we had to do and tried to find six authors or topics we were already acquainted with for each paper on which we had to do three questions. We huddled over books of criticism and made notes and re-read texts we had skimmed through in first and second year. Marty lingered over Henryson. 'It seems so appropriate,' she said, 'that poor Criseyde should end up a whore and a leper.'

I picked up with Matthew where we had left off. Marty was sleeping regularly with a fifty-ish business man who gave her a great many expensive presents. 'He's sterile,' she said. 'That's why his marriage broke up. You've no idea how comforting I find that, even though Greece was entirely my fault. I still use my gadget, of course, just to make assurance double sure and all that.'

Ruth came in to see me on the first Sunday of term, on her way back from church. 'You must think of me at Easter,' she said. 'I'm hoping to be received.'

I waited.

'You have to make a General Confession,' she said. 'I'll have to tell the priest all my sins, every one, for my whole life.'

Her eyes sparkled. 'Then I can go to Communion and be one with God.'

'I'm very pleased for you,' I said.

'It's wonderful, isn't it? I can start again. I can do penance. I've made a lot of mistakes, you know.'

'Haven't we all?' I said.

'You should do something about them,' she said. 'Life's very short. It's such a wonderful chance to start again. God's been very good to me, giving me the gift of faith.'

'Yes,' I said. 'I've often wondered why he doesn't spread it around more.'

'Oh, you mustn't question Him,' Ruth said. 'We can't hope to understand Him with our finite minds.'

'Yes,' I said, 'that's the whole trouble.'

She looked at me sorrowfully. 'You should open your heart and be humble,' she said.

'All right. Look, you may be right; I don't know. You go ahead if it suits you. But are you sure you're going into this religion because you believe it's true and right, and not just because it makes up for everything that went wrong between you and Marty? That's all that worries me. You seem to have a different approach from any religious person I've ever known. I knew Catholic girls at school. None of them talked like you. I only want you to be clear in your own mind why you're doing this.'

I paused. I had felt bound to say it, just once, after so long as a silent observer. Ruth looked at me and the pale green eyes that had once been alert and interested, long ago in first year, were blank and expressionless, as if covered by a film of glass.

'Oh, I shall still pray for her,' she said, 'and all the dreadful things she's done. She's lived a wicked life, you know, but God may be merciful since it was through her I came to Him.'

At the end of term I broke off with Matthew, knowing that Claire would return in April. It was a surprising wrench for

I felt – a word I had never expected to use in this context – fond of him. I accepted the fact that nothing could be clear cut and simple again, once you were no longer a child. At least I had learnt that much.

Marty was going to Scotland with her business man. 'It doesn't work yet, you know,' she said to me, 'but at least I'm not scared and it's comforting. I think that's a start, don't you?'

'I'm sure it is,' I said.

'You see,' she said, very seriously. 'If I don't have this my whole life is changed. When I'm middle-aged I may feel quite different, I'm prepared to believe that, but right now this is the most important thing. And nobody wants their whole life changed overnight, do they?'

I worked all through the Easter vacation. It was the first I had devoted entirely to work. I spent a week with Anne, who was also working hard and was a restful companion, since she did not come up with diverting asides about sex, the way Marty did. She only spoke about herself once, during one of our few breaks for food and drink.

'It's funny how much more you fight when you're married,' she said.

'Do you fight – you and Keith?'

'Oh yes.' She smiled. 'We didn't much, before we were married; there was never enough time, so we always made the most of being together. But now we do, only it doesn't matter. We learn something every time. We improve. It's so fascinating, watching it grow and working at it. I hate fights but I think they are necessary – some of them, anyway.'

'You've obviously been studying your favourite subject pretty hard.'

She laughed. 'Yes, I have. I mustn't become a bore about it. Please hit me or something.'

'Don't be silly,' I said. I thought about it. 'Of course, you've been married a year now.'

'Yes, we have just had our first anniversary. Keith's been a wonderful help with my work, going over things with me. I'm so glad we got married when we did. And we were very lucky to get his degree out of the way first.'

The summer term brought a new atmosphere of stress. We counted weeks.

'There'll be a heatwave,' everyone said. 'There always is. Just you wait and see. In June when we're sweating over our papers.'

Warm weather in May seemed a cruel mockery to those of us who could not study in the open air. As the time passed, ideals were abandoned and aims became strictly feasible. We realized at last how much we would go into finals without knowing. At school we had been convinced we would somehow know everything. But of course to the university this was only a first degree, though for most of us it would also be our last.

Marty was gay, more cheerful than I had seen her for many months. She had met an American from the Embassy and discarded her business man. 'He's so sweet,' she kept saying. 'I do like him.' I met him once and was so overwhelmed by his charm and accent that I could hardly glimpse the character underneath, though he seemed intelligent and was certainly attractive. Marty appeared excited. 'Perhaps it's going to be all right,' she said. 'Oh, God, I hope so.'

Ruth wandered around looking calm but not, as far as I could tell, doing very much work. Jeanne was frankly terrified and had resorted to prayer in a normal fashion. She was also somewhat distracted by her July wedding plans. I felt fatalistic; I worked steadily but without inspiration. Soon it would be too late for anything. There were days when I did nothing as a form of escapism, wanting not to believe it was really so near. But on the whole I more or less covered the work I had set myself.

I had good luck cards from Tom and Matthew on our opening day. The first exam was such cold-water shock that

I nearly panicked and ran away. We conferred over lunch, drinking our special-treat orange juice. The condemned. We had started, at any rate. We were, of course, numb to a large part of it. Perhaps it is like that in death. But you cannot, I feel, dread something increasingly over a period of years and then be fully conscious when it finally hits you. Some safety valve of insensibility takes over.

When it had finished, when the solid week of it was over and at last we could do no more to help or hinder ourselves, we were hysterical. We drank brandy in Marty's room and dropped an egg down the well of the stairs. It was obscurely satisfying. Then limpness set in and we lay around in what was left of the hot weather that had reached its zenith, of course, during our big week, so that our hands had stuck to the paper and our pens grown wet and uncontrollable. How fast we had written and what a lot. It all faded from the brain with astonishing rapidity. Brilliance or rubbish, we would never remember exactly what we had said. But it was over. They had taken the weight off us and we could float to the ceiling. We slept a lot and made up for the nights we had stayed up till three still pumping our brains full of information.

On the last night I sat up late with Marty after she came in from seeing her American. We drank tomato juice (coffee had become associated with working vigils and induced temporary nausea) and talked. She was staying in London and I was going home.

'Please write,' I said. 'You're so bad about letters.'

'I'll try. But we won't lose touch anyway, somehow.'

We looked at each other.

'Oh, Marty,' I said, 'whatever happens, I'm glad we came. I have loved it, in spite of the bad parts. I'm glad we were here.'

'So am I,' Marty said.

TWENTY-EIGHT

AUGUST. That funny in-between month. I'm at home helping my mother to face up to Martin's wedding in a fortnight's
time. She won't be quite alone even then, because I'm doing
a secretarial course in the autumn. It's always useful if you're
not going to teach.

Anne is going to teach; she's quite keen on the idea. She
got an upper second; Marty and I got lowers, Ruth and
Jeanne both thirds. I have just had some cake from Jeanne's
wedding so I don't suppose she's worrying about not having
done better. They've gone to Switzerland for their honeymoon.

Dad and Philippa had a son in July. I'm very pleased for
them. It really doesn't hurt any more which is an enormous,
surprising relief. I think I owe Matthew something, and
Marty.

I wish Marty would write. I've only had one postcard from
her in all these weeks. But it said, 'Life is worth living again,'
so I must be patient. I'm glad for her; I couldn't expect the
abortion to transform her life, or rather, I should rejoice that
it didn't, I suppose.

Anne writes regularly, bless her, but she and Keith are
going to Nigeria next year, so I won't see her after that, for a
while. So I suppose I'm just waiting. I'm being quite useful;
Mother really does need someone. I saw Peter the other day
and there wasn't a flicker. I felt so proud of myself.

It will happen sometime, I know. One stage of my life is
over and another must begin. There will be someone I can

share it all with, if I wait. And it must be someone who will find everything he wants in me, so that I can grow.

It will happen; I'm not being too idealistic. I shall meet the right person one day; after all, people nearly always do, don't they?

MORE ABOUT PENGUINS
AND PELICANS

For further information about books available from Penguins please write to Dept EP, Penguin Books Ltd, Harmondsworth, Middlesex UB7 ODA.

In the U.S.A.: For a complete list of books available from Penguins in the United States write to Dept CS, Penguin Books, 625 Madison Avenue, New York, New York 10022.

In Canada: For a complete list of books available from Penguins in Canada write to Penguin Books Canada Ltd, 2801 John Street, Markham, Ontario L3R 1B4.

In Australia: For a complete list of books available from Penguins in Australia write to the Marketing Department, Penguin Books Australia Ltd, P.O. Box 257, Ringwood, Victoria 3134.

In New Zealand: For a complete list of books available from Penguins in New Zealand write to the Marketing Department, Penguin Books (N.Z.) Ltd, P.O. Box 4019, Auckland 10.

Andrea Newman in Penguins

A BOUQUET OF BARBED WIRE

Peter Eliot Manson is in love – with his own daughter. Confused, he hides behind a guilty affair with his secretary. Within a few short summer months a whole family is turned inside out. *A Bouquet of Barbed Wire* gains the tense momentum of a thriller as convoluted relationships lead to tragedy.

ANOTHER BOUQUET . . .

Prue is dead, but Gavin and Manson cannot let her go. Her presence lingers in the tangled relationships of the people who knew her. And the shifting aftermath of Prue's death takes a new, tragic course.

THREE INTO TWO WON'T GO

Andrea Newman turns the eternal triangle on its head. The angles are not all equal, three into two won't go – and somebody has to lose.

ALEXA

In answer to a call for help from her friend Christine, Alexa arrives in the household only to tangle with the husband Paul . . .

Now a powerful television production.